THE SCOTSMAN

"If you must know," Madeline said, "I, that is, you . . . how shall I explain myself? You are not from among the Society here, and in wedding you I would not have to expose the true nature of my father's *situation*."

"Proud to the last," he offered provokingly.

Her spine stiffened a little more. "Have it as you will. I am in need of a husband of some substance. I am proud, but not so proud that I have come to you. The choice is yours. Will you renew your addresses, or not?"

Sir Roger was furious, but kept his temper tightly in check. Did she think to command him so easily or that she was so tempting a morsel? Well, she had a lesson or two to learn, it would seem, about him and about offended Scotsmen in general.

"I might be persuaded," he said at last. "I have conditions, however, which you might not like." Her gaze became almost shrewd, an expression that intrigued him suddenly. He desired more than anything to take her in his arms and kiss her, something he intended to do today regardless of how strongly she might protest against the notion.

BOOK YOUR PLACE ON OUR WEBSITE AND MAKE THE READING CONNECTION!

We've created a customized website just for our very special readers, where you can get the inside scoop on everything that's going on with Zebra, Pinnacle and Kensington books.

When you come online, you'll have the exciting opportunity to:

- View covers of upcoming books
- Read sample chapters
- Learn about our future publishing schedule (listed by publication month *and author*)
- Find out when your favorite authors will be visiting a city near you
- Search for and order backlist books from our online catalog
- Check out author bios and background information
- Send e-mail to your favorite authors
- Meet the Kensington staff online
- Join us in weekly chats with authors, readers and other guests
- Get writing guidelines
- AND MUCH MORE!

**Visit our website at
http://www.kensingtonbooks.com**

A DARING COURTSHIP

Valerie King

ZEBRA BOOKS
Kensington Publishing Corp.
http://www.kensingtonbooks.com

To Keith and Norma Mathieson and family,
for a wonderful time in Britain,
for new friendships

AUTHOR'S NOTE

The town of Chilchester and its surrounding villages, hamlets, castle, manor houses, and valley exist only in my imagination. The general sense of the place I have taken from the old county of Sussex.

One

"You were not so kind at our last meeting," Sir Roger said, one haughty brow lifted faintly.

Madeline Piper stared at Sir Roger Mathieson, unable to credit he could be so ungentlemanly as to have reminded her of their last encounter but a month past. Presently, she stood on the walkway of Pelworthy Castle's tall curtain wall, a gentle breeze tugging at her bonnet and toying with the golden curls surrounding her face. She should have been deeply content, for the castle had been a favorite haunt of hers since childhood and the views of Chilchester Valley below were unequalled. Her heart, however, beat erratically, her knees wobbled, and her mouth had grown very dry. She had merely exchanged civilities thus far, but Sir Roger had not been so receptive as she had hoped. Indeed, she could see that he meant to be difficult.

She drew in a deep, silent breath and attempted to calm the pounding of her heart. "I had not meant to be unkind," she responded stiffly, "the last time we spoke."

He barked his laughter. "You threw a clock at my head."

Madeline compressed her lips, vowing to keep her temper at all costs. "If you will recall, I had been sorely provoked," she responded reasonably.

"Because I offered for your hand in marriage? You consider that a *provocation?*"

She felt a blush climb her cheeks. "Well, yes, of course, that . . . and . . ." Oh, dear, this was not going at all as she had planned. The set of his chin was as mulish as ever, and if she did not have a care, she would fail in her quite specific, albeit odious, purpose in coming to the castle in the first place. "I wish we might forget our last exchange."

"I might be willing to," he responded with a suspicious light in his eye, "if you will give me the kiss I asked for but was summarily denied when last we met."

Her ire spiraled up to the tip of her skull and nearly exploded into the air. "How dare you!" she exclaimed.

"Just as I thought," he remarked, leaning negligently against one of the few portions of the castle that was not in a completely decayed state. He crossed his arms over his chest, undoubtedly for emphasis. "So what the devil do you want with me, Miss Piper? For I cannot credit that you have called merely to be polite. Though perhaps I have been mistaken in you. Do you mean by this visit to acknowledge me and to perhaps begin drawing me into Chilchester society?"

Madeline whirled away from him, not for the purpose of taking her leave, but to regain her balance. How easily he could set up her back. No man, certainly no *gentleman*, had ever done so before. At least her present anger had had the good effect of calming her nerves. Only, how was she to proceed? She did not know, for she had never been required to go a-begging before.

Sudden, unexpected tears stung her eyes. She blinked them back quickly, refusing to surrender to them. She would not become a watering-pot for any man, let alone the horrid *Scotsman* who had so brazenly invaded her pristine neighborhood. Why, he was even taking what had been a charming ruin of a castle and rebuilding it stone by stone! Horrid, horrid man!

Only this was not the day to be either scrupulous or hen hearted. She was the daughter of Lucretia Cowdray Piper of the Kent Cowdrays and Horace Piper of Fairlight Manor. Her mother had been deceased these many years and more, but her legacy of proper conduct had been firmly instilled into Madeline's head. She knew her duty on every score and intended to do it now, even if in doing so she violated numerous other scruples. There were, however, certain pecuniary circumstances which made it possible to set aside the general precepts of the *beau monde*. Sudden financial need, no matter the cause, always overrode the most stringent of tonnish dictums such as the avoidance of an alliance outside of one's station in society.

Madeline shuddered faintly. Wedding *a Scotsman* was so far removed from all that she had been taught was proper and decorous that she felt tinged with some un-named malady at the mere thought of it. However would she endure such a terrible fate?

Endure it she must, however, and, after straightening her spine, she turned back to Sir Roger, a little surprised to find a rather concerned expression on his handsome coun-tenance. She could not imagine its source. Perhaps some errant thought or other about the cost of the refurbishment of Pelworthy Castle had tripped through his head. What-ever the case, she knew what she must do, and so she said, "I have reconsidered your kind and quite generous offer of a month past and, if you are still inclined, I would be happy to accept of your hand in marriage." Her voice had not broken once during this speech, but her knees had returned to feeling watery and useless. She could not tell by his ex-pression how he had received her declaration.

Sir Roger met her gaze, every feeling bristling in re-sentment at her words. He was suspicious and angry, yet at the same time drawn to the beauty standing so proudly before him. She was of medium height and elegant in every manner and gesture. She had been groomed to secure a handle to her name if ever a lady had been thus directed. Her eyes were an unusual green, large, and thickly fringed with long lashes. Her brows were arched in a patrician manner further bespeaking her breeding. Her nose was straight, her lips a delightful shape which, when easing into a smile, had more than once set his senses reeling. He had early in his acquaintance with her concluded that when Madeline Piper smiled she was the fairest of creatures on God's great earth.

He had had a *tendre* for her since first seeing her upon his arrival in the charming Sussex valley. The town of Chilchester and several surrounding villages were cradled in the downs, like many Sussex neighborhoods. Pelworthy Castle had been his object for many years, a ramshackle collection of stones erected on the hillside and waiting for a new master to restore its turreted charms to a form nearer to more glorious days. The very day that he had purchased the castle some five months earlier, he had been walking the perimeter of his newly acquired property only to return to the bailey and find a great beauty, covered in a dark green wool, seated on an ancient horse-block, tilting her face skyward, her eyes closed as she bathed in the weak winter sunshine.

He had not known who she was at the time, nor had he even the smallest notion why she was there. He had seen only the secretive smile on her face and had been enchanted. Who was this beauty who had come to visit the owner of Pelworthy the first day of his arrival in Sussex? A goddess? A wool-draped fairy? A ghost?

He had watched her for a long moment, a cold blast of arctic wind battling past the crumbling curtain wall and buffeting her green bonnet. She did not even seem to notice, but kept her thoughts and her gaze upward into the heavens. Blond curls, having escaped the bonnet, danced over her cheek.

He had approached her at last and quoted a new poet, John Keats:

> *For, indeed, 'tis a sweet and peculiar pleasure*
> *(And blissful is he who such happiness finds),*
> *To possess but a span of the hour of leisure,*
> *In elegant, pure, and aerial minds.*

She had jumped at the sound of his voice. She had stared at him as though he had been the specter, not she. "Who are you?" she cried.

"I am master here," he said, gesturing in a broad sweep of his hand to the broken walls banked in shaded places with mounds of February snow.

She rose to her feet. "Then it is true. Pelworthy is sold?"

"Aye," he responded.

"You are the Scotsman, then?" she inquired, her chin lifting, her lovely smile long since vanished. In her green eyes, he saw past her present disgust and detected a glimmer of loss so profound that he was at once surprised and curious.

"I am," he returned firmly, proudly. "I am also the Englishman who has purchased the castle. My mother was a native of Sussex. I must confess, however, that of the two heritages, my northern roots call to my soul more often, more powerfully."

He watched her swallow—nervously, he suspected. She was a proud one, easily seen in the resolute set of her shoulders and spine.

"I must go," she said. "I beg your pardon for having trespassed on your property. I hope you will forgive the intrusion, but I was used to come here since I was a child and wished to say good-bye."

"You need not offer your farewells. I hope you will come as often as you desire. I am certain the castle will be missing you as well."

At that, a glimmering of her former smile appeared at the edges of her mouth, but quickly disappeared behind her careful reserve. She dropped a curtsy. "Good day, sir."

He bowed and let her pass without inquiring after her name. He felt certain she would be offended were he to attempt to do so. He also knew that such a beauty could not be unknown in the nearest village.

The months that followed had been a stormy sea which had battered him severely. He had begun repairs on the castle immediately, which had endeared him to stonecutters and masons, but not in the least to the *haut ton* of Chilchester society. The doors had been lodged firmly shut against him from the beginning. No attempt on his part had prevailed to permit him the smallest entrée. Miss Piper, a prominent member of that Society, had all but given him the cut direct.

He had not expected better, the prejudices of small, country neighborhoods being what they were, profound and deep-seated. Even the permanent resident in his house, Lord Anthony Stephens, the son of the Earl of Selsfield, had not pried open even one societal door for him. In the face of such opposition, however, he found himself oddly pleased, for he had come to stay, and one day Chilchester Society would accept him, happily or not. He had known all too well the manner in which a group of narrow minds could set themselves steadfastly against even the most charming and intelligent of individuals.

His mother had been such a one, and her only crime had been that she had married a Scotsman.

To have, then, the lovely Miss Piper ask him, quite

against her will, to marry her, was an interesting turn of events full of promise. His offer of a month ago he had laid at her feet because it pleased him to torment her in precisely that manner. Of course, he had begged permission from her father to pay his addresses to her and had often wondered just what reason Mr. Piper had to allow the proposal in the first place. This he doubted he would ever know, or at least thought he would not—until now. So, Madeline Piper desired a husband, and not just any husband. She desired him. But why?

"Are you in love with me?" he asked provokingly.

She seemed to recoil. "Of course not. This would be a marriage of convenience. If you must know, certain unfortunate circumstances have arisen that have made it necessary for me to seek a husband."

"I see, but why me?" he asked, pressing the point.

A faint blush arose on each creamy cheek. "I will not insult you by telling whiskers. Because of your wealth, of course."

"I see. And when did it become necessary for Miss Piper to marry for such a reason as this? I had been given to understand your dowry is considerable."

"The difficulty is not mine, but my father's. A recent *embarrassment,* if you will."

He believed he understood, yet found himself surprised. He had heard nothing untoward concerning Horace Piper, not a single jot of servants' gossip that would have led him to believe he had suffered a severe reversal of fortune. Regardless, Mr. Piper's daughter was standing before him speaking of quite the opposite. "You have several suitors who would be willing to do the job, Miss Piper, and who would undoubtedly have sufficient largess to redeem whatever vowels your father has promised. Again, I must ask, why did you choose me?"

At that, her demeanor grew rigid and haughty. "I should

have known you would press me with ungenteel questions."

"I will not be fobbed off by such a remark. I demand a clear answer of you. Why did you choose me, when a dozen others would do as well?" Was it possible she was in love with him? The flaming glare which she cast on him did not, however, support this notion.

"If you must know," she said, if haltingly. "I, that is, you . . . how shall I explain myself? You are not from among the Society here, and in wedding you I would not have to expose the true nature of my father's *situation.*"

"Proud to the last," he offered provokingly.

Her spine stiffened a little more. "Have it as you will. I am in need of a husband of some substance. I am proud, but not so proud that I have come to you. The choice is yours. Will you renew your addresses, or not?"

He was furious, but kept his temper tightly in check. Did she think to command him so easily or that she was so tempting a morsel that she thought he would grasp at the chance to husband her? Well, she had a lesson or two to learn, it would seem, about him and about offended Scotsmen in general.

"I might be persuaded," he said at last. "I have conditions, however, which you might not like." Her gaze became almost shrewd, an expression that intrigued him suddenly. He had been so little in her society that in truth he did not know a great deal about her except that he desired more than anything to take her in his arms and kiss her, something he intended to do today regardless of how strongly she might protest against the notion.

"Such as?" she inquired.

"I have lived in Sussex for nigh on six months, Miss Piper. I am generally extremely fond of Society, but have had little here. I would expect to have many doors opened to me were I to court you."

She seemed horrified. "You cannot possibly think—"

"Oh, yes, indeed," he countered. "I would expect you to bring me into fashion."

"But it cannot be done! You do not know what you ask!"

"I believe I do know," he responded.

She shook her head, her green eyes appearing wild. "Bring you into fashion? Good God!"

"If you are clever enough, it could be done."

"I suppose I might manage an invitation or two were it to become known that we were betrothed."

"No," he drawled. "Not betrothed. You and I will have an understanding that must remain secret. No, you must bring me into fashion while I court you over, let us say, the next month. That would place the date, if I am not mistaken, near Lady Cottingford's harvest ball, which I would expect you and me to attend."

She blinked several times, and for a long moment he felt certain she might faint. "Lady Cottingford's harvest ball? You are not serious. Surely you understand even I have never attended so prestigious a fete. The . . . the guests are comprised primarily of her London acquaintances, the Park Lane set—Wellington, Byron, and the like. Even the Regent has been known to attend."

He shrugged. "It sounds quite hopeless, then, so I suppose I will have to reject your offer, Miss Piper, for it will be the harvest ball or nothing."

Madeline stared very hard at the man before her. He still leaned against the wall, and his arms were yet locked over his broad chest. Even leaning as he was, she still had to look up into his face. His light blue eyes flashed over her, his thoughts reflected in each purposeful glint. It seemed clear to her he was enjoying her discomfiture immensely.

"I believe you must have gone mad. Either that or you have no proper understanding of what you ask."

"I have a proper understanding," he responded coolly.

"And I am not mad. If you want my fortune, this is my price—to be brought into your Society and to attend the harvest ball with you—and your father, of course."

"There are but a handful of Chilchester families who receive such an invitation. The Pipers never have, not in all these years."

"But I know how intricately you are connected to all the families in the vicinity. From the first of my acquaintance with you, I understood that fact quite to perfection. Now you must decide how desperately you want me—or, rather, my fortune. That, my dear, is the price."

A smiled flickered over his lips, reaching to his eyes, which laughed merrily at her expense. Why shouldn't he laugh at her? she thought gloomily. She had been brought low by events of the past few days, lower than she had ever imagined possible. She had reviewed all the gentlemen to whom she could have applied to relieve her father of his sudden financial embarrassments. Two of her suitors would have seen to the matter quite nicely, except how could she explain that she had never meant to choose a husband in the context of a marriage of convenience? Such a notion had always been of the most abhorrent to her.

Now her situation was quite different. Certainly she had her dowry, a quite respectable eight thousand pounds, but this paled in comparison to her papa's debts. If he did not receive relief quite soon, involving a figure four times that amount, Fairlight Manor would be sold at auction to pay his outrageous gaming debts, acquired only recently in a fortnight's jaunt to Brighton.

She still could not credit it was true. The Pipers were all but ruined. All her dreams were gone, vanished in a roll of the dice. How had this happened to her?

She gave herself a shake. These hopeless ruminations would not do in the least. Better to tend to the matter at hand. "So what you are saying is that I am to bring you into fashion, culminating in an invitation for both of us to attend the harvest ball, along with my father? Have I understood you correctly?"

"Precisely. But, come! Do not be so downcast, Miss Piper. Surely you are made of sterner stuff. I believe with a little effort you could achieve these desired objects. You must have a little more confidence in your abilities."

At that, she ground her teeth. "I have sufficient confidence in many things, but there is an old proverb about a sow's ear which troubles me greatly at present."

He clucked his tongue. "My dear, if you wish to win my heart, or at least my pocketbook, you ought to refrain from insulting me."

"Then I would beg you not to be so provoking."

He nodded. "Very well. I shall make such an attempt for your sake."

"Thank you for at least that much, Sir Roger."

He smiled and appeared quite mischievous, an expression she found rather appealing. "There, you see," he said, "we shall do famously. We have already had our first quarrel and survived it quite nicely."

"Bring you into fashion," she murmured, trying not to imagine just how difficult, how impossible, such a task would likely prove. "Very well, I shall try."

He leaned forward slightly and in a low voice said, "If you succeed, Miss Piper, I believe you would find me an agreeable husband."

Something in his expression, in the piercing quality suddenly present in his blue eyes, diverted her thoughts down a different path altogether. He would be her husband, and she his wife. She would be the mother of his children and all that such an arrangement entailed.

A new blush made its way up her cheeks, only this time she was not so much embarrassed as quite stunned by the thought that such a man, deeply sun bronzed from having resided in India for over fifteen years, broad of shoulder and chest and in every sense a quite physically powerful man, would by her own permission be granted command of her. Her lips parted and she sucked in a shocked stream of air. How could she ever allow this?

She lifted both hands, a certain panic flooding her. "Forget that I have even broached the subject of matrimony with you, Sir Roger!" she cried suddenly. She turned away from him abruptly, intending to leave. "I never should have come! What was I thinking? There must be another way! Something! Anything!"

As she moved away from him, she did not get far, for he caught her arm swiftly in a powerful clasp, at the same time rising to his full height. "Miss Piper, wait!" he cried sharply. "I beg you will not run from me. I am no monster, as you seem to believe."

You might as well be, she thought, checking the words before they spilled past her lips.

"Only tell me what has suddenly overset you," he added.

She turned back to him. "How can I marry you?" she cried. "When you are . . . you are a . . . a Scotsman? Every feeling must be offended. Do you not see as much?"

He still had strong hold of her arm. "That is not what you were thinking just now. I would wager my fortune it was not. Tell me the truth. Why did you suddenly take fright, when before you were as bold as Hercules accomplishing one of his twelve labors?"

How could she tell him? "I . . . I did not think, I did not realize until just this moment, what marrying you would . . . would involve."

A slow smile overspread his lips. "That is what I thought," he said softly. "But you are mistaken in thinking you would dislike it."

Before she knew what was happening, he released her arm, only to catch her up in a powerful embrace. She could not even breathe. She knew what he was about to do and a protest did rise to her lips, but before she could utter the words, his lips were upon hers. She had thought she would dislike it immensely, for he was brutish in so many ways, but there was nothing sinister about the soft feel of his lips on hers, a sensation which gave her pause.

Perhaps in this moment curiosity prevailed, for she allowed the kiss to continue. Could she bear the touch of a man—for she could hardly call a Scotsman a gentleman—so decidedly beneath her notice?

At first, she appraised the gentle assault in a purely objective manner: arms like a vice; lips soft, even a little moist; a tender search over hers as though he was asking a question. What question? Could she tumble in love with a Scotsman, perhaps? Never, of course. Only why could she no longer frame her thoughts so clearly? Why was she coming to feel so oddly disconnected from herself?

He drew her to himself more closely still, but how was that possible, and why were her hands drifting over his shoulders—and what was this sigh that seemed to pass through her entire being like a welcome summer breeze?

Madeline had never been kissed before, not once in her six and twenty years. She had always supposed that adjusting to it would require a great deal of time and effort. However, she found the current experience so uniquely pleasurable that there drifted through her presently lethargic mind the thought that she could remain within the circle of Sir Roger's arms forever.

When he drew back, the cloud of unexpected desire which had held her captive disappeared like a morning mist when the sun rises high in the sky. She blinked and saw that there was laughter in his eyes and a smirk on his lips.

"Oh, what a wretch you are!" she cried indignantly.

"As I told you before, Miss Piper, you are mistaken in thinking you would dislike being my wife."

"I think you a horrid beast," she retorted, scowling at him. "And now, I must away. I must tell Papa that your intention is to court me with the understanding that should I succeed in bringing you into fashion as well as acquiring invitations to the harvest ball, that you would then be willing to marry me and to discharge the sum of his debts. Have I the right of it?"

"Precisely."

"Good day, then," she returned crisply. With that, she whirled about purposefully on her heel and began a quick march toward the nearest turret so that she could make good her escape. She could not bear the thought that he might attempt to kiss her again, for there had been nothing so lowering in her entire exchange with Sir Roger than the fact that she had enjoyed his kisses quite against her will. Very lowering, indeed!

Two

As soon as Madeline began her trek back to Fairlight Manor—a very short two miles from Pelworthy Castle—and was certain Sir Roger could not hear her, she let out a low, frustrated growl. Quite unladylike, but she felt certain the nearby robins and titmice would not expose her. She could not remember having been more frustrated in her entire existence than in this moment, when the course of her life had been so completely disrupted—first by her father and his newly acquired vice, and now by Sir Roger, who was refusing obstinately to cooperate!

She had been so certain he would readily embrace the notion of a forthcoming marriage with her it had never once occurred to her he might not be completely delighted with idea. Instead, he had been beastly from beginning to end, even going so far as to take her in his arms and force a most unwelcome kiss on her.

She felt her cheeks blush anew, not at the memory of the kiss but at how much she had actually enjoyed it. She pressed her hands to her cheeks and willed the heat and color to disappear. She felt in this moment that she had somehow betrayed herself in a manner that was entirely unforgivable. It was one thing to do one's duty. It was quite another to relish the idea of it, especially with a Scotsman. What would her mother think of her were she alive today?

She began to walk more quickly, every nerve of her

body uneasy and tense. She should have pushed him away. She should have adjured him never to trespass her lips in such a fashion again. She should never have gone to him in the first place. Foolish, foolish errand!

And now his demands!

There must be something else she could do to right her fortunes. Once more she considered going to Mr. Calvert, Captain Bladen, or even ridiculous Harris Rockingham, who followed her around like a puppy, for each were in possession of considerable fortunes. Yet even as these possibilities crossed her mind, she dismissed them. She had known each of these gentlemen for years, and Harris had been a playmate from childhood. How could she then approach them about her suddenly straightened circumstances, nonetheless offer herself as barter for a fortune in order to relieve her father of his sufferings? Every feeling was offended at the very thought of it. No, for the present, she must submit to the pursuit of Sir Roger's immense wealth.

Glancing around, she realized she had crossed the first mile of the descent to her home. She turned back to look at the castle, now visible on its lonely prominence. The walls were ragged, ivy cloaked, and still charming in their antiquated way, but one of the turrets was nearly restored, the vestiges of the former ruined state visible in the difference in coloration between the new and the weathered stones. A wagon laden with stone was making its way slowly up the hill.

A feeling of intense loneliness swept over Madeline, a surprising sensation given the ire which raged in her spirit, and yet quite familiar. As her gaze lifted from the castle and swept over the clear blue of the July sky, she knew precisely the moment she had begun to feel as though she walked alone on the earth—the moment her mother had passed from this life. As the eldest of four daughters, the responsibility of Fairlight Manor had fallen on her shoulders.

And she was responsible. She always knew her duty, and she always did her duty. But how wonderfully different everything would be if her mother were still alive. For one thing, she never would have permitted Papa to gamble away his fortune on holiday in Brighton!

This would not do, however, this maudlin dwelling upon the sadness of the past. She whirled around and began her march back to Fairlight and to the future, a future in which she must somehow accomplish the impossible, and that within less than a month's time, for she must somehow acquire three invitations from Lady Cottingford or her family would be in the basket, indeed!

She worked backward in her mind, trying to find some pathway by which she could accomplish this extraordinary feat. Who would she have to involve, to call upon to support her? How could she gain such support when it involved a Scotsman?

She shuddered at the mere magnitude of the labor before her. Which of the leading hostesses of the neighborhood about Chilchester would be willing to support her in her bid for three invitations to the harvest ball? None, was the simple answer which returned to her, since each hostess cherished the hope of receiving an invitation this year herself.

Unless—here Madeline's heart leaped—unless she did not make it known that this was her object. She began running lightly down the final incline to the border of her father's property. There were several hostesses of whom she could make considerable use to promote her cause, even if she must be as wily as a fox about the business. Elizabeth Crawley for one, Lady Hambledon for another, and her own grandmother, should she be hard-pressed. Another she probably would be required to approach was Harris Rockingham's mother, a veritable dragon of a woman, but one who possessed considerable influence.

Yes, she finally began to see a way that the object might be achieved by means of a few select favors requested. A soiree here, a picnic there, and the deed might just be accomplished.

The most pressing difficulty, however, reared its head, causing Madeline to stop dead in her tracks once more. Sir Roger. Even if she were exceedingly careful in every stratagem, how the deuce was she to secure an invitation to Lady Cottingford's harvest ball for Sir Roger?

She squeezed her eyes shut. And how on earth had it happened that her simple country life had suddenly become so very complicated?

"Call him off, Mathieson!"

Sir Roger snapped his fingers. His faithful hound, Churchill, drew up sharply next to him and settled onto his haunches. Sir Roger set aside the receipt for the most recent shipment of stone and glanced at Lord Anthony, whose white complexion had grown quite pink. Beads of sweat were visible on his forehead. "Will you never learn?" Sir Roger asked, a smile tugging at the edges of his mouth.

"Oh, the devil take it!" Lord Anthony cried. "You know very well that beast of yours takes delight in tormenting me! And look at this, another pair of breeches ruined!"

"I have no sympathy for you, as you very well know. You need to be firm, masterly. He senses he is able to dominate you, so he does." He glanced at the fawn-colored breeches. The knee of the left one had been ripped quite nicely and now hung in a pretty fringe over the front of Lord Anthony's glossy top boots.

His friend of a decade and more glared at Churchill, and for this small gesture was rewarded with a faint baring of teeth and a soft growl. "Enough!" Sir Roger stated.

Churchill looked up at him adoringly and wagged his tail, which swished behind him over the carpet.

Lord Anthony moved away from the vicious dog and bent over to tuck in the offending shred of fabric.

"No!" Sir Roger cried as Churchill lunged forward, intrigued by the new mark. He could only laugh. His friend was hopelessly dim-witted and the easiest of targets for so fearless a creature as the hound still sitting obediently beside him.

There was nothing for it, however. He rang for his butler, Shipley. A few minutes later, Churchill trotted proudly beside Shipley, being led to the kitchens, where Cook spoiled him mercilessly.

"There, you see," Sir Roger said, his smile still threatening his lips, "even Shipley, who is as old as Pelworthy, can manage Churchill."

Lord Anthony merely scowled heavily, then threw himself into a chair near a massive stone fireplace. "What did 'the Paragon' want?" he asked, pulling an apple from his pocket and beginning to munch. "Tell you again what a scapegrace you are?"

"Worse," he responded. "She has suffered a change of heart—and circumstances—and wishes to marry me."

Lord Anthony choked on a bite of apple and did not stop coughing and sputtering for a full minute.

"Good God, man! Are you all right?"

"Yes," Lord Anthony wheezed. "What did you say to her? You mean to leg-shackle yourself to the proudest, most disagreeable, most priggish creature in Sussex? If you do, you are more addled even than I!"

At that, Sir Roger grew thoughtful. He took up a chair opposite his friend, who once more began to chomp on his apple, and considered this remark. He had once believed her to be quite prudish, but after this most recent kiss, he was no longer certain. He had been stunned by the way she had leaned quite scandalously into him and wondered if she was a lady of some experience after all. However, the shocked expression on her face afterward had convinced him she had merely responded to him, a not unhappy notion, but had been unaware of it until after the fact.

At the same time, he had also been surprised by his own reaction. He had always taken great delight in kissing the ladies, but in accosting Miss Piper he had meant to subdue her a little. Instead, he had found himself astonished by how he had felt holding her in his arms, as though the earth had become a vibrant drum beneath the soles of his boots. He could have kissed her forever.

Until, of course, she drew back and looked at him as though he was as hideous as Vulcan himself. His original purposes had been renewed in that moment as all his former ire returned to him. How much he would delight in bringing Miss Piper down quite a few pegs over the coming month. This would at least be some measure of retribution for the many indignities his own mother had suffered at the hands of an English neighborhood.

"To answer your question," he said, watching a trickle of juice ease down his friend's chin, "I have not made up my mind. I would have, of course, a month ago when I offered for her, but now . . ." He rose from his chair, whipped his kerchief from the pocket of his coat, and offered it to his bacon-brained friend.

"Obliged," Lord Anthony murmured and wiped at his chin.

"You are welcome," he responded, smiling, then resumed his seat. He had met Lord Anthony, the youngest son of the Earl of Selsfield, while in India. He had been quite a misfit in a land of heat, of ambitious and shrewd businessmen, and of an ancient people whose habits were to his lordship quite incomprehensible.

Sir Roger had picked him up from a filthy gutter. The poor young man had been completely foxed and robbed, of course, of his last tuppence, having been abandoned by a group of dastardly English *gentlemen* who thought the escapade a quite amusing lark. A fast friendship between the two men had ensued. Whatever Lord Anthony lacked in mental acumen or even to some degree social perception, he made up for in loyalty. Sir Roger had never known so determined a friend as Lord Anthony.

"What I don't understand, old fellow," Lord Anthony said, a deep frown on his brow, "is why you did not tell her to take herself off and be done with it."

Sir Roger leaned back in his chair, a sense of satisfaction overtaking him like a cool breeze on a hot day. "Because that would not have been half so amusing as the prospect of being able to watch her grovel before every one of her acquaintances."

Lord Anthony shook his head and stared at the half-eaten apple. "I must have a clear answer, because you are not making the smallest bit of sense to me—do you intend to wed the chit?"

"Good God, no! I had rather cut off my nose first!"

Enlightenment dawned on the young lord's lethargic brain. "You intend to make a great deal of sport of her. Oh, I see." He then scowled anew.

"What is it now?" Sir Roger inquired amused.

"Not at all the thing, Roger. Miss Piper is a lady."

Sir Roger dismissed his friend's chivalrous scruples. "She was also the lady who threw a clock at my head because I deigned to offer for her hand in marriage."

Once again Lord Anthony frowned. "She shouldn't have done that. Quite beyond the pale. Ah, well, what is Cook preparing for dinner?"

* * *

Madeline took up a seat at her writing desk and began to ponder the impossible once more. She knew she had to begin with Elizabeth Crawley, who was hosting a soiree two days hence on the first of August. She, her father, and her sisters were already invited and, of course, planning to attend. However, it seemed to her if she was to have even the smallest chance of succeeding with Sir Roger, he would also need to be invited and the very difficult task of bringing him into fashion launched that very night. Only how to achieve it? she wondered.

She drew forward pen and ink and began making lists of those who would be likely to attend, how many would be shocked by his presence, how many would be indifferent, and the handful who would actually be welcoming. One of these, in opposition to his wife, was George Crawley, Mrs. Crawley's husband. She felt the key, therefore, to be Squire Crawley and his generally known good opinion of Sir Roger's worth. Of course, it was one thing for a man to extol the virtues of another of his fellow creatures and quite another to invite him to hunt on his lands.

Once more the sensation of how hopeless the task really was rose up to threaten what little confidence she possessed. She left her chair and began to pace her bedchamber, back and forth, back and forth. How was Mr. Crawley to be so moved that he would actually insist that his wife extend an invitation to Sir Roger? How?

The Crawleys were the most prominent family of the town of Chilchester, living just at the edge of that thriving community. There was nothing in the old market town which Squire Crawley did not know nor have some hand in, whether directing the course of the weekly markets or guiding parish business. Every socially adept lady of Chilchester sought Mrs. Crawley's opinion and every man of sense laid his concerns before the squire. How, then, to persuade them both to draw Sir Roger into their circle, and that within two days?

Finally, Madeline drew the only conclusion she could. She must speak with the squire, the sooner the better.

After nuncheon, she drove her father's gig the five miles to Wistfield Hall, the squire's ancient family seat, and was ushered without the slightest delay into Mr. Crawley's study. She took up a seat. He offered her a sherry, which she accepted gratefully and tried to still the nervous thumpings of her heart. She found the sherry was of some use, but only a very little.

"The lanes appear dry today," he offered, glancing out his window. His study was situated overlooking the lane so that he had an uncommon view of an orchard and a hill, as well as the main road to Chilchester, down which a steady procession of vehicles could be seen lumbering.

"Nicely so," Madeline responded, holding her sherry carefully in her gloved hands. "I drove my father's gig, and it was quite pleasant."

"Good, good," he murmured. He had remained standing and now looked down at her, a frown puckering his brow. He was a large man and still held to the old-fashioned use of a powdered wig. "You know, Miss Piper, in all these years, you have not once called on me in this manner. I must say, I am quite intrigued. All is well, I trust, at Fairlight?"

"Yes," she offered in just such a way that caused his frown to deepen. She added hastily, "However, there is a matter of some concern which . . . which I felt I ought to lay before you."

"I see," he said, taking up his chair behind his desk. A formality now seemed established, as well as a sense that whatever was spoken in this moment would be kept confidential. He clasped his hands before him and stared hard at her.

Madeline drew in a deep breath. How was she to begin?

She glanced away from his piercing stare for a moment and sipped her sherry. She felt her hand tremble and lowered both glass and hand to her lap.

"You may tell me anything, Madeline," he said softly. "You must know that. I have known you since you were small enough to bounce on my knee."

At that, she could not help but smile. "So you have. It is just . . . Mr. Crawley—Squire—I cannot tell you all. I can only beg something of you that I fear will not be received well by this house."

He chuckled. "My dear, you could not have raised my curiosity higher in this moment. Pray, put me out of my suspense and make your request. I promise you, short of telling me to pluck every hair from my eyebrows, if it is in my power, I shall grant it. You are, you have always been, a favorite of mine, even if . . . well, that hardly matters."

"Even if?" she inquired, a little surprised.

"Do you mind a digression for a moment?" he asked.

She shook her head. Now she was intrigued.

He huffed a sigh. "You ought to have been to London by now, seen something of the world. Our Society is not all that it should be."

"Whatever do you mean?" She had always loved Chilchester society, at least until Sir Roger's unsettling appearance in the valley.

He sighed heavily again. "That you have not the faintest notion what I mean is the very trouble, I fear. Well, well, I suppose that is neither here nor there, though I tend to lay the blame at Horace's door. I dare say Lucretia would have done better by you, and you know how much I take issue with your grandmother's opinions on just about every subject."

Madeline was indeed stunned by all these rather surprising revelations. She had not known of Squire Crawley's strong resentments concerning her father and her grandmother. She did however agree with him on one score. Her mother, Lucretia, would have made certain she had had more than one Season by now, probably several. However, she had never really felt the lack of them and so could not truly appreciate the significance of the squire's wish that she had had a London experience or two.

"At any rate, my dear, let me encourage you that should you have even the smallest opportunity to visit the metropolis, then do so, for you will be in for a shock and a delight." These words were spoken with a smile, and she knew he meant them to be an encouragement to her. Given her current troubles, however, in particular her father's perfidy in Brighton, she thought his advice somewhat frivolous. He, of course, could know nothing of that, so once more she wondered just how to broach so delicate a subject.

Finally, she began. "You have been so good as to speak plainly with me, and so I shall return the courtesy. I have a request. Would you please extend an invitation to your soiree on Saturday night to Sir Roger Mathieson? I have a particular reason for making this request, only I cannot elaborate at this time."

She found that her hands were trembling again and for that reason hastily drank the remaining sherry.

"Sir Roger!" he cried. "But you detest the man!"

She had the good grace to blush. "That is all in the past, but more I cannot say."

He grunted and scowled and stared at her. "Sir Roger? Good God! I fear my wife would have a fit of the vapors were I to make such a suggestion."

"Yes, I know, which is why I do not make this request lightly and also why I came to you first."

He pursed and puckered his lips, sucked in his breath, and let it out with a swooshing sound. He drummed his fingers, crossed and uncrossed his legs, and tugged at his powdered wig. He scratched his chin and twisted his face into a variety of grimaces.

Finally, he rose to his feet. "I'll do it!" he responded, thumping his desk hard, "but you had best leave now, for I do not mean to hesitate upon telling Mrs. Crawley what is expected of her, and if you do not wish to hear the beams shattering from the shrillness of her protests, then you should hurry away."

"Thank you, Squire!" she exclaimed. She was so happy, so inutterably grateful that it was all she could do to keep from throwing her arms about his shoulders. She could not believe it was true. Sir Roger would be attending the Crawley soiree!

She left as she was bid, and at the very moment she had turned the gig in the direction of the avenue, a peculiar wailing sound could be heard coming from beyond the front door. With a prickle of conscience, she slapped the reins firmly against the haunches of her fine driving horse and at once began moving at a brisk trot down the lane.

At dinner that evening, Madeline had just lifted a spoonful of soup to her lips when her youngest sister, Hope, blurted, "Maddy, is it true that you begged Squire Crawley to force his wife to invite Sir Roger to her soiree Saturday night?"

Madeline did not sip the soup on her spoon. She was certain she would have choked if she had. She could not credit that a scant three hours had passed since she had spoken with the squire, and already word of her purposes there had reached Fairlight. She glanced at her father, who frowned slightly and nodded to her.

"Yes," she responded to Hope's question. Hope was just eighteen and full of opinions about everything.

"I think it famous!" she cried. "I have always thought

the disinclusion of Sir Roger was ridiculous, and now we are to enjoy his company!"

"I think it dreadful," Charity returned, staring at Hope as though she had sprouted horns atop her guinea curls. "Once he is permitted to roam Society at will, what will follow? The French woman who lives in a cottage at Elsbourne village?"

"She is of aristocratic descent," Mr. Piper offered, ladling deeply into his bowl of soup.

"I have never met her," Prudence said in her soft voice, "but Geoffrey Gilbert says she is the kindest creature imaginable. I believe she was disappointed in love once."

"Who gives a fig for the Frenchwoman!" Hope exclaimed. "Only tell me, Maddy, is Sir Roger to attend? I mean, will he attend? And why did you make the request to the squire?"

Madeline felt flustered. The entire business was so new to her that she had not yet arranged all her thoughts or planned just how she was to explain her extraordinary conduct. Since their father's pecuniary difficulties were to be kept from her younger sisters, at least for the present, she knew quite well she could hardly tell them the truth. Clearing her throat, she finally said, "Over the past several weeks, I have come to be of the opinion that the man who is sparing no expense in restoring Pelworthy Castle ought to be given a place in our extended neighborhood. It does not seem right otherwise. And besides, his mother was English, which must count for something."

Prudence shook her head as though bewildered. "But you have always said you detested the repairs he was making, that the castle was perfect as it was."

Madeline withheld a sigh and dipped her own spoon. She felt no explanation could suffice, so she said, with a slight shrug of her shoulders, "I have changed my mind."

All three sisters stared at her for a moment, then turned to exchange glances with one another. In true feminine spirit and sympathy, they each expressed their view of the matter.

Charity, the next eldest said, "It is a woman's prerogative to change her mind."

Prudence chuckled softly. "I changed my gown three times before dinner."

Hope looked off into space. "I am forever changing my mind about which of my suitors to encourage."

Madeline could not believe how easily she had passed this first of what undoubtedly would be many tests of her sudden shift in attitude toward Sir Roger. Her father, next to whom she was seated, caught her eye once more and lifted his glass of claret to her. She had informed him earlier of her conversation with Sir Roger, of the knight's demands and of Squire Crawley's unquestioning support of her request that he be invited to Wistfield Hall on Saturday night. Her father had been delighted, as well he might, since Sir Roger's fortunes would repair his own.

"I do not understand."

Madeline glanced at one of her most persistent suitors and wondered just how she ought to go about hinting him away. John Calvert was a stalwart gentleman of slightly portly dimensions and owner of Gumbers Lodge near the village of Balfriston. He had ridden over to call on her after dinner specifically to discuss the rumors he had been hearing all afternoon. His sister had accompanied him.

"Indeed," his sister said, "neither John nor I could credit you had done anything so foolish. We felt obligated to come to you directly and hope we have not inconvenienced you."

These soft words following her harsh criticism did little to allay Madeline's temper. Pamela Calvert Spight, a widow of thirty-three, lived at Gumbers Lodge with her three children. She was very thin and exceedingly proper.

Her husband had perished at Waterloo, a fine captain of a dragoon regiment, a death which had been made sport of in recent months by unnamed gentlemen who said he hadn't been shot as reported but was in hiding from his wife. Mrs. Spight had a snake's tongue and bite.

Madeline might have offered a more appropriate rejoinder, but she recollected quite quickly that she would need to be exceedingly diplomatic with everyone during the coming weeks if she hoped to gain invitations to Lady Cottingford's harvest ball.

She therefore drew in a deep breath and began a speech she had written and rehearsed shortly after dinner. "I comprehend your feelings completely," she said. "Indeed, you both must know me well enough to comprehend that I have until today shared your sentiments completely. However, it has come to my attention that Sir Roger has no intention of leaving our vale, and far from quitting Pelworthy, has continued the repairs on the castle to such an extent that I believe he may have a majority of the work accomplished by Michaelmas—at which time"—and here she prevaricated—"it is my understanding that he intends to give a Christmas ball which the Earl of Selsfield himself means to attend."

Her guests stared at her in wide-eyed disbelief.

"But I thought Lord Anthony had been rejected by his family," Mr. Calvert said.

"It is no such thing," she said. Although it might have been true, she simply did not know. This was one more matter she must discuss with Sir Roger, and she thought it would be best if she requested he call on her tomorrow to discuss the truly tangled web she had begun weaving about herself.

"How do you know these things?" Mrs. Spight queried, shaking her head. "I was speaking with Lady Hambledon only this morning about Sir Roger and Lord Anthony. She said nothing of the matter, and I have always known her to be abreast of the latest *on-dits* where her peers are concerned."

Madeline felt her fingers begin strangling one another. Few things irritated her more than Pamela Spight speaking as though she knew everything. She was, in her opinion, a platter-faced mushroom with more hair than wit who pretended a keen confidance with the baroness that simply did not exist.

Despite her dislike of Mrs. Spight and her pretensions, she answered politely. "I chanced upon Sir Roger this morning on one of my rambles, and we had a very long discussion of these matters. He was ever so kind as to have given me a proper hint concerning these critical matters."

"And you believed him?" Mr. Calvert asked, incredulous.

At that, Madeline stared at her faithful suitor. "I had no reason not to," she countered. "I have made no secret of my dislike of Sir Roger's lineage or even of his presumption in purchasing Pelworthy Castle and beginning his modernization of what was for me a favorite childhood haunt, but he has never given me cause to disbelieve anything he has ever said to me."

Mr. Calvert scowled and shook his head. "This is most unsettling. I wish you had consulted me, Miss Piper. Indeed, I wish you had. I am certain I could have quashed any such hopes on his part or Lord Anthony's without offending the Earl of Selsfield."

Madeline was astonished. "Since you are not acquainted with his lordship, I do not see how."

Mr. Calvert appeared flustered, throwing up a hand. "I feel you should have at least given me a chance to unravel this difficulty before you acted so hastily. Good God, to think of Sir Roger Mathieson at Wistfield on Saturday night. It is not to be borne."

"It is to be borne," Madeline responded firmly, thinking she was speaking as much to herself as to her guests. "And it will be borne. The Earl of Selsfield is too powerfully connected to be given even the smallest offense. You can imagine, I am sure, the repercussions were he to arrive in Sussex and be ignored by every important family in the valley."

These words caused the blood to drain from her guests' faces, and for that reason she thought it prudent to call the private conversation to a close. "But come, my sisters and father will want to see you and will, of course, want to hear your opinions on the matter. Cook has prepared a ginger-bread cake."

She had hoped this offering would soothe Mr. Calvert and his sister, but Mrs. Spight shook her head. "Have you forgotten, Miss Piper? Ginger always makes dear brother bilious!"

Three

"Miss Piper is here?" Sir Roger asked of one of his footmen. He let the heavy head of the sledgehammer slide to the stone floor next to his foot. He was in the dungeon, breaking up several superfluous partial walls erected sometime in the sixteen hundreds, which his architect had deemed ready to be dismantled. There was only one way to achieve the desired result, and whenever he had the chance to engage in a piece of challenging physical labor, he did so—not quite the usual activity for a gentleman, a circumstance which in this moment caused him to smile broadly.

"Bring Miss Piper to me," he commanded.

"Sir?" his footman asked, his eyes startled like a rabbit caught in a box trap.

"You heard correctly. Bring her here. See to it at once."

"Very good, sir." The servant turned and fairly ran back up the spiraling stone staircase.

Sir Roger once more picked up the sledgehammer and began swinging at the remaining stones of the wall he was dismantling. He laughed aloud, thinking his entire experience in Chilchester Valley thus far would undoubtedly be worth every trial merely to see the expression on Miss Piper's face once she arrived in the dungeons. He could not imagine what her thoughts might be once his man began leading her into the bowels of the castle.

A few minutes later, Madeline descended the spiraling

stone steps quite slowly, her hand touching the cold wall for balance. She wondered if the footman had gone mad to have directed her to the dungeons of the castle, for she could not imagine that Sir Roger would have actually insisted she meet him here. It was dangerous, dirty, and not in the least how she had expected to be received.

In the distance, she could hear the steady sounds of a hammer smashing at stone and could even taste the resulting dust on her tongue. Clearly a laborer was at work, so why had she been brought here? For one thing, she could think of no rational reason why Sir Roger would be in the vicinity of so much dirt and, for another, why he would ever have exposed her to such wretched conditions.

When she reached the bottom of the stairs, she glanced in the direction of the steady, rhythmic pounding and saw only a lone workman toiling with a large hammer, steadily swinging at a pile of rubble which might have at one time been a wall. He wore a white kerchief tied over his nose and mouth and the dust roiled about him, visible from the light of two lanterns hung on the wall behind him.

Just as she thought. She had been led here by an imbecile. She rolled her eyes, thinking Sir Roger had hired a complete nodcock for a servant. Then her eyes began to see more clearly in the dusty gloom, and all at once she realized that the tall workman was none other than Sir Roger himself.

She could not credit it was true and blinked several times in order to make certain her vision was not deceiving her. To say she was shocked did not even begin to express all that she felt in this moment. Sir Roger Mathieson was hefting a sledgehammer over his head and again and again driving it against the stone of a partially demolished wall. But why? She could not understand what he meant by doing such low work or why, in particular, he had summoned her to witness it.

Somehow it seemed in perfect keeping with her general

view of the Scotsman, and disgust surmounted her stunned
sensibilities. She very nearly turned on her heel in that moment, forgetting what she had achieved only the day before
in securing the invitation to Wistfield on his behalf and re-
linquishing any desire or claim to his hand in marriage.
She might have left instantly had he not, in that moment,
caught sight of her and called to her.

"Come, hither, Miss Piper," he said, pulling the kerchief
below his chin. "Though I can see by your disdainful countenance that I have offended you, I promise you that what I
am engaged in is but a little honest labor, hardly a crime."

She saw an answering contempt in his eyes already reflected in the sarcastic mode of his speech and she felt her
temper, as always in his presence, prickle the very roots of
her hair. In this moment she utterly detested Sir Roger
Mathieson. Indeed, she despised everything about him and
wished him to the devil. "I have no intention of speaking
with you in this environment. Have you no decency at all?
You are not even properly clothed."

"I am wearing a shirt and breeches, and if you were lifting this sledgehammer time and again, believe me, you'd
strip down to your shift as quick as the cat could lick her
ear."

She sucked in her breath, her anger reaching new
heights. "How dare you!" she exclaimed hotly. "Of all the
vile, wretched men on earth, without the smallest degree
of sensibility or understanding, you are quite the worst."

She suddenly wished she were a man, that she might
challenge him to a bout of fisticuffs, and by the sudden
flaring of his nostrils thought he was in that moment of a
similar mind. Suddenly, he tossed aside the heavy hammer
as though it had been a dry stick, whisked away the kerchief from about his neck, and began marching toward her.

She began backing up uneasily at his approach and felt
a measure of panic slide through her. At the same time, her

gaze was caught by his thin, linen shirt, soaked with sweat and open halfway down his chest. She could see a soft mat of black hairs covering his sun-bronzed skin.

She felt very dizzy suddenly and short of breath. Even in a state of relative undress, he was remarkably handsome. His face, though partially covered in stone dust, had a chiseled appearance, with strong lines slanting across his cheeks and jaw. His blue eyes blazed with fire, and she felt oddly as though she was seeing a vision from another time and place, a fierce clansman descending on her in a state of Celtic wrath. She understood now why Emperor Hadrian had built a wall across the breadth of northern England in an attempt to keep the Scottish Picts from razing English towns, villages, and farms.

She lifted her hands as though to protect herself, to ward him off, but he advanced on her steadily nonetheless. She knew an instinct to turn and run, but she could not seem to get her feet moving properly.

"What are you so afraid of?" he barked, laughter and anger mingling in his expression. "Most of the men on earth dress in this manner to do their work and are proud of it. If you are to be my wife, you will see me in less than this in a few weeks' time, eh? Or did you come here to tell me your mission is utterly hopeless and Madeline Piper of Fairlight Manor in the parish of snobbish little Chilchester has quit before she has even begun?"

She was not certain which of his words startled her more, that he spoke of his worldly experiences, which reminded her of how little she knew beyond her own small Society, or that in his venomous counterattack he had just made it clear how very little he thought of her, of her abilities, even of her persistence. She knew her mouth had fallen agape, but she could not draw it shut—just like Pelworthy Castle's drawbridge, which she knew to be rusted permanently open.

"Just as I thought," he sneered, turning his back on her, and dismissing her with a flip of hand. "Return to your flowery bedchamber and pen your tidy letters to your aunts and cousins and friends, practice your pianoforte, paint in your watercolors and whatever else you do with your time. I have work to do here."

She gave herself a shake, her intention of leaving having been dismissed entirely. Did he think to be rid of her so quickly, so easily? Then he knew very little of her. He might be a beast of a man, but she at least could show him what it was to be civilized. Besides, she knew her worth, even if he did not.

She watched in silence as he returned to his station and retrieved the sledgehammer. He began whacking at the stone with a vengeance, his kerchief still in a small heap on the floor. Whatever he thought of her, there was one thing she could see they shared in common—she set up his back as easily, as quickly, and as thoroughly as he set up hers.

Somehow this realization calmed her, and her thoughts fell into order. She began walking toward him, watching the dust from his labors rise and swirl before the two lanterns.

She drew her own kerchief from her reticule and held it to her mouth.

When she had reached his side and he, deigning to notice her approach, had lowered his sledgehammer, she said, "I hope we might be able to set aside our quite substantial differences of opinion for a moment to discuss a matter of business. Will you at least speak with me for a few minutes?"

He paused for a long moment before finally nodding, his expression grim.

"I came to tell you that I was able to procure an invitation for you as well as for Lord Anthony to Mrs. Crawley's soiree tomorrow night."

At that, he frowned heavily. "You did what?"

She drew in a deep breath. "I gave your requirements a great deal of consideration yesterday and felt that the best course would be to apply first to Squire Crawley for his help and support, since he has great influence in Chilchester. Naturally, I did not relate the particulars to him and, as a gentleman, he did not press me for information. He mentioned that he felt our neighborhood was not quite up to snuff and in the end, despite what proved his wife's fervent opposition to your presence in her home, agreed to the scheme." She could not help but smile a little. After all, she had slain her first dragon in the form of Mrs. Crawley and in this moment, with Sir Roger's mouth unhandsomely agape, she felt a very nice measure of victory. "Do you mean to say nothing?"

"I—we—Lord Anthony and I are to attend Wistfield tomorrow night? Have I heard you correctly?"

"Yes. I am certain a written invitation will be forthcoming shortly. Mrs. Crawley, whatever her reservations, would not be backward in such an attention."

He sneered his disbelief.

At that, Madeline straightened her shoulders as the dust settled a little more on the surrounding stones. "She may not approve of what her husband has agreed to, but she will do what is proper, since his assent has been given."

"I suppose I will have to trust you in this."

At that, he tilted his head slightly and leaned on his sledgehammer. "Had you shown me this much courtesy, Miss Piper, any time before the present, I vow I should have tumbled violently in love with you. I will not pretend that I am not astonished at what you have already accomplished."

"Did you think me without resources?" she inquired, sensing the depth of his ill opinion of her.

"Yes, I believe I did. If that is all, I shall return to hammering at my stones."

He started to lift the sledgehammer again, but she caught his arm. "I have not finished. There is more." Here, her heart began pounding loudly in her chest and she wondered just how he would accept her forthcoming confessions and requests. "I fear I have told a whisker or two in order to support my sudden shift in position where you are concerned, and I was wondering if it would be possible for us, once we are wed, to give a ball at Pelworthy sometime during Michaelmas to which we would invite the Earl of Selsfield. Naturally, for the present, you would be giving the ball, since our betrothal is to remain a secret for a time, but it would be quite helpful if you happened to drop a hint or two tomorrow evening." These words, which she spoke with considerable assurance, nearly made her swoon. They were full of certainty of their marriage and of his acquiescence to what was a quite presumptuous request. She rather thought he would laugh at the absurdity of it all rather than confirm they would one day be husband and wife.

"Good God," he murmured, losing hold of the hammer completely. The handle landed with a loud thump on the stone floor. "Have I heard you correctly? A ball at Michaelmas to which Lord Anthony's father is to be invited?"

"And his wife, siblings, whatever you desire—or did you think that once we were wed, I should not desire to offer an appropriate number of entertainments to our friends and family? After all, I will be the mistress of Pelworthy Castle and Lady Mathieson as well. Much will be expected of both of us."

For the first time in her acquaintance with him, he seemed truly confounded. "I had not thought," he stammered, "but I suppose a Christmas ball will do. As for

Lord Selsfield, I suppose he would be willing to attend, but that can be settled at a later date."

"And Lord Anthony? Would he be willing to join you at Wistfield tomorrow night?"

"Yes, of course, unless he has a previous engagement of which I am not aware. He is as fond of Society as I am."

"I hope he will, for I daresay there will be more than one hopeful lady present tomorrow night who will want to make his acquaintance. There has always been a great deal of curiosity fixed on him in general. Will you do this for me, then? I know it is grievously presumptuous on my part, but if it were known that there would be a ball, it would do quite well, for instance, in softening the lacerated sensibilities of Mrs. Crawley."

"I fear I do not give a fig for Mrs. Crawley's sensibilities."

"But you would wish your wife to be comfortable, would you not, Sir Roger?"

At that, he once more seemed stunned and answered with a mere nod of his head.

"Then may I consider the matter settled?"

"Yes," he responded, although it appeared he had been struck by his own sledgehammer.

Finally, she smiled. "Then I thank you, Sir Roger." She wondered if there was anything else she needed to discuss with him, but nothing came to mind. "I know that we have had our difficulties, but I hope we will do better."

"I, too," he responded quietly.

She had meant to bid him good day but instead she found herself caught by his thoughtful, if slightly perplexed, stare. After a moment, though she really did not know precisely how much time had passed, a slow smile overcame his features. A dizziness invaded her senses, though she could not quite understand the source of it. With a start, however, she realized she had felt the same way when he had kissed her atop the curtain wall. She became aware yet again of his sun-bronzed chest and the powerful muscles beneath his shirt which allowed him to heft the oversized hammer as though it was a feather. She knew the strangest impulse to remain standing where she was forever, or certainly for the next few minutes, in hopes that she might be able to watch him raise the hammer overhead once more and bring it slamming against the stone.

"Is there something more?" he inquired softly, taking a small step toward her. His smile grew broader still.

She shook her head. "No," she murmured, hoarsely. "I suppose I should leave you to your labors."

At that he grinned, gave her a knowing look which caused a blush to rise on her cheeks, then turned to retrieve the hammer.

Once more, she held the kerchief to her mouth and began slowly backing away. She watched the hammer rise and fall, the sound almost deafening in the underground chamber. How strong must a man be to heft such a weighty tool? she wondered. Goodness, very strong, indeed!

Finally, she gave herself a shake and turned on her heel. Perhaps there was something to admire in a gentleman's physical prowess. However, he never should have had the servant bring her to the dungeons in the first place. That had been rude beyond permission.

She straightened her shoulders, content in her principles. However, that did not in the least prevent her from taking one last glance at Sir Roger before she began her ascent, a circumstance that caused her to feel dizzy all over again.

Saturday morning, Madeline had been gathering raspberries for over an hour in a particularly pretty tangle of wild vines to the south of Fairlight when one of the servants sought her out, quite red-faced and out of breath.

"What is it, James?" she inquired. She thought with horror that some accident had befallen her father. "Is Mr. Piper well? Grandmama? My sisters?"

He was gasping for breath. "S-sorry, miss. Everyone is well." He gasped another deep lung full of air and continued haltingly, "The house, miss, is overrun, I fear."

"Mice?" she asked, startled anew.

"Nay, miss. Gentry."

She stared at him and understood immediately what had happened. "Worse yet, I see."

The servant, a man in his thirties and quite quick witted, burst out laughing, then immediately schooled his countenance and murmured an apology.

Madeline began trudging back to the house, ordering her thoughts and practicing her speeches yet again. When she reached the drawing room, she was not surprised to find no less than ten personages of some influence, if not rank, present in her home and glaring at her with no small degree of disapprobation.

Her father, she noted, sat in the wing chair nearest a decanter of sherry and though it was not yet eleven, was sipping happily, a broad smile on his lips. She realized that he was delighting in all this nonsense and felt suspicious suddenly, though of what she could not precisely say.

Her sisters each bore a different expression. Charity appeared as though made of stone, Prudence regarded her with compassion, and Hope's eyes were dancing.

The delegation of the local gentry was led by no less a personage than Albinia Rockingham, her daughter, Julia, and her son, Harris. The latter was one of Madeline's most ardent suitors. Presently, he stood beside his parent, his features stormy, as usual. Of all the young gentleman of her acquaintance, none was so opposed to Sir Roger's presence in the valley as Harris.

The usual contingent flanked Mrs. Rockingham on both

sides—their hostess for tonight's soiree, Mrs. Crawley; her stodgy son, James; and her two daughters, Mary and Cressida. Only Randolph was lacking, but since he was of a rebellious nature and thought most of Chilchester society ridiculous in the extreme, it was not to be expected that he would join his family on such a call as this.

In addition to the Crawleys, Captain Richard Bladen, Pamela Spight, and John Calvert had arrived to add their voices of dissent. The last personage present, however, was the only one to truly unnerve Madeline. Sylvester Gilbert was present and, as heir to Viscount Lord Cottingford, every word of today's conversation would be related to Lady Cottingford, whose prestigious harvest ball was the very reason she had kicked up such a dust in the first place.

"Good morning," she called out cheerfully as she entered the drawing room, fortifying her nerves by turning away from Mr. Gilbert. "I am sorry to have kept you waiting, but I was picking raspberries in the southern pastures. To what do I owe the honor of such an unexpected, yet of course welcome, visit?" She smiled hopefully, but there was such a dreadful quiet permeating the entire chamber that her heart began pounding in her chest. This was not at all propitious.

She took up a seat opposite Mrs. Rockingham, who puffed her massive bosom quite ominously and whose brown eyes had taken on a painfully severe expression. "I believe you know very well why my family and I have come. You have given us a shock, my dear! A dreadful shock! I only wonder that you sit there so composed, as though nothing untoward has happened, particularly when you know very well that you, and you alone, have been the cause of that northerly pollution now threatening to descend on the entire valley." She drew in a powerful breath. "Naturally, I have come here to put a stop to it at once!"

In this moment, Madeline cursed Sir Roger anew. How

dare he force her into such a wretched predicament? She had been perfectly willing for the sake of her family to relinquish all of her Society forever in order to right their fortunes, since that was what appeared to be required of her in begging for Sir Roger's hand in marriage. Now, however, with his present demands of social inclusion, she was forced to endure a great many palpitations. He was the cause of this, not she, and yet she must continue. She glanced at her father, who encouraged her with a nod and a dip of his chin.

She met Mrs. Rockingham's hard stare, fully cognizant of the fact that she was the next lady to whom she had meant to apply to help gain Sir Roger's entrance into Society. She had not thought she would face her second dragon so soon, particularly when the first was still quite well and standing firmly beside her in the form of Mrs. Crawley.

Ordering her thoughts, she recalled her rehearsed speech to mind and began. "Though Sir Roger is of an unfortunate parentage, in truth his mother was English, and by that circumstance alone he does have a claim to certain permissions among us. Recently, I have had the opportunity to view the present refurbishments of Pelworthy and must report that his most recent efforts include transforming the dungeons into a vast wine cellar." Here she paused, for her conscience was prickling her mightily—again. When, she wondered, would her prevarications end? "I understand he has already ordered hundreds of bottles of wine from France for his forthcoming Christmas ball, which it has also come to my attention that Lord Anthony's family and quite famous and well-connected father intend to attend. I felt that any oversight might be seen as a grievous offense. Perhaps I should have applied to you first, Mrs. Rockingham, and in that I now see that I have erred, but it would seem Squire Crawley and his wife have been most gracious in opening their hearth and home to our newest neighbor."

Since these statements, littered with falsehoods, were received with many intakes of breath and small cries of astonishment, she felt she had accomplished her first objective, which was to shock her audience.

After a stony silence, Mrs. Rockingham finally responded, "I don't give a fig what his potential connections might be. I know the man to be ungentlemanly and a veritable brute. The last time I saw him on Chilchester's High Street, for instance, he had the audacity to ask me if I would mind if he wore his kilt to the next assemblies!"

For some reason, this made Madeline want to smile, for she could conceive of nothing that would have set up this lady's back more quickly than what she suspected had been delivered as a rather roguish remark. She bit her lip rather hard, however, to keep her amusement from showing. She also wondered if he intended to wear his kilt this evening and thought she might be wise to pen a note advising him against any such thing.

"So you find all of this amusing, do you?" Mrs. Rockingham cried, rising to her feet.

"No, indeed, ma'am, I do not," she countered quickly, also leaving her chair. "I beg you will not go before having a cup of tea."

The crowded chamber began to bustle in signs of departure, but Mrs. Rockingham for some reason seated herself again. "A little tea would suit me perfectly. As it happens, I have not yet breakfasted, having been entirely overset by Mrs. Crawley's news."

Madeline smiled. "And Cook prepared one of her famous lemon cakes, which I know you to enjoy. Would that be welcome to you?"

"Yes, thank you."

Madeline met Charity's gaze and nodded to her. However much her next eldest sister disapproved of her current efforts involving Sir Roger, she was also precise in matters of housekeeping and quit the chamber to see to the tea and cake herself.

With so many unexpected visitors and a corresponding number of teacups to assemble, it was not surprising that within a few minutes, a parade of Fairlight's servants appeared to set up the tea service and dispense the cake in a speedy manner. This interlude had the benefit of allowing Madeline a few minutes to collect her thoughts.

Once Mrs. Rockingham had eaten half her cake and had begun sipping a second cup of tea, Madeline felt inclined to broach the subject again.

"I do appreciate your concerns. Indeed, I most certainly do. Until very recently, until I learned that Lord Anthony's father would descend upon Pelworthy Castle at Christmastide—yes, it is true—I had thought I would never be called upon even to speak with Sir Roger, let alone beg for invitations on his behalf. As his nearest neighbor, and with the full support of my father"—she let these last words settle upon her father's shoulders as the entire assemblage turned to glare at him—"I felt compelled to begin the process. Was I truly wrong in doing so, ma'am?"

Mrs. Rockingham turned from Mr. Piper to Madeline and huffed her displeasure again several times. Since each huff was punctuated with another bite of lemon cake, her countenance soon appeared to grow rather mollified.

"I begin to comprehend your extraordinary conduct, Miss Piper, but you were wrong to begin the business before discussing it with those of greater influence and experience. As for Lord Selsfield's supposed impending appearance at Pelworthy, that remains to be seen. For the present, for the sake of propriety, Squire Crawley's invitation cannot be rescinded, but please do not broach so important a subject with any of the gentlemen again. They do not have the same understanding of such matters as we do." Here she glanced at Mrs. Crawley, who nodded fervently in agreement. "As for Sir Roger, should he be of a pliant, obsequious countenance this evening, then we can settle precisely to which of the lesser events he could be invited. Should he prove otherwise, I promise you my doors will be permanently closed to him, the Earl of Selsfield or no!"

With this pronouncement, she clattered her cup on her saucer, settled both with a loud thump on the table next to her, dabbed her lips with her linen napkin, and rose to her feet. Those still drinking their tea were forced to gulp the remainder. The traveling court had been brought to an abrupt conclusion, and there was no doubt Mrs. Rockingham believed the departure of the entire party to be requisite in this moment.

Madeline released a very deep sigh as she, too, rose again to her feet. She could not remember the last time that she had ever been so happy that a guest had departed her home before, except perhaps a month past when Sir Roger had first offered for her and in her temper she had thrown a clock at his head.

As the party began filing out, Harris Rockingham and Captain Bladen drew her aside.

"M'mother was beside herself, Miss Piper!" Harris cried. "You can have no notion! Thought she would have a fit of the hysterics, but all she could say was, 'And you hope to marry this ridiculous girl?' I said you weren't a girl but a woman. Still, she would continue ranting about your wretched character."

"You were very good to support me, then, in the face of her disapproval," she responded facetiously.

Her tone was lost on him. His brown eyes bulged alarmingly and he ran a finger just inside his neckcloth, as though the inoffensive white linen had begun strangling him. "That's what I thought," he responded. "But I love you, Miss Piper, as you very well know, and would go to the ends of the earth for you. Only you should not have made Mama so mad."

"And you would not wish to anger her further by keeping her waiting." She offered her hand to him. He took it and, in true puppy-like fashion, lifted her fingers to his lips, with Captain Bladen observing his conduct all the while, and placed a kiss on her fingers. When he appeared rather heartsick and opened his mouth to begin a new speech, she jerked her hand from his. "Good day, Harris."

"Yes, yes, I must go, but I shall see you this evening."

She smiled perfunctorily and watched in some relief as he flourished an absurd bow and quit the chamber.

She turned, therefore, to the third of her most devoted swains. "I hope you were not so badly shocked as everyone else," she offered.

Captain Bladen narrowed his eyes, as though attempting to comprehend every nuance of her statement. He was a calculating man, something that had always troubled her, and yet in every other respect he was her favorite. He had offered for her twice and had made it his object to intervene whenever Harris Rockingham's attentions became overzealous. That he was able to do so without injuring the young man's pride was greatly to his credit, although the significant difference in their respective ages of Captain Bladen's two and thirty years compared to Harris's meager two and twenty perhaps accounted for this power over his younger friend.

"The shift in your attitude was so sudden and so complete," he responded in a low voice, "that naturally I was concerned, even shocked, I must confess. You were not precisely restrained in your previous disapproval of Sir Roger's purchase of Pelworthy."

She sighed, thinking that such a luxury as disapproving

of Sir Roger's ownership of her favorite childhood haunt was receding rapidly into the past. "I suppose I was not."

At that, he laughed. "Miss Piper, you were used to say that you would perish before ever you permitted Sir Roger entrance into Chilchester society."

She felt her cheeks grow warm. Had she really been so harsh? Of course she had, for in those days she felt utterly secure in her family's station and fortune. But all that was gone, and now she must recant as graciously as possible. "It will be of no use to pretend with you," she murmured. "Circumstances over which I have not the smallest control have changed. Though I can say nothing further, it has become imperative to my family's happiness that Sir Roger be brought into the fold, as it were. I hope—I trust—that you will be able to support me in this?"

He seemed utterly shocked. "What has occurred? You have given me the worst suspense."

"I can say nothing at present. Perhaps in time."

"Sir Roger has injured you in some manner," he cried.

"No, no, it is no such thing, I promise you. Oh, dear. I should not have spoken."

"I would have learned the truth at some point. Only why do you keep me in suspense? Why will you not tell me what is going forward, what has happened to have forced you into recognizing Sir Roger when before you would rather have poked out your eye first?"

At that, she could not help but laugh. "Pray, do not press me. It is nothing that many a young lady prior to myself has had to endure, and I promise you the trouble is not to be laid at his door, but on this subject I refuse to say anything more. May I rely upon you to keep our conversation confidential?"

"Of course." He was still watching her and scowling.

"If you do not smile in this moment, I shall pinch you dreadfully," she said.

"Oh, very well. I see that with this I must be content."

"Come, I shall walk you to your horse."

After bidding good-bye to the last of her guests, Madeline went directly to her writing desk and began a lengthy explanation of what had transpired in her drawing room, specifically informing Sir Roger that he was to let everyone in the party know that he intended to turn the dungeons into a buttery and that he must instantly make arrangements to purchase a large quantity of wine from France and also to make certain he had no intention of wearing his kilt tonight.

"Another missive from Miss Piper?" Lord Anthony inquired, having just walked in from the stables, his riding crop in hand.

"Yes, indeed," Sir Roger responded, chuckling. He had not considered wearing his kilt, but now that she had mentioned it, he thought there could be no real harm in it, since he had no intention of making her task easier tonight. On the other hand, he was truly beginning to enjoy the depths to which the proper Miss Piper was sinking in having already told so many whiskers.

"Why are you smiling? You look like a simpleton. Oh, no, no, no!" He turned on his heel suddenly and began to run. From across the chamber, having bounded into the drawing room from the nether regions, Churchill had caught sight of his prey and was now in earnest pursuit.

Sir Roger knew he was being callous in the extreme in not immediately calling his dog to heel, but he waited a very long moment until from the hallways beyond he heard Lord Anthony's muffled plea, "Mathieson, call off your dog!"

"Churchill, come!" A moment later, the contented beast

trotted proudly into the chamber, Lord Anthony's riding crop clamped in his jaw.

The cursing which followed, but which grew fainter after each expletive, told him that poor Lord Anthony was retiring for the present to his rooms.

He was therefore at liberty to sit before his writing desk and to compose a succinct message.

> *Dear Miss Piper,*
>   *What a grand notion. A wine cellar it will be, and consider the bottles ordered. Assuming Chilchester society grows as painfully thirsty as any other at Michaelmas, will five hundred suffice?*
>
> Yours, etc.,
R.M.

He then summoned his valet and ordered his kilt pressed. The Highland regiments serving in the Napoleonic wars had made the appearance of the tartan fashionable in some circles, but not in Sussex, it would seem. He could not help but smile. The expression on Madeline Piper's face—of consternation, embarrassment, and certainly of anger—would be worth every snub he had received for the past six months and would go a long way to atoning for the clock she had thrown at his head.

Four

With the summer sun still rather high on the horizon, Madeline crossed the portals of Wistfield Hall that evening in a state she had never experienced before. She was suffering a profound fit of the nerves, a circumstance completely at odds with her habitually poised and confident demeanor. What was this thing she had done, she wondered, not for the first time since dressing for Mrs. Crawley's soiree. How had it come about she had actually agreed to bring Sir Roger into fashion?

She had gowned herself simply, as was her style, in white beaded muslin, with her golden curls coiffed into a tight ring of braids at the crown of her head. At least in her grooming she felt reasonably certain she would not offend any of the high sticklers, a circumstance which might have served to help calm her nerves, except that one of her sisters had taken exception to her choice.

Hope had met her at the top of the stairs, glanced at her from head to foot, and subsequently wrinkled her nose. "Must you always dress as though you are being sacrificed to the gods instead of attending a night of amusement?"

She had been stunned by her youngest sister's rather severe criticism and had not known how to respond to her. Even her father had nodded in agreement before she slipped her silk cape over her shoulders and stepped aboard the family traveling coach. She had made the five-mile journey to Squire Crawley's home in silence, the chattering of her younger sisters soothing her agitation at Hope's unexpected disapproval.

Now, as she greeted her stony-faced hostess, who was still unforgiving for what she undoubtedly felt was a profound degree of social treachery, she made her way to the drawing room, wondering if Sir Roger had as yet arrived. A quick glance at the numerous familiar faces told her he had not and, quite without thinking, she released a very deep sigh of relief. She realized now that she had been hoping he would not come at all, that he had been only taunting her with the threat of his presence and perhaps had from the first known his acceptance in Chilchester society was as ridiculous as it was impossible.

She was greeted immediately by Cressida Crawley. "Is it true, really true?" she asked, having left her circle of friends to wrap her arm about Madeline's and walk further into the chamber with her. "Do both Sir Roger Mathieson and Lord Anthony intend to come this evening?"

"I believe so," she said, wishing, hoping it was not true.

"I am all amazement, and I must confess quite excited, for I have only seen Sir Roger at a distance when he shops in Chilchester, though I have often seen him driving his curricle along the highway. And as for Lord Anthony, did Hope tell you that I sat very near him in services only Sunday last? He is quite handsome."

"Yes, I believe he is," she responded politely. She drew near the windows overlooking the drive and regarded the enlivened features of her companion. Cressida had light brown hair and lovely brown eyes. She was clearly in a state of excitement.

Cressida leaned very close and whispered, "You should have seen Mama just before our first guests arrived. She was twirling in circles and flailing her arms, heaping every manner of abuse upon Papa's head for having allowed you to beguile him into issuing the invitation in the first place. Papa laughed at her, however, which only served to heighten her hysterics. Of course, you always were one of Papa's favorites. Did you not know as much? I can see by your expression I have surprised you, but if you must know, he always praises you to the skies and even told Mama that if you approved of Sir Roger, he knew he would as well."

"Indeed? He said as much?" she asked, shocked.

"Yes. And there is something more. Mrs. Rockingham sent a note to Mama saying that she would arrive very late and stay but a quarter of an hour, at which time she would take her leave, that she was only attending for the sake of their friendship and that regardless of promises of a ball at Michaelmas, she still had no intention of recognizing Sir Roger or his exalted house guest."

Madeline's heart sank. None of Cressida's revelations gave her much hope at all. "These are not glad tidings," she said.

"No, indeed." She glanced past Madeline's shoulder, her gaze becoming fixed at some object on the drive. "Oh, dear," she murmured. "And I can see there is worse to come. Do but look, Miss Piper!"

Madeline whirled about and gave a small, startled cry, for there, just descending an elegant coach, was Sir Roger wearing a kilt.

"Oh, my," Cressida murmured in a very odd tone.

Madeline watched him in stunned silence, taking in the sight of the leather shoes, the thickly knit stockings worn to the knees, the plaid kilt, an unusual belt which she believed was called a sporran, the dark blue coat worn without tails, a matching plaid sash, a white neckcloth and shirt, and on his head a small blue cap with ribbons dangling behind.

He did not immediately approach the house, but rather moved in the direction of the horses and spoke with his coachman for a long moment. Behind him, Lord Anthony finally descended the coach, looking very dashing in a black evening tailcoat, pantaloons strapped beneath his shoes, and a finely tied neckcloth.

Beside her, Cressida sighed. "He is even more handsome than when I saw him in church and I must say, Madeline, Sir Roger looks quite magnificent. Do you not think so? I visited Scotland once. The land is ever so pretty but quite rugged. Does he not appear as though he has just emerged from the highland mists?"

Madeline stared very hard at Sir Roger, and for the oddest moment thought she heard the cry of distant bagpipes. She did not know how it was, but even though the Scottish kilt was as far from breeches as a man could wear, there was something quite warrior-like, even formidable about Pelworthy's current resident knight in this moment. There was certainly nothing squeamish or nervous in his demeanor. He stood tall and proud as his coach ambled in the direction of the stables and he began his march to the front door, the first of Chilchester's many bastions he meant to breach in the coming weeks. She felt dizzy, just as she had in the dungeons, as though the mere sight of him had some inexplicable charm over her. The sound of ancient battles, English and Scottish, resonated in her ears. What had her father said only that afternoon—that the English had banned the kilt in 1745, an act later repealed, with the intent to suppress the Scottish spirit. This spirit, she thought as Sir Roger disappeared beneath the portico, could never be suppressed.

A moment later, a shrill cry was heard coming from the entrance hall.

"That sounded like Mama!" Cressida exclaimed.

Mary Crawley burst into the chamber and shouted, "Sir Roger is wearing a kilt, and Mama fainted!" The look of excitement on her face made it perfectly plain to the entire assemblage that she was not in the least in fear for her mother's health. The chamber erupted noisily as some of the guests moved swiftly in the direction of the entrance hall, while the rest expressed their wonder both at the fainting of Mrs. Crawley as well as the decision by Sir Roger to have challenged Chilchester society so boldly by having worn his kilt in public.

Only a handful attempted to enter the hall, the rest remaining discreetly in the drawing room to await events. During these few minutes, the previous sight of Sir Roger began to dull in Madeline's mind, and instead of seeing images of his strong figure sporting a kilt, she began to see the unnerved body of Mrs. Crawley lying prone on the planked floor of that good lady's entrance hall.

All her former ire toward the Scotsman rushed over her again. She had specifically requested that if he owned a kilt to refrain from sporting it this evening. She knew his intelligence to be far too great to have either forgotten or dismissed the request. Therefore, only one meaning could be attributed to his betrayal of her simple petition. He had worn his kilt for no other purpose than to set up her back, thinking it would be both amusing to him and infuriating to her to ignore her instructions.

She moved away from the drawing room window, easing toward the deeper recesses where she would not be so easily seen when he entered the chamber. Harris Rockingham drew up beside her just as Sir Roger and Lord Anthony appeared upon the threshold.

"Unforgivable!" Harris cried beneath his breath.

Madeline glanced at him and saw that he was scowling, his gaze riddled with sword points as he glared at Sir Roger. "I could not agree with you more," she responded.

"M'mother will fall into a decline at the mere sight of him," he said, shaking his head. "I only wish you had allowed me to guide you. Now do you see how mistaken you were in inviting him here?"

Madeline withheld the biting remark poised on the tip of her tongue. Harris Rockingham, a full four years her junior, was ridiculous in most settings, particularly when he played the part of a suitor with claims upon her. In this moment, however, she felt ready to scratch his eyes out for even attempting to puff his chest at the expense of her pride.

Returning her gaze to Sir Roger, she watched as Squire Crawley, dignified in his powdered wig, introduced Sir Roger and Lord Anthony to the assemblage one by one. Sir Roger bowed, smiled, and was all politeness. How hypocritical of him to be civil now when he had all but ruined the entire party by wearing his kilt.

She found she was grinding her teeth and gave herself a shake. It would not do to be quite so furious upon greeting him, for he would likely sense her temper and exploit his advantage over her. Instead, she schooled her features and when at last the trio arrived before her, she was able to smile primly upon him.

"How do you do, Lord Anthony, Sir Roger. A pleasant evening, is it not?"

"Quite," Lord Anthony responded with a broad smile. "Only I hope Mrs. Crawley is feeling better. The entrance hall was rather hot. This room is much more comfortable."

To this innocent speech, she nodded in response, but turned and lifted a brow to Sir Roger.

The squire was quick to interject, "My wife often faints when she becomes overheated, but she is with her maid now and I have little doubt she will return to us shortly."

"Is there anything I might do?" Madeline inquired, feigning innocence.

At that, the squire smiled. "I believe you have done enough"—he lowered his voice—"but I do not mean to complain, for I have not had so much fun in years."

To his credit, Sir Roger pretended not to comprehend the squire, and for that she felt he was at least attempting to behave as he ought. How much worse had the gentle-men triumphed together over Mrs. Crawley's sufferings, however absurd they might be.

He then introduced his youngest daughter. Cressida, quite full of her youth and innocence, addressed Lord Anthony. "I saw you in church Sunday last. You were wearing a brown coat."

He turned to her and nodded. "I was? Can't remember, precisely."

"You were. I remember because there were deep notches cut in the lapels."

"Yes!" he returned brightly. "Now I recall quite to perfection. Mathieson called me a dandy because of them."

"Oh, no, not a dandy," Cressida said in an adorably sincere fashion. "Not in the least, for you did not wear clocks on your stockings or sport a dozen fobs. Papa says this is how one can tell if a man is a Pink of the Ton."

Lord Anthony, still addressing Cressida, began telling her of the Green Man and how this gentleman had taken to wearing only the color green in every aspect of his attire, which prompted the squire to bow politely to their group and move away that he might attend to his other guests. After a few minutes, when Cressida offered to show Lord Anthony her mother's recent purchase of a Broadwood Grand pianoforte, Madeline found herself alone with Sir Roger. Indeed, she was grateful for the opportunity, since she had two or three words she desired to offer him, just a strong hint or two on the subject of decorum and honor.

"In the future," she whispered harshly, "I shall expect to be warned when you mean to wear your kilt or anything else of a Scottish nature."

He appeared to ponder these words. "Odd. I cannot think of anything else, or was there something specific you had in mind? Bagpipes and my woolen nightshirt, perchance?"

Madeline lifted her chin to him. "I suppose I ought not to have expected any great degree of propriety or even consideration from you."

"Because I am Scottish?" he offered helpfully.

"No, because you are the most odious, provoking gentleman I have ever known."

"Why, this is progress," he cried, appearing quite elated. "Did you indeed just call me a gentleman? Somehow I had the strong impression that the terms 'Scotsman' and 'gentleman' were entirely incongruous in your thinking."

"I might not have thought so before making your acquaintance, but I am presently convinced of it."

He pressed a hand to his heart. "You wound me, Miss Piper. Indeed, you cannot know how dreadfully."

"Oh, do stubble it. Here is one of my sisters, who happens to think it high time you entered our Society. Prudence, have you met Sir Roger?"

"No, I have not, but I am happy to do so now."

The introductions were more formally applied, after which Madeline drew away from them both and sought out a large bowl of punch, where she received a cup from Mrs. Crawley's maidservant.

She sipped the tea and lemon concoction and wondered if it was possible Mrs. Crawley had added rum to it, for it did not in the least taste innocent. It was, however, quite good, and she remained near the punch bowl for some time, until she became aware that the maid was sighing over and over. When she glanced at her, she saw that she was staring at Sir Roger.

"Are you of Scottish heritage?" she could not help but inquire, albeit secretively.

"No, miss," she responded softly. "But I do so love a man in a kilt. I do not know what it is, but he is that handsome anyway, Sir Roger is, and I must say . . . oh, but I should not."

Madeline turned into her slightly to keep the conversation from being overheard. "Go on. I am all curiosity."

The maidservant hesitated, but only a moment. "He has a nicely turned leg, as me grandmama was used to say."

At that, Madeline choked on her punch and moved away. How strange to think that a single man should evoke so varied a response from everyone he met. Glancing anew at Sir Roger, in particular at the hem of his kilt, she had to agree with the maid. He had a nicely turned leg, indeed.

Mrs. Crawley eventually returned to her soiree, if not nearly so steady on her feet as was usual for her. Madeline noted that her arrival was somewhat unpropitious, for at that moment Sir Roger was surrounded by some of the gentlemen and relating an anecdote which caused the crowd to burst into a brief shout of laughter. Mrs. Crawley could not have been content to learn that her abhorred guest was actually being quite properly received and enjoyed.

For herself, Madeline was relieved on this score. Having not been much in company with Sir Roger, she had no true knowledge of his manners. It would seem that whatever his flaws of birth and, to some degree, breeding, he could at least keep the gentlemen nicely entertained.

Later, after she had just told Harris Rockingham to please not renew his addresses in public, she was a little surprised to find that Sir Roger was this time surrounded by some of the ladies, speaking in subdued tones, smiling every now and then and with whatever subject was at hand, evoking question upon question from his enchanted audience. Passing by, she heard Mary Crawley ask, "And did you actually capture the tiger?"

"Yes, but not without the aid of a hundred servants, two nights without sleep, and several exotic traps."

The ladies expressed their awe in a joint sigh. Madeline walked on, feeling strange again whenever she was presented with some facet of Sir Roger's disposition or abilities. She could not credit that this had been her doing, that he was for the first time venturing upon the fringes of tonnish Society in Chilchester, and all because she needed his fortune.

Later, while she was discussing the progress of Harriet Wisborough's confinement with Mary Crawley, a sudden hush fell over the crowd. As one, the two ladies turned toward the fireplace, where Sir Roger had just bowed to Mrs. Crawley, who in turn began wafting a fan swiftly over her face. Her cheeks bore two bright red spots, and her eyes were darkly hostile.

"Madame," he began politely, "I know that there have been some rumors about a ball at Christmas at Pelworthy, and I wish at this time to announce that these rumors are, indeed, true. Without a mistress yet established in my home, and in particular with the impending arrival of Lord Selsfield at Christmas, I was hoping that I might prevail upon you to offer me your wisdom and guidance as to the general management of the event. Would you do me the honor of rendering me such aid?"

A feather could have been heard to settle upon the planked floors of Wistfield Hall in that moment. All eyes were settled upon Mrs. Crawley, whose color had now receded and who had stopped fanning herself entirely. "You . . . you seek my advice?" she asked, clearly startled.

"Indeed, very much so, unless it would be too inconvenient. The principal rooms will be completed and furnished by that time, but there is so much more to giving a ball than a proper sofa or two."

"I should say there is!" she cried, as one with a great deal of experience.

Madeline watched a war rage over the features of her hostess as well as within every limb. Mrs. Crawley squirmed, wiggled, and shifted in her seat. She sighed, she lifted her eyebrows, she murmured several, "Oh, dears."

Madeline believed she understood her thoughts. Such an honor was not without considerable distinction. At the same time, she would surely offend every high stickler in the valley if she agreed to the request. Yet how could any lady resist the opportunity of meddling so forthrightly in the general affairs of another house, let alone a renovated castle?

Mrs. Crawley's bosom swelled, and it appeared her decision was made. She gestured with her fan to the chair nearest her. "Do get up, Mrs. Spight, and let Sir Roger sit down. We have much to discuss." The obsequious widow, always anxious to please her hostess, fairly bolted from the chair. Mrs. Crawley continued, "So it is true, then, that the Earl of Selsfield, who is known to dine frequently at the Pavilion when in Brighton and at Carlton House when in London, is to grace our valley and your castle? It is quite, quite remarkable . . ."

A general hubbub rose to obliterate the remainder of her thoughts on the subject, but Madeline continued to stare in their direction. She confessed she was utterly stunned that Sir Roger had made so magnanimous a gesture to his hostess, not only restoring peace at Wistfield but solidifying their future relations as well, perhaps even to the end of time. Was there a hostess alive who would not wish to be the guiding force for a ball given in honor of a peer of the realm?

She began to smile, and some of her uneasiness departed. Her shoulders relaxed, and for the first time since her father had told her that she would need to wed a fortune in order to save the Piper family from financial and social disaster, she actually felt hopeful. Perhaps he was not so bad a fellow as she had thought.

She could only smile, however, for Mrs. Crawley would probably not draw breath for half an hour. A just punishment, she thought, for so vile a creature as Sir Roger Mathieson.

While Mrs. Crawley continued assaulting Sir Roger's

ears with dozens of suggestions for a proper ball, he happened to glance at Madeline and received from her an approving nod. His hearing grew dull and his vision became centered entirely on the prim lady now smiling happily. In that moment, he felt his heart constrict almost painfully in his chest. She was never more beautiful than when she smiled thus, and it seemed to him a rare thing for her to smile. He wondered why she withheld her smiles generally. He determined that before the night was through he would ask her just such a question.

An hour lapsed before an opportunity presented itself. He had been observing a game of speculation in which she was one of several participants. Her face had gradually grown quite pink in the heated drawing room, and by the time the game drew to a close, she was fanning herself vigorously.

"I must have some air," she announced, rising to her feet.

Evan Hambledon took up her place immediately, seating himself beside Cressida Crawley.

Sir Roger approached her and offered his arm. "I should be happy to escort you to the terrace. There is, I believe, a cooling breeze from the south just now."

"Thank you," she murmured politely, taking his arm. He thought she seemed embarrassed.

Once outside, he guided her slowly the length of the red brick without uttering a word. The hour was late, the sun had but recently set, and there was a pretty reddish glow on the western horizon.

"Where does that path lead, I wonder?"

"Beyond the gate is an herb garden. The kitchens are not far."

"Take me there," he commanded softly.

She drew their progress to halt. "No," she stated simply. He felt her try to withdraw her arm. "But we are betrothed," he murmured against her cheek, refusing to let her escape him.

"No one knows that but you and me and my father, and even then only conditionally."

"Then if we are found out, I shall permit an announcement to be made so that your reputation is not in any manner sullied. For the present, however, I cannot see how dastardly it would be to take a tour of Mrs. Crawley's herbs."

At that, a smile glimmered at the edges of her mouth.

"Come," he said, knowing by her expression that he had already won the day. "I promise I shall conduct myself properly and you may identify each plant for me, since I am woefully ignorant of the names of the various herbs."

She chuckled, and when he tugged on her arm, she did not resist but allowed him to guide her down the shallow steps, along the path, and beyond the creaking gate.

"It smells of heaven," he murmured.

"Yes, I must say it does. A summer's labor, I believe."

"What is that plant?" he gestured near her skirts.

"Sweet marjoram, and the one beyond is thyme. That weedy creature is parsley, but the delicate, honeyed fragrance so prevalent throughout is woodruff."

He did not allow her to get one word further, but caught her up in his arms and kissed her hard on the mouth.

She resisted and drew back, her hands planted firmly on his chest. "Sir Roger!" she whispered. "You . . . you said you would behave properly!"

"Is it not proper to kiss one's betrothed?"

She gasped. "You are the most incorrigible man," she cried, yet she did not struggle from his arms as he had expected her to.

"You smiled at me tonight," he said, holding her fast, but respecting her wishes. "You smiled at me, and then I remembered why I had offered for you a month past."

She frowned slightly. "Not just because you wished to enter our Society?"

"I would never offer for a lady for such a reason. Do you think me addled?"

"I do not understand. You cannot have offered for me because of my smiles."

"I can think of no better reason."

"Character, sense, fortune?" she offered, staring at him as though he had gone mad.

At that, he gathered her a little more closely to him. "I far prefer my reason, particularly since your smiles are all loveliness."

"That is no reason to offer for anyone," she chided, but her tone had grown very soft.

"Will you allow a kiss, Madeline?"

"I suppose it is my duty," she whispered.

He could not help but smile. "Yes, it is most definitely your duty." He did not ask again, but kissed her gently for a very long time, until he felt her arms relax and drift away from their protective place on his chest. For the moment, he forgot all the unkind things she had ever said to him and reveled in how wonderful she was to kiss. There was a promise of sweetness in her embrace that he knew he would want to taste forever.

Madeline felt herself leaning rather scandalously into Sir Roger. This time, her arm snaked its way about his neck and the former quite tender kiss became something new, something bold and demanding. She did not quite understand what was happening, but a moment later, her knees simply failed her. Were it not for his strong hold on her, she would have fallen into the parsley.

"Oh, I am sorry. I do not know what happened to me."

He was chuckling. "Nor do I."

"We should return to the party."

"No, we should never return. My home is but a few

miles distant—four, I think. I could carry you there in my arms, and keep you forever in one of the towers."

She did not know what to make of him, nor did she understand why such ridiculous words were acting upon her stomach in just such a manner as to make her feel quite deliciously nauseated. It was most astonishing. But even more inexplicable still was the sudden impulse she had to say yes, she would go with him! Really, it was quite remarkable.

"You could not carry me four miles," she countered, pressing gently against his arms and forcing him to relinquish his hold on her.

He allowed her to withdraw from him, but continued to stand very close to her and whispered in her ear, "I could—and I would, if you would but say the word." A spate of gooseflesh traveled at lightning speed down her neck and arm. She drew in her breath. How was it possible that even though he was no longer holding her in his arms, she still felt as enthralled as ever?

"You are being nonsensical," she whispered, wishing suddenly that she could remain in Mrs. Crawley's herb garden for another five minutes—or five days, even.

He brushed a kiss against her cheek. "I am being perfectly rational."

She giggled. She never giggled. She felt young, younger than she had felt in many, many years—eleven, to be precise. Certain memories rose up of a more innocent time in her life and how she had often felt just this way, as though her feet had wings and when she walked it was as though she was running, and when she ran it was as though she was flying. That was before, during the time when her mother had been alive and as the eldest she was the first to be permitted into her mother's world. What a lovely adventure it had been, but only for the briefest of times.

A penetrating sadness began to work in her. Tears started to her eyes.

"What is it? How have I offended you, my dear? I would not have done so for the world just now. Only tell me what is wrong?"

She stared at him, feeling as though she was looking at a specter and not the man to whom she was betrothed, if secretly. Her gaze fell to his kilt, and she took a step backward. What was it her mother used to say, "Proper attire reflects character, taste, and general breeding"? What did a kilt say of Sir Roger?

"We should return within," she murmured turning away from him, but he caught her arm, preventing her.

"Not until you tell me what is amiss."

"I was remembering my mother," she said, lifting her chin. "She died a very long time ago, but there are moments when she returns to me as if her death occurred but yesterday. Can you understand?"

He nodded slowly. "Yes, I believe I do." He was frowning.

"May I return now?"

"Of course."

The short journey to the terrace and to the drawing room occurred in silence. Madeline forced a smile to her lips and as soon as she was able disengaged herself from Sir Roger. She did not know how it had come about that kissing him had led her to become engulfed in feelings of grief over her mother, but so it had. Such sentiments hardly belonged at a soiree, however, so she strove to quickly bury her feelings. She led Sir Roger to Squire Crawley, and within a few minutes the Scotsman was telling his host about the nature of his improvements at Pelworthy. "We are currently rebuilding the south curtain wall with Sussex flint work to match the original. My architect believes the stone to be of eleventh-century work. The barbican is in excellent condition . . ."

She moved away and approached a nearby group, begging to know if anyone would care to join her in a round of whist. Within a few minutes, with Evan Hambledon as her partner, she was happily employed arranging her thirteen cards.

She passed an hour winning and losing trumps, but in the end, she and her partner won enough trumps to have given her a gentle glow of triumph.

Afterward, she rose to her feet, feeling that another cup of punch was in order, when Harris Rockingham approached her. "I will call him out, if you like," he said in an urgent undertone, drawing her aside.

Madeline felt her cheeks begin to flame instantly. Had Harris seen her kissing Sir Roger in the herb garden? "Why . . . why ever would you wish to do that?" she stammered.

Harris rolled his eyes. "Because of his wearing of the kilt, of course. I was never more astonished at the man's effrontery than tonight. My eyes bulged in my head. How could he have insulted our Society as he did? It is indeed beyond bearing, and I will call him out for you, if that is your desire." There was something so childish in his passionate demeanor, in the manner in which he held his hand to an imaginary sword hilt, to the way his brown eyes flashed darkly, that she nearly lost her countenance.

"I beg you will not," she responded quietly but firmly. "He should not have done so, but beyond causing his hostess to faint, it seems to me he has been received well enough."

"Is that what you think? I fear you are mistaken. There are several of us quite willing to put an end to him."

She started. "What? You wish to slay him so that he might not go about in Chilchester society?"

"Good God, no. I only meant to put an end to his mushroom ways." He then waved at John Calvert and Captain Bladen, who both joined them immediately. "I was just telling Madeline that not everyone present is enamored of

Sir Roger and that several of us are willing to thwart his intentions of forcing his presence in our midst."

"Are you forgetting that I insured his invitation tonight?" she asked.

John Calvert, his expression severe, said, "I wish that I might be able to forget it. I, we, simply do not understand what truly prompted you to see that he was invited."

Madeline felt ill of a sudden. She could hardly tell them the truth, and yet in this moment she was sorely tempted, since she could see that though she had already started down this path, the three gentlemen standing before her were prepared if need be to pull her back into her former, more decorous, secure existence—only would any of them be able to rescue the Pipers from their present misfortune?

Captain Bladen was reputed to have inherited a tidy sum from his uncle, which was invested in the funds, so it was possible that he would have the resources to help her, but she did not know the extent of his wealth. John Calvert was remarkably well shod, but she knew his parsimonious disposition and she could not imagine his professed love for her exceeding his desire to keep his pocketbook flush. As for Harris, he would enjoy a very handsome income indeed once he inherited Dallings Hall, but since his parent was a robust gentleman of fifty years whose own father had not paid his debt to nature until he was five and eighty, it seemed unlikely that he would be of the least use in righting her family's fortunes.

As much as she was tempted to join her swains in their protests and wishes to keep Chilchester society as happily insular as it was before, she still felt her best course was to continue with her secret betrothal to Sir Roger. He was, after all, conducting himself admirably this evening, except perhaps for having stolen a kiss from her. But even in that, she could not fault him wholly, since they were engaged—or almost so.

"I am not certain how to answer you, Mr. Calvert, except to reiterate my reasons of Thursday night. He is refurbishing Pelworthy Castle and has already planned a Christmas ball to which one of the most august personages in all of England has been invited. I simply do not see how we can continue ignoring what appears to be his permanent presence in our valley. I have also been given to understand that he is quite well connected in London." Another whisker. Oh, dear. She seemed to have grown a penchant for telling lies almost from the moment she agreed to Sir Roger's terms for their betrothal.

"What connections?" Captain Bladen asked, his brow furrowed sharply.

"I do not know," she responded. "It was merely something I heard from Lord Anthony, I believe."

"That simpleton?" Harris cried.

Madeline bit her lip, for she rather thought that was like the pot calling the kettle black. "Yes, Harris, but you must remember that though he is not quick witted, he has known Sir Roger for a great many years and must by his length of association be acquainted with any number of facets of his friend's life. Until it is proved otherwise, I can only believe what I have been told." She paused, feeling yet again a certain degree of horror that she was beginning to tell her whiskers with such ease. She continued, "There is no reason why Lord Anthony would prevaricate, I'm sure. So you see, I feel under some obligation as my father's eldest daughter and as the nearest neighbor to Sir Roger to welcome him into our Society, or at least to attempt to do so. Would any of you truly ask me to conduct myself differently under these circumstances?"

All three gentlemen scowled, glared, and mumbled their complaints, every now and again turning to grimace at Sir Roger. Madeline caught his eye more than once and saw that he was quite amused with her predicament. Sir Roger already knew of her most loyal court.

"I don't give a fig for how much money he's thrown at the castle, I think he looks ridiculous in that kilt!"

"Aye, aye," the gentlemen intoned.

Madeline sighed heavily and suddenly wished the evening might end so that she could return to her home and retire to the serenity and quiet of her bedchamber. She glanced at Sir Roger again, her gaze sweeping once more over his coat, sash, kilt, and stockings. Her mother's words floated through her head anew, "Proper attire reflects character, taste, and general breeding." Why could Sir Roger have not honored her request that he leave off wearing his kilt altogether?

When Mary Crawley approached their group and begged the gentlemen to play at commerce with her and her mother, Madeline moved to join Cressida Crawley, who was talking in an animated fashion with Lord Anthony. She arrived in time to hear Cressida gasp faintly. "My lord," she murmured, "did you know there is a tear in your pocket?"

"What the deuce?" he cried, turning to his left, lifting his arm slightly and examining the small rent. "Churchill again!"

"Churchill? You mean one of the Duke of Marlborough's family?"

"Sir Roger's horrid dog! Worst beast ever born! Cannot see me without attacking my clothing! Yesterday, he tore my riding crop from my hand. I found it chewed up in the stairwell leading to the east turret."

Cressida's complexion became perfectly white, her brown eyes opened as wide as they could possible be, and a faint cry escaped her lips from behind her hand.

"There! There!" he cried. "Did not mean to give you a fright. He's a good sort, just likes to play and tear at my coats and breeches whenever he sees me."

Cressida shook her head and lowered her hand. "I must confess, Lord Anthony, that I do not like dogs. I know I should not say so, for it seems so wrong of me to even speak such blasphemy, but they frighten me. You can have no idea!"

"Oh, but I believe I do," he said. "Churchill may not mean to rend me limb from limb, but when he is chasing me down a hall—" He did not continue, but shuddered eloquently.

"I feel for you, indeed, I do," she cried sincerely.

Madeline, who would not have disturbed the ebb and flow of this conversation for the world, watched in some fascination as Lord Anthony's expression softened. "We seem to have a great deal in common, Miss Cressida. Noticed it from the start."

Cressida blushed rosily. "Indeed, I begin to think we do."

Madeline drifted away, thinking never had there been so propitious a beginning to a romantic entanglement than in this moment. She wondered what the end of it would be, however. She knew Lord Anthony to be as poor as a church mouse and that Cressida's dowry, quite handsome at twelve thousand pounds, had given rise to the notion in her mother's breast that one day her lovely daughter would make an excellent match. Lord Anthony might be extremely well connected, but he did not have a feather to fly with.

How difficult the entire business seemed to her suddenly. If only she could return to the halcyon days of her innocence and security, when her deepest thoughts were about which sonata to practice on the pianoforte and whether the bonnet she had seen in Chilchester the day before would truly suit her. How desperately she longed for that life, when her mother had been alive and before her father had lost his fortune in Brighton!

Five

Sir Roger, who was standing in a group of several of the gentlemen and listening to Randolph Crawley's description of his recent journey to Paris, let his gaze drift over the guests. Several had seemed to take to him, though he could not help but comprehend that many of those were of a determinedly rebellious nature, like Randolph. Others glared at him whenever his gaze chanced to meet theirs, like the trio situated by the window.

Harris Rockingham was one of the most vocal, never ignoring even the smallest opportunity to snort an insult whenever their paths drew near. Sir Roger was not so green, however, as to be drawn in by such a halfling's ridiculous antics and had succeeded thus far in keeping his countenance indifferent. Beside Mr. Rockingham were two other gentlemen to whom he had been presented this evening, Mr. Calvert, owner of Gumbers Lodge, and a Captain Bladen, who had struck him as a rather deep one, a man he instinctively distrusted. It had not escaped his notice that these gentlemen were the primary members of Madeline's court. If he was in any manner serious in allowing his courtship of Madeline to draw to a successful conclusion, he could only laugh at the men who had already been cut out of the race.

These thoughts naturally led him to wonder where Madeline was at the moment. His gaze found her not far distant, drawing away from Lord Anthony and one of the Crawley chits to stand near her father. He sipped his glass of iced champagne and watched her for a moment over the rim of his glass. How sad she appeared to him, almost despairing—only why? Did she loathe him so very much that she must suffer a depression of spirits because she might become leg-shackled to him?

He was struck with the sudden realization that from the time he had entered Chilchester Valley generally she was not as content as she had made attempts to appear. She was always gracious and smiled politely, as was expected of her, but genuine smiles of amusement and delight were, for the most part, far from her expression.

He found himself intrigued. Why were her spirits so hindered from happier expression and what could he do to encourage her liveliness?

The group about him burst into laughter as the point of Mr. Crawley's anecdote reached its peak. He offered his own smiles, though he had no way of knowing what the subject had been. He was about to excuse himself that he might attempt to engage his prospective bride-to-be in a conversation about her smiles when a bustling at the entrance to the drawing room drew every eye to that location.

He turned as well and saw the imperious countenance of Mrs. Rockingham fill the doorway. He had the impression that were she to speak, flames would leap from her mouth and smoke steam from her nostrils. The entire assemblage fell into servile silence. Some of the younger ladies even felt obliged to offer distant curtsies.

He was at once on his guard, particularly when her hard gaze began a sweep of the guests and, upon finding him, came home to roost. Her brown eyes narrowed and her lips pursed as she took in the sight of his kilt.

Mrs. Crawley hurried to her side, ready to efface herself before so much consequence, but Mrs. Rockingham waved her back. The latter then began a march toward him. Harris joined her ranks, along with her husband and daughter, Julia, all of who followed obediently in her wake.

Sir Roger, amused by the lady's obvious belief in her supreme importance, bowed politely upon her approach.

Mrs. Rockingham glared at him, but did not offer a single word in greeting or conversation. He felt obligated by every sense of self-respect to remain equally silent.

Finally, the lady opened her mouth. "And this is how you would repay Mrs. Crawley, by taunting her in her own home? Is this how you were taught to behave the gentleman?"

"I swooned at the sight of him," Mrs. Crawley added helpfully, once more drawing near.

Mrs. Rockingham raised her hand again, and Mrs. Crawley begged pardon for having dared to interrupt her superior. "I gave you more credit, Sir Roger. I had thought you would know better than to have accepted Mrs. Crawley's invitation. You would have been better served to have refused and so avoided my necessary and quite public opinions on the subject. You have crossed every boundary of decency this evening in having polluted the halls of Wistfield with your presence here."

He could not resist. "Not every boundary, surely?" he inquired innocently.

"Do not dare to defy me!" she exclaimed. "You may have been able to somehow persuade Miss Piper, who is of a hopelessly compassionate and tender nature, to have granted you an entrée into our Society, but she does not have the power to grant your continuance here."

"And you do?" he asked, still feigning innocence.

"Of course I do. There are others, but you will not get far without my blessing, I assure you. I had been willing to allow you some entrance into the less exalted homes in our neighborhood. Farmer Quince, for one, has an occasional party you could attend without giving offense, and I would have been content to guide you in such matters, but the moment I saw your horrid costume, I knew that I would never offer you even this portion of my consequence. No, Sir Roger, you have proven yourself unworthy this evening and I intend to make certain that tonight is the last any of us will see of you. What, then, do you have to say to that?"

He sipped his champagne, intending to give the appearance that he was actually contemplating her tirade. Finally, he smiled and said, "Not a great deal, I fear."

Her bosom began to swell. He wondered just how frequently she employed the puffing of her chest in her attempts to intimidate the weaker of her acquaintance. Seeing the widening of Mrs. Crawley's eyes, followed by several frightened gulps, he knew his hostess had more than once felt the full effects of Mrs. Rockingham's self-bloating.

For himself, he found her ridiculous in the extreme.

"You would speak to me thus?" she cried.

"I wish only to make it perfectly clear that I resent your insults and I think it excessively rude that you have kept your hostess waiting these many hours and more before presenting yourself in what you must have known would have been a most trying situation for her."

"Do not think to turn me aside by accusing me of not knowing how to go on in Society. You are the contemptuous one—wearing a kilt, no doubt to overset us all!"

At that, a smile glimmered on his lips. "Only one," he murmured.

"I do not take your meaning, but if you are referring to me, I promise you, you have chosen the wrong object upon which to play such a prank."

"I was not referring to you, madame."

"I should think not."

He turned to Mrs. Crawley, "Nor you, madame, and I do beg pardon if I have offered you any insult. I do take a great deal of pride in my Scottish roots, something my mother encouraged me to do. I hope Mrs. Rockingham's obvious displeasure will not affect your willingness to help me in making arrangements for the Christmas ball."

"What?" Mrs. Rockingham thundered, turning to glare at her friend. "Have I heard correctly? Have you indeed agreed to be of use to this man?"

Sir Roger watched as Mrs. Crawley's color receded dangerously. He felt it necessary to intervene. "She took pity on me, ma'am," he said. "I hope you will take pity on the entire assemblage and for the moment forget my presence here. There are many guests ready and anxious to greet you."

He then bowed and began to move away, but she would not permit it. "I am not finished with you, yet, Sir Roger!"

"But I am," he responded, once more bowing. His temper had begun to mount. His initial amusement at her demeanor had worn thin quite rapidly in the face of her cutting remarks, and he knew himself well enough that if he did not make good his escape, he was likely to give an unhappy answer to her diatribe. He added in a quieter tone, "You would do well, I think, to let the matter drop for the moment. If you wish, I would be happy to call upon you and discuss anything that would give you pleasure or at least a portion of relief."

"You will never see the portals of Dallings, if that is what you are suggesting. I had heard you were nothing short of an encroaching mushroom, but heretofore I had not thought so badly of you. I saw nothing of the mushroom in you until tonight! Again, I say, you ought to have stayed home. Better still, you ought never to have purchased Pelworthy. When I think of that lovely, ancient dwelling having fallen into your hands, every feeling is offended."

Once more, his ire tickled the inside of his skull. "You have quite said enough," he responded politely and again tried to move away.

"Not so fast, Sir Roger! Let me ask you this: Have you no sense of obligation or decency? Did your mother not teach you the essentials of breeding and manners? Did she not instill within you a basic sense of right and wrong? Would she not in this moment be ashamed of her spawn? But what, then, I suppose could be expected of her, when she had married a Scotsman and forsaken every principle of good breeding herself!"

At that, Sir Roger felt his temper soar into the highest reaches of his spirit and his mind. He turned stiffly back to her. "You may insult me as much as you choose, for I understand to perfection that you cannot help the narrowness of your thinking, but the moment you offer even the smallest slur on my good mother's name, you go beyond the pale. You may take every sour remark you have just uttered to me and stuff it up your creaking corset for all I care. Good night, ma'am." He bowed to Mrs. Crawley, "Good night. You have shown me a great deal of kindness, and for that I shall always be grateful."

He glanced at Madeline and, seeing the stony expression on her face, offered her an ironic bow. He thought in this moment that she resembled Mrs. Rockingham in nearly every particular.

He gestured to Lord Anthony, who immediately offered hurried farewells to his host and hostess.

Madeline watched him go, her mind feeling so stunned that she soon realized she had simply stopped breathing as, she believed, had much of the assemblage about her. His words, the fire of his demeanor as he had confronted one of Chilchester's worst dragons, had shocked everyone into a state of severe silence.

"I believe I shall faint," Mrs. Rockingham suddenly cried, releasing the chamber from its suspense.

Everyone began chattering at once as Mrs. Crawley led Mrs. Rockingham to a chair near the refreshments. She fanned the offended lady and offered her a cup of punch.

Then a curious thing happened. Madeline began to hear snickering and giggling from nearly every quarter. Even one or two gentlemen released loud guffaws.

"Stuff it up her corset, indeed!" Randolph Crawley snorted from somewhere behind her. "Wish I had thought to say such a thing to the old bat the last time she gave me a dressing down in public."

Madeline felt the horror of the situation descend on her in a sudden sweep of mortification. She was the one who had taken the awful pains to invite Sir Roger to Wistfield, and she would be the one to suffer every imaginable difficulty because of it.

"And you see nothing wrong with such rudeness?" her father whispered beside her.

"Nothing wrong?" she cried, also keeping her voice low. "I was never more shocked to hear such words roll from Sir Roger's tongue. How can you even—"

"I was not speaking of Sir Roger, my dear. Believe me, as much as your grandmother and I brangle about nearly everything, I would never tolerate so many public insults from her or any lady, not even from the queen herself! So I ask you, Madeline, is this what you admire in our Society? This sort of cruel attempt at domination that would use a gentleman so harshly?"

She wanted to answer him, but he turned away from her. She was left to stare at Mrs. Rockingham, who was weeping into her kerchief and allowing at least five ladies to minister to her wounded sensibilities. Mrs. Crawley had moved away from her, however. Squire Crawley had taken up a place beside his wife and was speaking into her ear. She could not imagine what he was saying to her, but she had never seen so arrested an expression on Mrs. Crawley's face before.

Madeline felt a strange panic course through her suddenly. Everything was changing. She could feel it in her bones. Tears stung her eyes, and her heart began to race. She did not want anything to change, not again, but so it would seem it had. How? Why?

If only Sir Roger had been able to maintain his temper. He had managed the first portion of Mrs. Rockingham's dressing down quite beautifully. Indeed, Madeline had been struck by his composure, even his indifference to her remarks. In that moment, she had felt rather dizzy watching him square his shoulders and meet the dragon without even the smallest flinching or squirming as so many others had before him. He had even seemed amused and had had the presence of mind to make a subtle reference to her in the midst of everything. If only he had continued and not permitted his sensibilities to be overset. A true gentleman would not have allowed his temper to be touched, even if the memory of his mother had been insulted.

She felt very confused and tired of a sudden. Searching out her father, who had moved to converse with Evan Hambledon, she tugged gently on his sleeve. When he turned toward her, she queried in a low voice, "Might we go home, Papa? This has been a very long day."

"Of course," he responded, but there was little sympathy in his tone. She still could not credit that he had championed Sir Roger over Mrs. Rockingham. Was it possible he saw Sir Roger as more than merely a mode of salvation for his own gaming recklessness?

As her sisters gathered near and as a family they began to depart the soiree, Madeline once more lifted her gaze to her father. His cold expression still surprised her. She glanced back at the assemblage, many of whom were also beginning their departures, and she could not help but think of her own mother, who would have been absolutely horrified at what had just occurred.

Her next eldest sister, Charity, drew close. "I am still so very stunned, Maddy. What do you think Mama would have had to say to such an event?"

"A great deal," Madeline responded on a whisper.

"A great deal, indeed," Charity returned.

Just before she passed from the chamber, she noticed that Harris Rockingham, Captain Bladen, and John Calvert were grouped together talking in an animated fashion. She felt her heart sink further. She knew their thoughts well, that each was in complete agreement with much, if not all, that Mrs. Rockingham had said to her betrothed. She could only hope that their heads would cool and that whatever mischief might be brewing would be squelched with a more proper consideration of events on the morrow.

A few moments later, as her family was quitting Wistfield, Squire Crawley caught her elbow and held her back a trifle. In a low voice, he said, "Do not permit these absurdities to affect your course, Madeline. You are doing a very good thing here."

To say she was shocked was hardly to give an accurate name to the feeling of astonishment which possessed her in that moment.

"But his incivility was beyond bearing," she countered.

"As was hers, though I believe he had the greater claim to feeling wounded. Forgive him, my dear. He is worth a hundred of her, trust me in that."

She did not know what to say, and began to feel as though she was a very small boat in the midst of tall waves which pushed her about from every direction.

"Good night, Mr. Crawley."

"And for God's sake, smile more, my dear. You look like heaven when you do!"

Later, as the coach bowled along the highway in the direction of Fairlight Manor, Madeline wished that her sisters would cease speaking of the evening altogether, of Sir Roger's kilt, of Mrs. Crawley's turnabout in favor of helping him with his Christmas ball, of Mrs. Rockingham's meanness of spirit, and mostly of Sir Roger's horrendous response.

"I still cannot believe he would say such a thing to Mrs. Rockingham," Charity cried, appalled. *"Stuff it up your corset?* It was so crude!"

Hope, however, began to laugh heartily. "I have never heard anything so horrible yet so amusing in my entire existence. I do so hope this does not mean the end of his going about in Society, for I have never been so well entertained."

"Hope, please," Prudence intruded gently. "You forget yourself, and most certainly you forget what Maddy must be suffering, since it was she who saw to his invitation in the first place."

At that, Hope tempered her laughter and offered an apology. "I am sorry, Madeline, if I have overset you." She pursed her lips, averted her gaze, contorted her face, then finally burst out laughing anew.

Madeline sighed heavily. Perhaps had the entire circumstance happened to anyone else, say to Pamela Spight for instance, she could certainly have shared in a little of Hope's amusement. For the present, however, all she could see was disaster looming on the horizon. She would no longer be able to persuade any of the hostesses to invite Sir Roger to an event, let alone either Mrs. Rockingham or

Lady Cottingford. No, it seemed to her that her campaign had been as short-lived as it had been disastrous.

She glanced at her father and shrugged hopelessly. He surprised her by smiling. "All is not lost," he responded, "Trust me in this. Mrs. Crawley will not quickly relinquish her chance to be a guiding force for a ball at which Lord Selsfield is to attend. And I, for one, will do all I can to see that he continues to receive a proper amount of invitations, although I am afraid I will not be able to persuade Farmer Quince to receive him."

Madeline's lips twitched. This reminder of the precise moment in Mrs. Rockingham's speech when she made his worth in her eyes so clear to the entire assemblage brought some of the amusement of the situation home to her. Farmer Quince was a very good man, indeed, but he never offered invitations to the gentry and certainly would never impose on a knight. Mrs. Rockingham had seemed a little addled in having even brought forward the ridiculous notion.

"Notwithstanding your lack of position with Mr. Quince," she said, "I am not so sanguine as you."

"You never were," he responded.

Madeline was surprised. "What do you mean?"

"You tend to take a dark view of everything, m'dear, and I wish you would not. I loved your mother very much, but she was of a similar disposition, and it was not her happiest quality. Sir Roger erred, there can be no two opinions on that score, but if you think half that room has not wished to say something of just that sort to Mrs. Rockingham, then you know nothing of the matter."

"But the point, the entire point, Papa, is that he spoke the words. In this, he proved himself to be ill bred."

"Ill bred!" her father shouted, causing all four of his daughters to stiffen in their seats. "The man was sorely provoked. Truth is, I should have said something to stop her. If you must blame someone, blame me for not having had the courage to tell her to go to the devil the moment she began her absurd speech!"

The Piper sisters gasped as one.

"Papa!" Charity murmured, aghast.

Prudence shook her head. "I wish that Mrs. Rockingham had not spoken so unkindly."

Hope, who was seated beside her father, slipped her arm about his and smiled up into his face. "Randolph called her an old bat!"

At that, Madeline bit her lip as her father burst into loud laughter.

Madeline watched her father for a long time. She thought that for a man who had lost his fortune so recently, he was more relaxed and happier than he had been in many, many years. She realized she knew very little about him, after all, and that she could hardly in this moment comprehend why he was not more distressed over his circumstances, particularly since the evening's events, regardless of his opinion, had all but obliterated his present chances to see his fortunes restored. No, she did not understand him at all.

She turned her gaze out the window, and watched the hedgerows light up, then fade from view as the coach lamps moved by. She could not imagine just what was to be done now to win Mrs. Rockingham's support when Sir Roger had all but ruined the possibility of that good lady ever forgiving him.

Sir Roger glared at his friend. "Would you please stop laughing?" he cried.

Lord Anthony was holding his sides and laughing in an almost hysterical manner. "B-but you have no idea! Sh-she looked as though you had slid a sword between her ribs!

Thought I would perish, indeed I did! *Stuff it up your corset!* Oh, dear God!" He was off again, laughing so heartily that tears poured in rivulets down his face.

Sir Roger chuckled. He could not help himself. He had lost his temper and made a complete fool of himself, besides offending every lady present and undoubtedly giving half the gentlemen at the soiree sufficient reason to call him out. He would otherwise have been quite content with the evening, since he had accomplished his first object, to steal a kiss from Madeline, and had had the additional delight of making the evening uncomfortable for her as well. The cold, disapproving expression on her face after he had quarreled with Mrs. Rockingham ought to have justified his conduct completely, only he could not revel in it. He had hurt her terribly, yet did she not deserve such ill treatment? Had she not insulted him as badly as most of Chilchester society?

Still, he could not rest in his victory.

As Lord Anthony's tears ceased to flow and his laughter subdued to on occasional chuckle, and as the coach began its plodding ascent to Pelworthy, his own thoughts drifted into the past.

He was reminded of having been in a coach with his mother many, many years ago, nearly three and twenty years past now. He had accompanied her on a visit to her aunt in a neighboring town ten miles distant from his own. The conversation had grown heated, and the subject, as usual, was the unyielding position the family had taken against her husband, Major Angus Mathieson. No matter how many victories he had enjoyed in the early years of the war with Bonaparte, his success could never overcome her family's abhorrence that Louisa Romney, of the Romneys of north Sussex, had actually married a Scotsman.

That particular day, she had left her aunt's home, restraining the tears which had started to her eyes. She had been calm at the beginning of the journey, but he knew her, that she had held one last hope that she might be able to return to the Society in which she had been raised, and that hope had been crushed.

"For the boy," she had pleaded. But Aunt Phillips had remained implacable. Neither of them had seen the Romneys since. His mother had died some seven years past.

The feeling which had been generated in him in that moment had remained to this day, an overwhelming need to revenge all his mother's hurt on such prejudice wherever he found it, even if it dwelled in the woman he had desired to make his wife.

As the coach finally drew to the front door, Lord Anthony quickly stripped off his coat.

Sir Roger thought it odd. "Why ever are you doing that?" he asked, laughing.

Lord Anthony shrugged as the footman opened the door and he descended the coach. "I am in no mood to be chased by your dog. I shall simply give him my coat and be done with it."

Sir Roger, jumping to the cobbles slung an arm about his friend's neck. "Tonight, I shall be before you, my friend, and shall call Churchill off before he has even begun. I owe you that much."

"What for?" he asked, craning his neck to look at his friend.

He released Lord Anthony. "For losing my temper this evening and exposing you to every form of ridicule this valley will undoubtedly heap upon my head, and thereby yours, through no fault of your own."

"I don't give a fig for that!" he cried. "You are my friend. She was damned insulting. Even I understood that much."

"You might not be so forgiving, Tony, if Wistfield's doors are closed to you forever."

"Eh, what's that?" he asked, suddenly appearing distressed.

"Thought as much," Sir Roger cried. "You are quite taken with her, are you not?"

His whole countenance softened like a bowl of porridge. "Pretty little thing. She hates dogs."

As the front door opened, Churchill's growl could be heard.

Sir Roger nudged Lord Anthony. "I wouldn't say disparaging things of the canine species of the moment," he whispered. "If Churchill takes it as an offense, even I may not be able to help you."

Lord Anthony's eyes opened wide, and regardless of Sir Roger's promises to be of use to him tonight, he extended his coat toward the faithful mutt.

Sir Roger took hold of the coat, called Churchill to his side, and not another growl was heard.

"Looked like a fish," Lord Anthony said, as the trio began their ascent to their bedchambers.

"Churchill?"

"No, Mrs. Rockingham, when she came the crab. Never seen eyes bulge like that. Thought they would pop right out of her head!"

At that, Sir Roger laughed outright. "You, my friend, have always known exactly what to say to me."

"Yes, I have," Lord Anthony responded.

Sir Roger cast a quick glance at him. He oftened wondered if there was a glimmer of brilliance in his friend that did not generally appear. In this moment, if he did believe what he said, then there was more to his friend than he had ever truly comprehended.

Six

On the following morning, Madeline awoke slowly, her mind caught between dreaming and waking so that she was acutely aware of the dragon Sir Roger had set upon with but a sword and shield in hand, astride a magnificent black horse. Part of his face had been painted with a bluish hue and his black hair had grown very long, like his horse's mane. He wore only his kilt and a loose muslin shirt. Even his feet were bare. Back and forth he battled the great beast, calling out incomprehensible challenges, his countenance lit with a fury she had heard was peculiar to the Scots. The dragon was a red and gold monster, breathing fire and roaring like a furious wind. She was surprised that he was not in the least afraid. Indeed, he seemed almost taunting in his demeanor.

A final bold slash and the dragon fell hard to the ground, flames extinguished, smoke curling from quiet nostrils. Sir Roger was not even injured, not the smallest bit, she marveled as he wheeled his horse toward her. A moment later, she was in his arms and he was kissing her quite furiously. But the kiss ended abruptly and a moment more he was laughing, astride his horse again, and racing off into the clouds.

Only then did Madeline's eyes open. Only then did she realize she had been dreaming. How real it had all seemed, the colors, the sounds of the beast, the feel of Sir Roger's lips on hers. She sat up and touched her lips, thinking and wondering. She had the same sensation she had experienced last night when she had realized that everything was changing without the smallest heed for her wishes.

She drew in a deep breath very slowly and calmed her nerves. She had been agitated since the terrible events of the night before, especially by her father's words on the return trip to Fairlight. Later, she had fallen asleep concerned that he viewed her as a lady who always saw things in a harsh, unforgiving light, for that was how she interpreted his use of the term "darkly." Did he possibly know how his comments affected her?

She folded her hands on her lap and stared at her fingers. She was six and twenty and unmarried, an apeleader by most standards. She was mistress of Fairlight Manor; all the servants deferred to her arrangements and sought her opinion even before her father's. When her mother had died so unexpectedly of a putrid sore throat, she had stepped into her shoes and cared for the manor, as well as all three of her younger sisters. She had become a sober young woman, certainly not given to frivolous activities or thoughts, but she hoped she was not so serious as to fail to enjoy a variety of things.

Besides, how could her father be so unkind as to lecture her about seeing things "darkly" when he was the one, through his wretched gaming in Brighton, who had cast the family into the most desperate straits possible? She thought it most unfair of him.

Yet even in light of these reflections, which ought to have been of some comfort to her, she could not be at ease. Sir Roger had asked her why she did not smile more. Even Squire Crawley had said something of a similar nature.

She felt such ruminations, however, to be of little effect and decided it was time to quit her bed and begin her daily routine. She rang for her maid, then returned to her bed, where she began slowly unbraiding her long blond locks. Her thoughts had become suddenly fixed on Sir Roger again, on the way he had appeared in her dream and how she had felt watching his efforts in battling the dragon. She had felt in awe of him in that moment and something more, something she could ill define.

At the same time, an inexplicable fright descended on her, like a cold sea wave washing over her. Her heart increased its cadence and she found it difficult to breathe. She could not keep the kilted image of Sir Roger, sword in hand, an expression of triumph on his face, from sweeping from through her mind. She struggled to find her breath and to keep it. What had her dream meant, truly, and why was she suddenly so fearful?

When a scratching sounded on her door, she jumped. She pressed a hand to her chest, realizing that her maid had arrived. At least the presence of her abigail would serve to divert the incomprehensible thoughts pummeling her brain. As her maid began arranging her coiffure into the familiar pattern of a loop of braids at the crown of her head with a few scattered curls about her face, she could not help but frown. What was it Hope had said to her only last night? *Why must you dress as though you are being sacrificed to the gods?*

She was not so prosaic nor so sour in temperament as all these comments seemed to bespeak, surely. Regardless, after she was presentable, she meant to seek out her father. She may have become confused about many things since last night's debacle, but of one thing she was perfectly certain: she could not wed Sir Roger no matter how great his fortune. Bringing him into fashion was a hopeless task, and even Lady Cottingford herself could not manage so monumental an object.

An hour later, she found her father playing at billiards. He smiled broadly when he saw her, his green eyes dancing as they usually did. "I see your expression. You've grown out of patience with me and mean to ring a peal over my head."

"What nonsense is this?" she cried, forcing a smile to her lips. Perhaps everyone was right. Perhaps she should smile more. "I did need to speak with you on a matter of some import, but not to come the crab, I promise."

He slung his cue and the balls clacked against the sides of the table. "You relieve my mind excessively. But how do you go on? Did you sleep well last night? My dreams chased me from midnight until dawn, and I must confess I woke up feeling as though I had wrestled with a bear."

Madeline thought of Sir Roger and the dragon, but decided it was best not to share anything of such bizarre nature with her parent. "I slept well enough. Indeed, I feel quite rested." Since her knees had begun to quiver, she thought it best to plunge on and bring forward the pricklish subject of her need to be married. "I was wondering, however, if you would not mind discussing our, er, difficulties. After last night, I have concluded that, regardless of the enormity of Sir Roger's fortune, I could not possibly marry him. His quarrel with Mrs. Rockingham precludes it, of course."

At that, Mr. Piper stood his cue upright and straightened his shoulders. "Do you mean to quit before you've begun? Yes, yes, I know his terms were rather harsh, but nothing you cannot manage, of that I am certain. Good God, Madeline, when you were but a chit of sixteen you took hold of the reins of Fairlight and brought us safely back to the stable. If you could do that, I have every confidence you could bring one handsome, if a bit surly, knight into fashion."

"But even you must admit that he all but ruined his chances of being invited anywhere by quarreling with Mrs. Rockingham."

"I did not say your task had not been made the more difficult, but I will always maintain that Sir Roger was badly
provoked."

She did not wish to entertain his arguments again. "Be
that as it may, I have been thinking that I might apply to
Captain Bladen. He is come into a snug inheritance, if all
the rumors are true. It is even bandied about that he is
preparing to purchase Maresfield House."

Mr. Piper leveled his cue again, took aim, and struck another ball. "I am persuaded the size of his fortune has been
exaggerated."

"It is numbered at over a hundred thousand in the
funds."

"He is a man of expensive tastes, Maddy. Have you not
seen the fine tailoring of his coats? And I vow I have not
seen a man in possession of more snuffboxes than he. I am
persuaded he would not like to give up his fortune, even
for your sake."

She wished he would not speak so crudely of his losses,
or even so indifferently, particularly when it was her future
which had been tossed into the wind because of it. "I
would at least like to apply to him," she offered. "With my
dowry, we are in need of less than thirty thousand pounds."
Her heart gave a hard squeeze as she spoke the dastardly
figures into the air.

He pursed his lips. "I will not permit you to quit your
campaign with Sir Roger, at least not yet."

"But I am persuaded I cannot love him," she stated
firmly.

"Now, puss, don't go lifting your chin to me. Besides, I
know you're telling a whisker. You've been head over ears
from the moment he first came to Chilchester."

Madeline blushed fierily. "It is no such thing, Papa!" she
exclaimed. "Oh, how could you think anything so vile?"

"Vile, you say," he countered. "Let me tell you, I should

welcome such a son-in-law into my home any day of the week, and should he develop even a particle of affection for you, I should think you would congratulate yourself one day out of two for your good fortune. He's not a man to settle for any of these weak little kittens we have about Chilchester. No, indeed! So why he has taken a fancy to you, I'll never know. Not but that you didn't have a great deal of spirit when you were a child, but now—"

"Papa!" she cried. His words had stung her deeply.

He tossed his cue onto the green baize and quickly rounded the table. "There, there! I did not mean to hurt you." He embraced her fully and she settled her cheek against his shoulder.

"But you meant every word of what you said," she mumbled into his brown coat. "Is that how you see me? A weak little kitten?" She drew back and looked into his eyes.

She saw the answer and felt ashamed, then suddenly withdrew from him. "How can you say any such thing to me, when I have borne all that I have borne these many years and more? Do you think I cherished the notion of having my girlhood obliterated in the wink of an eye? Do you think I relished the opportunity of speaking with Cook every day for the past ten years about menus and Mrs. Linch about linens and servants? Do you think it pleased me to talk to my sisters every night the way Mama was used to do when all I could think was how much I needed her? I will not permit you to call me any such horrid thing. If there is weakness, what of your recent ramble through Brighton's best houses, where you lost all that had been given to you?"

Far from offending him, as she had thought her heated words might, a slow, crooked smile twisted his lips. "I stand corrected in every essential."

"Then I shall go to Captain Bladen at once."

"You cannot," he cried as she turned toward the door.

She lifted her chin. "And why ever not?" she demanded to know. "It is what I wish."

He pursed his lips anew. "Because . . . because I told you a Banbury tale about the amount I lost. It is quite nearer to, well, twice the figure I originally confided."

Madeline's jaw fell slack and a sickening dread fell over her. "Twice!" she exclaimed.

He lowered his gaze and hung his head. "I fear it is true."

"Papa," she murmured, horrified. "You wagered more than even our estate is worth?"

He nodded, still not lifting his eyes to her.

"Oh, dear God," she mumbled. She could not discuss the matter further with him and quickly left the room. She was too shocked, horrified, and angry beyond words to even look at him. He had all but forced her into her present predicament with Sir Roger.

As she continued down the hall, she seriously considered returning to the billiard room and of telling him she meant to become a governess on the instant and that he could bear the burden alone of having disgraced his family so completely. However, she chanced to pass by the drawing room in that moment and saw three heads all bent over their various projects, Charity and her needlework, Prudence transposing a ballad into a more suitable key, and Hope pressing leaves she had collected near Balfriston yesterday.

She understood her duty all over again and addressed her sisters in her composed voice. "We will be leaving for services in an hour."

"Yes, Maddy," three voices intoned.

She moved on, her pace slow, her temper diminishing to a flicker. She would not complain in her spirit, not for one more moment. She was not the first young miss to have faced such a difficulty, nor would she be the last. Sir Roger it was then. She could only wonder what her mother would have thought of seeing even one of her daughters reduced to such stratagems and prevarications.

At noon, Sir Roger stood on the bottom step of the dungeons, his coat slung over his shoulder. He had come here with the intention of hefting the sledgehammer two or three hundred times in order to provide some relief for the aggravation he was experiencing. But as he glanced about the dark chamber, he saw not half-crumbled walls and dust drifted everywhere, but row upon row of wine bottles, hundreds of which he had been told to begin ordering immediately from France.

He could not help but smile. He gave Madeline Piper credit for that much. She had succeeded in opening at least one door to him, although she had done so by making use of a whisker or two. Of course, he had done his best last night to seal that door shut again, so perhaps he would not have to order the wine after all.

Realizing that he could not begin smashing another wall just yet, he turned around and began to mount the stone steps.

He regretted sorely his cutting remarks to Mrs. Rockingham, even if she had deserved every word. He had gone beyond the pale and had in that respect used Madeline very badly indeed. Though he had tried a score of times to assuage his conscience where she was concerned, he could not. Maybe a part of him desired her to feel the weight of societal disapproval, just as he had over the past several months, but still he could not be content. He felt obligated, perhaps because he had a certain affection for her, to make amends. But how?

Once descending the hill from the castle keep, he set his feet in the direction of Fairlight Manor.

When he reached the bridge which crossed River Fairlight, the southern boundary which separated Pelworthy from Mr. Piper's manor house, he caught sight of a young lady just rounding a bend in the lane, emerging from a thicket of shrubs surrounding an old elm. He smiled suddenly, for it was Madeline, sporting a pink bonnet and wearing a white summery frock. Had she read his mind? Did she know that he needed quite desperately to offer his apologies?

Watching the dirt lane as she was, she did not see him until she lifted her eyes. She stopped as one startled. Then, with a determined settling of her shoulders, she advanced toward him. He frowned, wondering yet again about her. He confessed he did not comprehend her in the least. Presently, she was as sober as a vicar on Sunday morning. Had she come to ring a peal over his head?

"Good morning," he called to her as she drew near.

"Sir Roger," she returned in blunt acknowledgment.

"Have you marched this way in order to give me the dressing down I so severely need?"

At that, she met his gaze fully. She seemed surprised. "Is that why you think I have come?" she countered, eyeing him carefully.

"You would have had every right to do so."

She shrugged faintly and turned away. She walked slowly to the apex of the stone bridge and looked down into the creek. "There are some trout here, if you have a fancy for a little angling."

He followed after her, not taking his gaze from her face. "You have not answered my question. I shall therefore ask another. Why are you so blue deviled?"

Again, a faint shrug. He felt a tug of annoyance. "I quarreled with my father," she said. "I had wanted to end my arrangement with you and had intended upon approaching Captain Bladen, but it would seem my father was not as forthcoming about his debts as he ought to have been at the outset, and Captain Bladen does not possess your wealth, unfortunately."

"I see. So you were unable to be rid of me."

She groaned faintly. "What a wretched business this."

He turned to stand beside her and let his gaze flow along the stream's length. In scattered places, a rock topped the water's surface and created a ripple in the otherwise smooth flow. When she remained silent, he said, "I was on my way to Fairlight just now. I meant to offer my apologies for my conduct last night. I am, I fear, particularly sensitive about having my mother's memory insulted in any manner. But I placed you in an intolerable situation. That, Madeline, I regret infinitely. Will you forgive me?"

He glanced at her and met her troubled gaze. "I suppose I must," she responded softly.

He could not help but smile crookedly. "Ah, yes, in seeking my fortune, I daresay you believe you would be required to do so."

Finally, a glimmer of a smile appeared. "No," she said with a sigh. "Because you are contrite and because . . ."

When she did not speak he watched her closely. He saw her lips twitch. "Now you must tell me your thoughts for I can see that they must be quite wicked in nature."

"You must promise to say nothing," she said.

"Upon my honor," he responded, intrigued.

Her eyes began to twinkle, a circumstance which served to catch his heart in a light clasp. "I have never seen Mrs. Rockingham so astonished in my entire life," she confessed. "There was a rather devilish part of me that could not be sorry for your sharp words. I fear she has deserved them forever."

At that he grinned. "Then I am not sorry I spoke." He

watched her for a long moment. The bridge was shaded by more ancient elms and dappled light played over her face as a breeze shook the uppermost leaves. "So I am forgiven?"

"Of course you are," she said, moving along the narrow bridge, heading to the opposite side. "I only wonder what you must think of me. I never thought to be forced into such a relationship with any man, and in truth I do not know precisely how to go on."

He drew up on the outside. "You had hoped for love."

"Of course."

"As had I."

At that, she glanced at him sharply. "Then why have you accepted my terms? You are not so old that you could not afford to delay marriage. I daresay you would likely tumble in love if you were sufficiently patient. Perhaps not here in Chilchester Valley, but you could increase the likelihood by spending more time in London or some of the watering holes—Brighton or Bath, for example."

"The London ladies did not please me."

"Now you astonish me. How could they not, when they represent the fairest of our island?"

He slung his arms behind his back. "Because London truly is a Marriage Mart, and I had no heart for the business."

"Yet you offered for me."

He chuckled. "But that is different. I liked your smile, when you chanced to offer it on those rare occasions."

She sighed in frustration. "You have described me, Sir Roger, as though I am always in the mopes, and I promise you I am not."

When she reached the end of the bridge, she turned down the path which led beside the stream. He followed along happily. He knew the banks well, that there was much beauty to be found nearby.

"Not in the mopes," he said. "You just seem so serious much of the time."

"I suppose I am. It comes from having become mistress at Fairlight long before I ought to have . . . if ever, in truth."

He continued speaking to her in this manner and learned much about her. When she grew comfortable in his company, she spoke of the death of her mother and the subsequent difficulties of assuming so responsible a role as she had, when previously her greatest concern had been the perfecting of scales on the pianoforte and her French lessons.

In turn, he shared with her many of his experiences in India, those at least that he could recount to a lady, and had all the pleasure of seeing her expression become as animated as her questions were pointed and articulate. When the stream began to widen and the land lost its shelter of elms, she suggested they turn back. As he did, he saw a horseman on the rise well beyond her, a stationary soul he believed to be watching them both. Of this, he said nothing to Madeline.

Returning back up the path, she asked, "Tell me of your mother."

"Do you truly wish to hear of her?"

"Of course," she returned sincerely.

"Very well. First, she was a brave woman. She married for love, never expressed the smallest regret because of it, but sacrificed all social happiness in having wed a horrid Scotsman." He watched a faint blush mar her cheeks. "So you have had that thought, eh?"

"Shall I spare your feelings, sir?"

"I beg you will not. Ours may be an unusual courtship, a rather daring one in some ways, but I want you to speak the truth to me, always."

"I see your mother's bravery has descended to you."

He chuckled.

"Yes," she confessed. "I did think you a horrid Scotsman, especially for having worn your kilt last night when I expressly asked you not to."

"I wore it *because* you asked me not to."

"I ascertained as much at once. I was as mad as fire, as well you know, but I shan't make that mistake again."

"I am found out," he admitted.

She laughed. "You are not so boorish as I had thought you might be, but I suspect you could be, so I promise I shan't give a fig if you pretend to behave the boor a thousand times over the next three weeks, for in that I do know the truth."

"You are a delight, Miss Piper."

"Do you mean to begin making pretty love to me?" she inquired.

He glanced at her and grinned anew. "I fear were I to attempt even the smallest line of a poem, you would bite my nose off. No, I shall simply hope that you will one day accustom yourself to me sufficiently so that we do not quarrel very often. I begin to think this day's ramble an excellent beginning."

She turned into him slightly. "And you are still set on Lady Cottingford's harvest ball? You will not relent in that?"

"Indeed, I will not relent," he stated firmly. "My children, *our* children, will be included in Chilchester society. Nothing less will suit me."

"Is that why you offered for me, then? Because you believed I could give you the entrée?"

He knew it would be completely unwise to confess more, so he nodded. "It is."

Once more, he saw her lips compose themselves into their former prim line. He was beginning to understand her a little.

"Very well," she said. "But first, Mrs. Rockingham's picnic. Oh, lord, how shall I ever manage that?"

On an impulse, he caught up her hand and placed a lingering kiss on her fingers. "I have every confidence you will manage it to perfection."

Seven

For two days, Madeline fretted about just how she was to achieve her most pressing object of obtaining an invitation for Sir Roger and Lord Anthony to Mrs. Rockingham's picnic. She turned the matter over in her mind a hundred times, whether brushing out her long curls at night, reading through the day's correspondence, or walking to Chilchester with her sisters.

On Tuesday afternoon, she chanced upon Mrs. Rockingham at the milliner's, but received so cold a stare that she knew even to commence the process of gentling the older woman's temper was a complete impossibility. Indeed, with such a beginning, she felt certain Mrs. Rockingham would not have a single word for her until Christmas had come and gone some five months hence.

This would not do, and yet she could not conceive of just how she was to finagle the critical invitation.

By Wednesday morning, she was feeling quite desperate. So much depended upon her success in this matter that her nerves were growing quite frayed with all her worrying. She was even considering approaching her grandmother for help. Mrs. Piper held tremendous influence in the valley, even though she did not go about much in Society. Still, one word from Eleanor Piper would be enough to set everything to rights, even with a recalcitrant Albinia Rockingham.

However, knowing her grandmother's staunch prejudices

against all foreigners—and to her a Scotsman was a foreigner—she held little hope that an appeal would be of much use.

Later that afternoon, she was reviewing the current state of the linen with Mrs. Linch when she received word that Harris Rockingham had come to call. A shot of hope burst through her, and she all but ran to the drawing room. Harris! Of course!

Caught in the grips of his calf-love, she felt certain he would be willing to help her, even though he had already expressed his severe disapproval of Sir Roger's presence in Chilchester.

Just outside the drawing room, she stopped, took a deep breath, and forced a smile to her lips. With a broad step, she swept into the chamber. "Good afternoon, Harris. What an excellent surprise! I had not thought to see you all week because of your mother's picnic."

"I stole away," he confessed, approaching her hastily in order to greet her. "How beautiful you are this morning, my dear Madeline."

At that, Madeline swept her hands behind her back. She felt certain if given the smallest encouragement he would to take them both up in his and plant wet kisses over her fingers, a circumstance she could not allow. "Do sit down and tell me what has brought you here."

"You, of course," he said fervently.

She first made as if to take up a seat on the sofa, but immediately thought better of it. Harris, seeing her first intention, was quite in her way, however, and jostled her as he first sat on the sofa, then rose abruptly when she moved the other direction. She felt his foot on the hem of her gown and heard the rip before she could balance herself.

"I do beg your pardon!" he exclaimed. "How clumsy of me! Have I ruined your skirts?"

"It is of no consequence, and it was entirely my fault. I

remembered at the last moment that I had strained my back and the sofa is not at all comfortable." She settled herself in a wing chair and gestured for him to sit opposite her. He did so readily, but his color was heightened from having torn her gown.

"I cannot conceive how I could have been so stupid," he cried. "Forgive me, Madeline? Perhaps there is something I might do to make amends. Shall I have a bolt of fabric sent from Chilchester, or London? Yes, perhaps I should go to London and search the shops on New Bond Street for just the right fabric."

She laughed. "It is not necessary. I shall give the gown to Charity, who, as you know, is famous for her ability to ply the needle. I beg you will not give it another thought. Besides, there is a favor I would ask of you, a very important one."

"Anything!" he exclaimed.

She drew in another deep breath. "I wish you to invite Sir Roger and Lord Anthony to your mother's picnic," she declared boldly.

So many expressions crossed the young gentleman's face in quick succession that she felt as though she was watching a violent wind pass through a tree. Every second which passed brought forth a new configuration of his features. He appeared to be shocked, disgusted, and quite angry, all the while frustrated that he had all but given his word to her and now must break it. "What you ask is impossible," he cried, rising hastily to his feet. He began marching to and fro, holding the hilt of his imaginary sword. "That man, that cretin, cannot be allowed to cross the sacred portals of Dallings Hall. It would be blasphemous!"

"Blasphemous?" she asked innocently, but her lips were twitching. Fortunately, her young swain was too occupied by his marching to take note of it. "I see. You fear your mother's wrath, then?"

"My mother's wrath? No. Yes. No. That is, you have not considered nor have you heeded any of my warnings against that fellow." He stood before her, his complexion enflamed. "He is not a gentleman, and someone ought to give the deuced fellow a hint!"

Madeline held her tongue. She wanted to warn him against ever uttering such an opinion in Sir Roger's presence, but restrained herself. Nothing would be served to begin brangling with Harris on the subject.

Instead, she offered to ring for some tea.

When he accepted, appearing nonplussed by her civility, he once more resumed his seat. She rose, gave a tug on the bellpull, and began speaking on indifferent subjects until a maid arrived. She made her request, and the servant departed. Madeline turned back to Harris, determined to keep the tenor of the conversation innocuous. "Is that a new coat?"

He looked down at the burgundy velvet and smiled faintly. "Weston," he stated proudly. "Can't say as he cared for the fabric, but the cut is perfection. A little buckram in the shoulders"—he cleared his throat—"that is, Weston wanted to puff me up like a Bond Street beau, but I said, 'No buckram, my good man.' He had to consent, of course. No one like Weston."

"So I have heard." She continued in this vein until all signs of apoplexy had disappeared from Harris's forehead. Only after two cups of tea had been enjoyed did she approach the subject from an entirely different direction. "Why is it, do you think, that your mother's dislike of Scotsmen is so great?"

He was quite at his ease now and shrugged. "She was in love with a Scotsman once," he said. "At least, that's what I've been told by my aunt. Of course, her good sense warned her away from him. After all, she could not have truly loved the man. Her brain must have suffered a momentary lapse, like a horse kicked hard with a new pair of spurs."

Madeline could see at once that Harris did not have even a particle of understanding as to what he had just related to her. She had no doubt whatsoever that had Mrs. Rockingham overheard her son's revelation she would have fallen instantly into a decline. Madeline, however, schooled her countenance to one of indifference. "She fears, then, that perhaps Julia might succumb were a Scotsman to inhabit our neighborhood?"

"Precisely. M'sister is something of a ninnyhammer and wouldn't know when she was being bamboozled."

"I see. Then I can most certainly comprehend your mama's abhorrence of Sir Roger's presence in Chilchester."

At that, Harris's brow clouded. "The man should be driven out, forced to sell Pelworthy."

Madeline sighed. Even though Harris had all but sworn upon his honor to grant anything she desired for tearing her gown, she understood now he would never relent where his mother's picnic was concerned.

Harris continued, "Which leads me to warn you against being seen with Sir Roger, as you were on Sunday."

"Seen together?" she queried, mystified.

"Yes, at Halland Creek. You were walking with him, unchaperoned." His complexion began to turn pink again.

Fearing that her swain would once more work himself into a temper, she felt she ought to give him a hint. "I am six and twenty, Harris. I believe I know how to manage myself."

"You are a lady," he cried. "You do not know the danger in which you are placing yourself!"

She withheld a new sigh. "Sir Roger is courting me,"

she stated bluntly. He might as well begin to comprehend
the truth of her situation, even if she was unable to relate
the whole of her family's troubles at present.

At her pronouncement, however, the earth trembled as
Harris set his teacup and saucer aside, rose to his feet, and
assumed the attitude of a prophet. His temper rose once
more, and she sank more deeply into the cushions of her
chair, preparing for the storm to break. She did not have
long to wait, for he immediately set about reading her the
riot act about all Scotsmen, about these wretched cretins
who try to pass themselves off as gentlemen but who secretly mean to seduce innocent young women, about vile
usurpers on English soil who pollute the land by purchasing castle ruins and committing the most heinous offense
of actually restoring them, of men who traipse about in
short plaid skirts so that anyone might have a look at their
knees, and on and on until he had quite literally worn himself out.

"Are you finished?" she asked quietly.

"I suppose I am," he cried with a solid huff.

She rose to her feet and shook out her skirts. "Then I
must bid you good day. I have delayed speaking with Cook
this hour and more, and I simply cannot keep her waiting
a moment longer. If she takes a pet, my father's turkey will
be decidedly undercooked, and that, as you must know,
will never do."

Though Harris seemed bemused by her speech, he did
not offer more than the mildest of protests, so that Madeline was able to usher him from Fairlight without the
smallest difficulty. Once rid of him, she leaned against the
front door and pondered the quite odd revelation that Mrs.
Rockingham had loved a Scotsman in her youth. How intriguing.

A moment later, however, she dismissed this interesting
news. These were Albinia Rockingham's private affairs,

which Harris should have had the good sense to keep private. In other respects, Harris had proven to be not the smallest use to her, and she was left with no great confidence that she would be able in the end to get an invitation to the picnic at Dallings Hall.

As she wended her way to the kitchens, however, she came to a simple conclusion. Though she had no desire to broach the subject of Mrs. Rockingham's wounded sensibilities with her grandmother, she was quickly becoming desperate. If she could on any score persuade Mrs. Piper to help her, these present difficulties would be solved in a trice.

On the following morning, Madeline dressed herself with extra care. Her grandmother was a high stickler, and every hair on her head must be placed properly in order to avoid the censure which would surely follow otherwise. When she informed her father that she meant to call on his mother, an oddly concerned expression crossed his face, but then quickly passed.

"Yes, of course, my dear," he said. "She will be pleased to have you call."

Madeline left wondering why he had seemed distressed, but as she walked the half mile to the cottage in which Mrs. Piper lived, she set her mind to arranging precisely how she was to place her request for assistance before the old dame.

The "cottage" in which Mrs. Piper had resided from the time of her husband's death some twenty years prior was a very fine house of some twelve rooms, in many ways grander than Fairlight proper. The dwelling had served any number of Piper dowagers for the past four centuries and had been built upon the original foundation of the stones of a quite ancient Norman moot hall. Mrs. Piper received guests on but rare occasions, a rheumatic complaint having restricted both her movement and her enjoyment of company generally. Madeline, however, called on her once a week as a matter of duty and form, if not a great deal of affection, a visit which she believed her grandmother relied upon for comfort and information.

Today, however, Madeline was not so easy as she might have been. She had heard her grandmother's views on every manner of societal dictum and could not conceive of just how she was to persuade her to help in bringing a Scotsman into fashion.

She entered the drawing room with a flutter in her stomach and approached the wizened woman of one and seventy years. Mrs. Piper was situated comfortably in a Bath chair and smiled at her. Madeline bent down and placed a kiss on her cheek. Her skin was cool, and a faint redolence of lavender greeted her senses. "Good morning, Grandmama. Are you feeling well today?"

"What a good girl you are, Madeline, to visit me," she said, smiling and patting her hand. "You always were, even as a child, though perhaps a trifle too high-spirited then. But the years have tempered you, and I could not be prouder of a granddaughter than I am of you."

"Thank you," Madeline stammered, surprised by so much unsolicited praise.

"As for myself," Mrs. Piper continued, "I am as well as can be hoped for, given the general creaking of my bones. Ring for some tea, will you, my dear?"

Madeline crossed the room to give a tug on the bellpull, then took up her usual seat near her grandmother.

"A fetching bonnet," Mrs. Piper announced. "And your curls are done just as they ought to be. These new fashions without the smallest semblance of order are a complete absurdity. Did I tell you I saw Harris Rockingham a sennight past while driving through Chilchester? I thought he was a Gypsy, his hair was so hither and yon. Albinia ought to take a stronger hand with that boy."

Madeline refrained from pointing out that Harris was two and twenty and as a young man who had already attained his majority had the right to wear his hair however he wished. Instead, she folded her hands politely on her lap and began the delicate process of waiting for the right moment to place her request before her grandmother. The rather one-sided discourse began, and Madeline focused her attention on the old woman, letting her talk and talk. She nodded politely, made a comment now and then which supported her diatribes, and generally strove to keep her mind from drifting away from whatever subject was at hand. When tea arrived, she prepared her grandmother's cup, then her own, and, after taking a sip, decided the moment had arrived to address the prickly subject.

"I was wondering, Grandmama, if you might help me with a very difficult problem." As succinctly as she could, she addressed her reasons for feeling that Sir Roger and Lord Anthony ought to be brought into Chilchester society, spoke of Lord Selsfield's supposed attendance at what was now a scheduled Christmas ball and added that even Mrs. Crawley had agreed to help the knight in planning the fete. "What I would like to know, therefore, is whether you would like me to take a message to Mrs. Rockingham on your behalf or whether you would like me to pen a note inviting her to come to the cottage and pay a call?" She was trembling at the end of this speech, especially because of the utterly stunned expression she found awaiting her on Mrs. Piper's face.

The very air in the drawing room grew as taut as the grim line of Mrs. Piper's lips. Madeline's heart sank. There would not only be no relenting in this woman today, but no compassion, no interest, no curiosity, nothing. She therefore simply sat back in her seat, sipped her tea a little more, and waited for the impending thunderstorm to hurl

bolts of lightning at her for daring to suggest anything so
vile as to come to the aid of a Scotsman.

Mrs. Piper's fury on the subject waxed long and thor-
ough. She even referred to the battle of Culloden of 1746
as one of England's finest hours and stated the repeal of
the Act of 1746, accomplished heinously in 1782, had
been a dark time, indeed. "Of course when I learned that
that man had so grievously insulted all of Chilchester society by wearing his kilt at Mrs. Crawley's soiree, I was
once more convinced that all tartans should have been
burned once and for all."

Madeline had not heard so much viciousness in a long
time, nor had she understood until this moment the depth
of Mrs. Piper's prejudices. The Scots, of course, were not
her only domain of hostility. The French held a particularly
low place in her esteem, as well.

Preparing herself a third cup of tea just as Mrs. Piper
finally came to the end of her tirade, Madeline was arranging her thoughts as to just what sort of apology might
atone for having made so odious a request in the first place
when suddenly her father appeared on the threshold.

Madeline was about to address him with a smile, even
thinking she had never seen so welcome a sight in her life,
when the cold expression on his face froze the curve of her
lips in place. She could see that he was angry, as she had
never before known him to be angry, but not at her. No, not
in the least. In truth, his gaze was fixed wholly upon his
mother.

His hat, which had dangled in his hand, he flung into a
nearby chair. A moment more and he approached his in-
firmed mother's throne. "Narrow and bitter to the last!" he
cried.

Mrs. Piper had never appeared so small nor so startled
in all the years Madeline had known her. She had ruled her

family with a strong hand, perhaps too strong, it would seem, for this bird had apparently come home to roost.

"Horace, have you lost your senses completely?" she asked. "Whatever is the matter with you, that you would storm in here in this fashion? Did you learn nothing at my knee?"

"I learned a great deal, Mama, as well you know, but nothing so horrid as your own prejudices."

Madeline settled her cup on her saucer, her gaze transfixed on her father, who appeared for the first time in his life to be ready to cross swords with his mother. What she saw shocked her, for in the past her father had always been entirely submissive to the great dame of Chilchester society. She could only wonder what had prompted him at this juncture in his life to give voice to opinions which she did not doubt for a moment had been withheld for a very long time.

Give voice, he did. Madeline watched him stand firmly before his parent and begin in a solemn voice. His complaints were numerous, from his mother's high-handed manner in Society in general to her constant criticisms of everyone around her and in particular to her machinations in his life, the latter of which appeared to hold the greatest resentment for him.

Madeline found herself bemused on several scores. Why at this moment was he giving utterance to his long-suppressed feelings, and why, in particular, had he followed her to the cottage, almost as though he knew what would transpire? In some odd, vague way, she felt that her father was making use of her secret betrothal to Sir Roger for purposes that were not yet apparent. Indeed, her suspicions grew quite profound when she recalled his manners generally from the time he had told her of his gaming losses in Brighton, even until Sunday, when he had forced her again into engaging her bid for Sir Roger's hand in marriage.

Something, she realized, was "rotten in Denmark," but what she could not imagine.

She was startled from her reveries when her father suddenly turned to her. "Come, Maddy, we are finished here."

She rose abruptly, took his arm, and marched beside him as, proudly, he quit his mother's presence.

Once outside and heading back to Fairlight, she attempted to engage him in conversation about what had just happened, but he refused to speak of it.

"I am far too happy in this moment to tell you anything beyond what you have just witnessed. Suffice it to say that my mother's mode of thinking has been outdated from nearly the time I was born. It was high time I spoke the truth to her."

Madeline grew quiet as her father began to whistle happily. He even laughed several times. Once they arrived at Fairlight, he looked about him and said, "Maddy, my dear, I will not be home for dinner this evening."

With that, he headed in the direction of the stables.

"Where are you going?" she called to his retreating back.

"None of your business, my girl. Not yours, nor anyone's!"

On the following morning, Madeline sat before her dressing table, aware of two things: first, that her father was still whistling, for she could hear him in the hall beyond her bedchamber; secondly, that Friday had stolen upon her without giving her even a hint as to how she was to achieve the impossible. How the deuce was she to persuade Mrs. Rockingham to extend an invitation to Sir Roger and Lord Anthony?

Her mind flew in several directions at once, from the astonishing dressing down her father had delivered to

Grandmother Piper to his odd conduct yesterday in disappearing from Fairlight until the small hours of the morning to Sunday's quite remarkable stroll with Sir Roger along Halland Creek. Whatever had been the origin of her secret betrothal with Sir Roger, the events which had succeeded it had thus far been extraordinary indeed.

Upon Halland Creek her mind, however, seemed to wish to settle. She had pondered her conversation with Sir Roger numerous times over the past five days, wondering at the degree of rapport which had existed between them during that leisurely hour. Having brangled with him so many times previously, she still could not credit that they had actually had a civil conversation, one that in several ways had pleased her very much. She had enjoyed hearing his stories of India, though she was convinced he had left a great deal out of several of his anecdotes. She smiled, remembering several awkward pauses in which he would clear his throat and take his discourse down another path altogether. The time had been pleasant, indeed.

And then he had taken her hand and placed a lingering kiss on her fingers. She drew her hand up to her mouth. For the oddest reason, she had thought of that kiss so often, the feel of his lips tenderly against her skin. These thoughts always reminded her of kissing him in Mrs. Crawley's herb garden. He was a powerfully built man, and yet he could be so gentle. Really, he was a most confusing gentleman.

If only he had not insisted upon Lady Cottingford's harvest ball as the price for his hand in marriage. She was persuaded she could accomplish many things by way of bringing him into fashion and certainly could achieve all that he might wish given sufficient time. However, with but two weeks now before the ball, she knew it would be an utter impossibility to gain an invitation without Mrs. Rockingham's blessing, because without that lady's cachet, she would not have the smallest chance of gaining an invitation to Lady Hambledon's fete in a sennight's time, and without attendance at the picnic, which Lady Cottingford always attended, she would not have even the remotest chance of speaking with the viscountess.

No, it was Mrs. Rockingham's picnic or nothing.

She forced herself to think harder and harder. There had to be a way. She would not let her family sink into scandal and obscurity, not with three younger sisters needing good husbands of excellent standing. No, she must get Sir Roger to the picnic, but how?

Her thoughts turned to Harris's revelations earlier, when he had spoken of his mother having loved a Scotsman once. She gasped. A bold plan pierced her brain in that moment, but could she possibly do this terrible thing merely for the sake of an invitation?

Did she have a choice?

No, she would do it, and she would do it now.

She rang for her maid, and within the hour was ensconced within her father's coach and traveling at a clipping pace the two miles to Dallings Hall.

The sprawling Tudor mansion of ancient stone did not lend itself to lightening Madeline's spirits. The dwelling had a dark, brooding aspect which from childhood had always caused her nerves to grow tense and wary. Given her present mission, she found she was frightened as she had never been frightened before. In one sense, her fears were ridiculous, since what could Mrs. Rockingham actually do to her once she heard her request? She certainly would not set her in the village stocks, nor have her flogged publicly, nor hurt her in any other respect. Still, the harm she could do to all the Pipers should she choose war in this moment instead of acquiescence caused even her ears to throb with her misgivings.

Once inside, Mrs. Rockingham received her quite imperiously, her expression smug.

She expects an apology, Madeline thought. For some reason this irritated her and at least a portion of her fears subsided.

The expected civilities were exchanged, inquiries of health and comments upon the weather and at least one cup of proffered tea drained properly. When a second cup had been stirred to Mrs. Rockingham's satisfaction, she said, "To what, then, Miss Piper, do I owe this unexpected visit, or do you mean to be shy with me today?"

"Shy, ma'am? No, I suppose I do not." She paused for a moment, then decided that directness was the only acceptable course. "Let me be very clear about what I desire of you, for it is a request. Would you be so good as to issue two invitations to your picnic tomorrow, one for Sir Roger Mathieson and the other for Lord Anthony?"

Mrs. Rockingham's brown eyes bulged unattractively. For several seconds she was utterly speechless, her mouth opening and closing like a fish cast upon the bank of a river. Finally, she said simply, "How dare you even speak that man's name in my home?"

Madeline had been prepared for a vast show of temper, so she again came directly to the point. "Because he is not the first Scotsman to have offended our valley, is he, ma'am?" She let her words seep deeply.

Once more, Mrs. Rockingham gulped for air. When she could breathe at last, however, she remained silent. It would seem she had understood her hints to perfection.

"I am hoping you will send for your writing materials and compose the invitations at once."

"You . . . you . . . what a dastardly girl you are become!"

"As you say, but I still require the invitations, although I will promise you that Sir Roger will be wearing proper breeches tomorrow, if that will ease your distress. Shall I ring for your maid?"

For a full ten minutes, Mrs. Rockingham sank into herself. When at last she lifted her gaze to Madeline's, she bore a hollow expression of dreams long forsaken. "I suppose you are in love with him?"

Madeline shook her head. "No, but I do hope to wed him."

Mrs. Rockingham frowned. "Why, if you do not love him? Why risk so much?"

For a reason she could not explain, she decided to confide in the older woman. "I do not believe I can speak of all that has happened, but suffice it to say that though I never thought to contract a marriage of convenience, it has now become requisite that I do so."

Mrs. Rockingham was aghast. "Are you saying that your father is in low tide?"

Madeline nodded.

"Good God. I have heard nothing of it. Dun territory, eh?"

Madeline withheld a sigh as she nodded again.

Mrs. Rockingham scowled. "But what of Captain Bladen or John Calvert? Either of these gentlemen would wed you in a trice."

"As I have said, our circumstances are changed."

"As bad as that?" she cried, clearly shocked.

"Worse."

Mrs. Rockingham was silent apace. "Only tell me one thing. How did you hear of my—my Scotsman? No, it is not necessary for you to reveal the source of it. I already know. My son, I fear, is a dolt."

In this moment, Madeline almost liked Mrs. Rockingham.

"Very well. Ring for Graff."

When the invitations had been written, sanded, and

sealed, Madeline took her leave. If behind her she left a quite sobered dragon, all the better, she thought.

She did not return directly to Fairlight, but passed the manor and began the ascent to Pelworthy. Bidding her coachman await her, she was told by a servant near the gatehouse that Sir Roger was in the western portion of the castle, somewhere near the keep, he thought. He said he would find his master at once, but Madeline had a different notion entirely.

"Thank you, but if you do not mind, I should like to surprise him."

"Very good, ma'am."

The servant bowed and Madeline moved in the direction of the turreted keep, which sat elevated on a hill covered in grass and surrounded by shrubs and trees. The keep had always been one of her favorite places, since from the top of the turret a view of most of Chilchester Valley could be enjoyed.

Climbing the rise, she was reminded of how, as a child, she used to pin her arms by her side and simply roll down the hill. She could not help but smile. How many times had she disappeared from Fairlight, run to the castle ruins, and engaged in hours of make-believe? Countless, if memory served.

As she reached the shallow doorway of the turret and began mounting the narrow, winding staircase, she was reminded forcibly of one particular occasion upon which her mother had come to fetch her. She had been but a child of ten—or was it eleven—when she had been pretending to fire arrows from a slit in the turret at an imaginary enemy and her mother had suddenly appeared.

Madeline did not think she would ever forget the stern, angry expression on her face and how she commenced a tirade that had left Madeline shaken and embarrassed.

"You are a young lady fully grown, or very nearly," her

mother had cried. "You should have left off these ridiculous jaunts of yours any number of years ago. I must forbid you from returning to Pelworthy. Do you not see that the entire neighborhood knows of your activities and that you are quite sullying the reputation of our family? The Pipers will never be invited to Lady Cottingford's harvest ball if you continue in this fashion. Really, Madeline, I must forbid it entirely."

Madeline stood on the turret now, a westerly breeze flowing over her heated skin and cooling her in the nicest manner. She had found herself unable to be entirely obedient to her mother and returned to the castle as often as she could without being caught, usually when her mother would leave Fairlight for a sennight's time.

Now, however, with her entire world having been turned upside down because of her father's gambling debts, she no longer thought she need have so many scruples. Besides, she was feeling wondrously victorious in having gotten the required invitation from Mrs. Rockingham. She picked up an imaginary long bow, plucked an arrow from a quiver that would have reached well past her waist, took careful aim, and fired at a shrub near one of the elms by Halland Creek. A man fell, a general cry went up, and the entire host of soldiers retreated in haste as far as the coast some eleven miles distant.

What would her mother say now? she wondered.

She leaned against the cool stone of the turret wall, still facing Chilchester Valley. Something was changing within her, something wonderful, she suspected, though she could not at present comprehend what it was precisely. She felt as though her soul was a caged bird, watching and waiting as a previously locked door began to open slowly. A feeling very much like hope began to rise up within her, but hope for what? In the most desperate sense, she should have felt quite the opposite, since she was all but consigned to the exigencies of a marriage of convenience. Yet she could not be entirely cast in despair. Something, indeed, was changing within her.

These thoughts, so contrary in nature, made not the smallest bit of sense to her, and yet she did not care. She smiled, deeply content as clouds scudded in small puffs across the sky. The blue of the sky beyond was as deep as the ocean was wide, with a delightful wind picking up strength and buffeting her bonnet and gown. She wondered if she had somehow gone mad, if all the pressures of the past several days had suddenly descended on her and bereft her of all ability to reason. She laughed aloud, and her laughter rippled over the turreted wall and down into the thickets, streams, and pasturelands below.

She realized she was happy and that, perhaps, for the first time in a very long time.

Sir Roger heard a woman's laughter and glanced about him in some surprise. The gentle ripples had seemed almost ghostlike in quality as the sounds bounced from the curtain wall to the gatehouse to the keep which he was approaching from the northwest. A stand of shrubs and trees which had grown up quite prettily at the base of the keep prevented him from seeing who or what was the author of such melodious amusement, and the thought that the castle was haunted entered his head not for the first time.

As he drew past the thicket, however, he looked up into the turret and saw the top of a bonnet. He moved backward several feet so as not to be quite so near the keep and he recognized not a ghost, but Madeline. He could not restrain his smiles. So she had come to Pelworthy, she had chosen to climb to the top of the turret before seeking him out, and she was even now standing and viewing the valley below without seeming to care who saw her or heard her.

This was most promising, he thought. Madeline was

breaking the rules of propriety, then laughing in the face of them. Most promising, indeed.

He rounded the base of the keep, that he might have a better view of her face. When he reached the easternmost facet of the turret, he could see her profile clearly. She was smiling as he believed he had never seen her smile before, secret ruminations visible in the expression of her exquisite face. He watched her closely and realized she seemed triumphant, certainly exhilarated.

He pressed a hand to his chest. These were the depths of her which she kept hidden from even her friends, perhaps even from herself. This was what he had seen in her so many months ago, what he suspected resided within her soul but which was kept locked away. If only he could coax this part of her forward so that her prim demeanor might be replaced entirely by so much fire and determination. Such a woman would command all of London, if she wished for it.

He climbed the grassy hill then entered the turret, mounting the steps two at a time. He arrived at the top to be greeted by green eyes that flashed fire and a smile that had come from ages past. He understood in a trice what had happened.

"You got the invitation."

"I did," she responded proudly.

He held her gaze for a long moment and could not seem to stop smiling. Finally, he ventured, "How the deuce did you achieve so impossible a task?" he asked, not holding back even a mite of his present admiration for her.

Her smile broadened until she was actually grinning. She seemed in this moment to be ten years younger, and he could not keep from advancing on her quickly and catching her elbow in his hand. He gave it a squeeze. "Do you also perform miracles?" he inquired. "Although I believe in achieving this you already have. Tell me, Miss Piper, how did you do it?"

She appeared to give his question serious consideration. "I am not certain if I should tell you, for you seem to actually approve of me in this moment and I fear dimming your present enthusiasm by revealing the truth."

He chuckled. "I cannot imagine anything you might have to say at present that would cause me to think less of you."

"Not even blackmail?" she asked, with a toss of her head.

"Blackmail," he cried. "Good God! What form of blackmail? What did you know of Mrs. Rockingham or any part of her family that would permit use of such a terrible weapon?"

At that, she grew even more serious. "I do not think I should tell you," she responded. "Perhaps once we are wed. For the present, I prefer to be quiet on the subject."

"Hmm," he murmured, narrowing his eyes slightly. "Blackmail and discretion, a very intriguing combination. Very well, I shall not press you."

"Thank you," she responded succinctly. She then withdrew the invitation bearing the Rockingham seal from the pocket of her gown and gave it to him.

He took it in hand, shaking his head all the while. "My God," he murmured.

She then looked about her. "You must forgive Mrs. Rockingham, you know, Sir Roger."

"And why is that?"

"Her family was once in possession of most of this land, including the castle, a gift from Henry VIII to one of her forebears. A few decades later, a most imprudent Rockingham opposed Charles II's return to the throne."

Sir Roger let his gaze sweep over the valley. "Then I understand her animosity toward me quite to perfection."

"Indeed, if you mean to keep your word to Mrs. Crawley and permit her to make the preparations for the Christmas ball then you ought, perhaps, to extend some corresponding honor to Mrs. Rockingham. She will have difficulty explaining your presence at Dallings otherwise."

He smiled at her anew. "You, my dear, are quite wasted in this hinterland. Your abilities suggest Mayfair, the courts of Europe, perhaps a diplomatic post. You seem to have been designed for managing quarrelsome parties."

At that, she sighed. "Only promise me to behave properly tomorrow and I shall be content."

"I shall do so most happily, barring any more unfortunate insults against either my parents or my lineage."

"Then I shall trust that once you are seen to be beneath Mrs. Rockingham's societal mantle, no one shall dare."

Eight

On the following day, Madeline moved onto the stone terrace of Mrs. Rockingham's house and placed her gloved fingertips on the balustrade. The afternoon was delightfully warm, a perfect temperature for the numerous events scattered over two rolling acres of lawn, trees, and shrubs. From east to west, her gaze took in a variety of games and entertainments. Whatever else Mrs. Rockingham might be, she was devoted to the children of the neighborhood and made every party at her home a pleasure for everyone.

Her summer picnics were no less engaging or elaborate. Tents were set up in imitation of the sorts of delights to be found at fairs, like ring tosses and marksmanship with bow and arrow. A small theater troupe was performing puppetry for a group of enthralled children. A very large oak toward the back of the property had been slung with several swings so that the squeals of delighted guests, both young and old, could be heard wafting across the green. In the center of the lawn was a small lake sufficiently deep and broad to allow for two or three small craft which anyone could commandeer or enjoy being piloted by several servants who kept the lake's edge guarded from the unwary. Finally, to the far right, Mrs. Rockingham's intricate maze bobbed with heads bent on discovering the solution to the backs and forths of the ancient design, all hoping to reach the center, in which stood a crumbling tower of Roman origin.

Her father and her sisters were already mingling with other guests. Charity moved to sit with a group of ladies beneath a protective tent, Prudence to help children in and out of the boats, and Hope to practicing her marksmanship with bow and arrow, a favorite sport of hers. Her father had a tankard of ale in hand and was talking in an animated fashion with Squire Crawley.

For herself, Madeline wished that she might trip lightly down the steps and engage in any of the proffered activities, but she could not. She understood quite to perfection that today's pleasures were to be replaced by the difficult business of somehow finding just the right moment to introduce Sir Roger to Lady Hambledon.

Beyond this needful objective, she could not allow even the smallest distraction, for if she did not somehow succeed in gaining that lady's approval as well as an invitation to her fete of Saturday next for Sir Roger, she knew there would be little chance indeed of securing the critical invitation to Lady Cottingford's harvest ball. She sighed faintly, realizing that her hope for her family's salvation had been placed on so fragile a sequence of events. Still, there was nothing for it. Sir Roger had demanded the impossible of her, and the impossible she must accomplish. She must do all she could to see that Sir Roger impressed Lady Hambledon favorably. As she glanced about, she wondered if he had as yet arrived, for she did not see him.

As though her concerns had somehow conjured him up, Sir Roger, Lord Anthony, several manservants, and any number of school-age boys emerged from behind the maze in what proved to be a raucous wheelbarrow race. The boys were steered by their ankles, hands to the ground toward a finish line some thirty feet distant. A group of ladies including Cressida and Mary Crawley, as well as young Arabella Spight of just thirteen years, ran behind cheering them on.

Madeline could not help but smile. Who did not love a picnic? And how kind of Sir Roger to take part in the contest. Indeed, knowing how much children enjoyed being noticed by their elders, she felt it was a very great kindness, greater perhaps than he knew. The thought struck her that he would no doubt tend to his own children in this manner, with attentiveness and kindness, and a strange warmth descended on her, one of admiration and appreciation.

She turned to her right, where most of the gentlemen were partaking of Mr. Rockingham's excellent ale, and noted that his son Harris, John Calvert, and Captain Bladen were grouped together and sneering at Sir Roger. She felt a twinge of anxiety. Of course they disapproved of him, but perhaps their present disgust was a warning that ought to be heeded. Perhaps Sir Roger would have been better served to have remained at a stodgy distance from the general festivities of the day.

A lady drew near her and spoke. "I think it wonderful," she remarked.

Madeline turned to find Lady Bladen at her elbow. She was the wife of Sir William Bladen of Somerset and her dearest friend. Captain Bladen was her brother-in-law. "Georgiana!" she cried. "I did not know you would be here today. How is that possible?"

Georgiana, mother of three young children and the daughter of Lord and Lady Hambledon, kissed her cheek. "How I have missed you," she cried. "Somerset is not so far when one examines a map, but apparently just far enough that making sufficient journeys to visit all my dear friends has become an impossibility. I was to glad to hear you had arrived. Only tell me how you go on."

Georgiana had been an excellent friend for years, but

had married five years past, berefting Madeline of her daily society. Madeline sighed. "Your expression alone tells me you have been apprised of some of our more interesting events in recent days."

The smile which suffused her friend's face was sufficient to comprehend her answer before ever she spoke. Laughter accompanied her words. "How has it come about, my dear simpleton, that you actually brought so much displeasure down upon your own head?"

"You disapprove of my having decided that Sir Roger ought to be included in our Society?"

Georgiana drew in a deep breath as her own gaze drifted in the direction of the wheelbarrow races. Randolph Crawley was now assisting in the game, and several more of the neighborhood misses were gathered about clapping their hands and shouting their encouragements. "I cannot say. It is all so odd. Why ever do you think he came to Chilchester in the first place? Having amassed such a fortune as it is purported he possesses, why did he not purchase a dilapidated castle in Scotland? I daresay there are as many of those to the north as there are here in the south."

"His mother was English," Madeline explained with a slight shrug. "I have the sense that he is equally as loyal to her blood as he is to his father's."

"He is quite a handsome man. I had just emerged from the drawing room when he and Lord Anthony arrived. I nearly dropped the vase of roses Mrs. Rockingham had asked me to bring to one of the tables out of doors. He robbed me of my breath, though I hope you will say nothing to my husband of it. He would tease me mercilessly otherwise."

Madeline glanced at Sir William, who had joined her father and Squire Crawley. "He is not so indifferent in looks, either," Madeline said.

"I am very fortunate," Georgiana said. There was just

such a softness in her expression that led Madeline to believe theirs had not only been a love match but that their marriage was still very much in a place of gentle affection. How she envied her friend in this moment.

She leaned close. "You asked why I had decided to at least attempt to bring Sir Roger into Chilchester society. I would tell you, my dear friend, if you promise the utmost discretion in what I have to say."

"Of course," Georgiana responded promptly, her expression instantly serious.

Madeline then poured forth the story of her father's gaming debts, of Sir Roger's proposal of five weeks earlier, and of her present pursuit of his hand in marriage. Georgiana's concerned frown deepened. "And all because of severe losses incurred in Brighton, you say?"

Madeline nodded. "I can see your disbelief."

"Yes, I suppose you might, but it springs from a different source than what you are thinking. I learned this morning from John Calvert that your father was purchasing one of his brood mares at quite a tidy sum."

Madeline was shocked. "Indeed?" she queried. "But that makes no sense. Unless—" Her heart skipped a beat. "Unless he is living upon the expectation of my marriage to Sir Roger."

"Perhaps he exaggerated his original losses to you. Perhaps they were not so bad as you think."

"That is impossible. I had suggested Captain Bladen as a better alternative to Sir Roger, but my father insisted that even though the captain has a tidy fortune of his own, it is not sufficient to repair our fortunes."

Georgiana stared at her a long time and finally queried, "Are you aware of how often you mentioned Sir Roger in your letters from the time he first came to the valley this past winter?"

Madeline did not understand why she had given the

subject such an odd turn. "I cannot have done so," she responded, bemused. "I rarely saw the man."

Georgiana nodded, then shrugged faintly. "It is all so strange," she said, casting her gaze once more in the direction of the wheelbarrow races. "I for one never could understand why he was not invited in the first place, particularly when he is fussed over so completely in London."

Madeline stared at her for a long moment. "I beg your pardon?"

"Well, Harriet was in London this spring and wrote in one of her missives that Sir Roger Mathieson was invited everywhere, that he was quite sought after by the matchmaking mamas."

"His fortune, of course."

"There is that," she drawled, "and he is quite handsome, but Harriet seemed to suggest he was invited because his manners were so engaging."

Madeline did not know what to think. Of course, she had experienced something of his charm, of the delight of his company, while walking with him along Halland Creek. On the other hand . . . "He wore his kilt to Mrs. Crawley's soiree. Did he ever do so in London?"

"Not to my knowledge," Georgiana said, laughing. "He does sound as though he has a great deal of bravado, this man. I would not want to brave Mrs. Crawley's displeasure in a similar manner. She is still as much a dragon as ever."

"As many of our hostesses are wont to be."

"I suppose they are. As for Sir Roger, I will say this much: I like him. I had the chance to converse with him for several minutes. He asked politely and with great interest after my family in Somerset and after the beauties of that county generally. I believe him to be very much the gentleman."

Madeline felt her heart ease slightly at her friend's praise. She was herself not so sanguine, since she comprehended well that Sir Roger was out of patience with much of Chilchester society and that he did not always strive to keep his temper in check. She could only hope that the man Georgiana admired would remain civil throughout the afternoon.

"You are looking well, Madeline," her friend commented, once more turning the subject. "I like this mode of arranging your curls very much. It suits you quite well, I think."

"Thank you," she said.

"Oh, do but look. Sir Roger is staring at you."

Madeline turned and found that he was indeed watching her. He smiled slowly, bowed, and then resumed his duties with an anxious eight-year-old who was bouncing up and down at his side, clearly anxious to begin the next race.

"He seems smitten with you," Georgiana murmured. "I know if he looked at me in that manner, I should believe myself to be an object."

"You are mistaken. He is merely as surprised by my hair as you were. He has never seen me without my braids."

Sir Roger slung his arm about the boy's neck and gave him a push. The other teams had lined up, and now he must make another dash for the finish line. A sizable group had gathered about their silly game, a circumstance which pleased him. He concluded that not all of Chilchester society was comprised of prosy old bores. Even Madeline had left off her braids, and this was for him a most hopeful turn of events.

When he had caught sight of her standing beside Lady Bladen, he had at first not recognized the young woman whose blond hair was caught up in a riot of lovely curls atop her head, curls that danced about in the soft breeze. He had even wondered who she might be until she smiled.

He could not credit he was looking at Madeline Piper, Madeline of the braids, his secret betrothed.

He had found himself stunned, a powerful feeling which took strong hold of his chest. How different, softer, more appealing she had appeared.

The race began and he slung the ankles of the boy, young Arthur Spight, urging him on with firm encouragements. The child inched forward until he gained his balance and understood his strength, after which he plunged ahead with remarkable speed. Sir Roger kept pace steadily, and before long the pair of them crossed the finish line and won the race. The child rose up, jumping in circles and crying out his victory.

"Well done, Master Spight!" Sir Roger shouted.

"Thank you, sir!" he exclaimed, then jumped in a few more circles.

Sir Roger glanced toward the terrace, but the ladies were gone.

"A dog!" Lord Anthony exclaimed suddenly.

Sir Roger turned around and saw his white-faced friend staring hard in the direction of the tents. On the lap of Mrs. Rockingham sat her favorite pet, a small dog by the name of Peaches, with rather long fur and a pink ribbon supporting a topknot. He could scarcely restrain a smile, but watched in some interest as Cressida Crawley approached Lord Anthony and took his arm. "There, there," the sweet young miss murmured. "'Tis only Peaches, and she is perfectly harmless, I assure you."

Sir Roger watched Lord Anthony emit a deep sigh. "I shan't have a moment's peace this afternoon."

Later, after the children had drifted away to other amusements, Sir Roger took the opportunity to approach his hostess. She was seated in throne-like splendor beneath a fine canopied tent. Her ladies-in-waiting in the form of Mrs. Spight, Mrs. Crawley, and twin spinsters, the Misses

Lamby, who resided in the nearby village of Romsbury, were grouped about her, each sipping ratafia. Peaches was asleep on her lap.

"I wished to thank you for your kind invitation," he said, addressing Mrs. Rockingham. "You have my eternal gratitude."

Mrs. Rockingham offered a cold smile. "You may speak as politely as you wish, Sir Roger, but it will take a great deal more to win my respect and a true place in Chilchester society. I have heard you have many acquaintances in London but even the riffraff can inveigle their way into the finest houses, or so I understand. I never could abide the place myself. I only request that you behave the gentleman while on my property, and then we shall see."

"I would not dream of expecting more than this from you," he said softly while offering a bow.

Her expression appeared arrested. "Indeed?" was her frosty reply.

He gave no response, however. Instead, he addressed an entirely new subject. "I have been given to understand that your family were at one time the owners of Pelworthy."

"You were not misinformed."

"I wish to ask you, then, if you would be interested in forming a historical society for the castle. My architects have in their possession at least a score of documents by which they have been making the necessary repairs to the castle, and I thought—" He got no further.

Mrs. Rockingham leaned forward on her pillows and pierced him with her direct stare. "Is this so? You have been consulting former plans and documents before refurbishing Pelworthy?"

"Of course."

"Of course? How easily you speak these words. There is no, 'of course' about it. I must say I am utterly astonished."

"You supposed, ma'am, that I was being arbitrary in the

renovations? I see no purpose in that. What changes I have made, such as removing a portion of the gaol in order to create a proper place to store my French wines, have all been a result of study and careful consideration."

She petted her sleeping dog and fanned herself. "Nevertheless, you have bereft me of speech, so you have. Well, this is something. A historical society for the castle?"

He could see she was intrigued by the notion, but he could only imagine the nature of the conflicts now waging a fine battle in her massive bosom. "Yes," he continued, "I suppose I am hoping to unearth more documents by means of your influence. Would you have any particular interest in such a project, or do I presume too much?"

"Of course you presume too much," she cried. "I am a very busy woman. However, I should like a day or so to ponder the matter. I shall send you a note Monday or Tuesday giving you my answer. But should I agree to it, I promise you the sacrifice will be very great."

"I have no doubt of it, ma'am." He bowed and moved away. He meant to seek out Madeline, for she was but ten yards from him. At that moment, however, Arthur Spight rushed up to him and asked if he would be so kind as to row a boat for himself and his younger sister, Sophy.

"I should be delighted."

Madeline watched him go, feeling greatly relieved. He was, in her opinion, conducting himself with both generosity and kindness and he seemed to have engaged Mrs. Rockingham in conversation without once offending her, a circumstance which would be useful in smoothing the path for introducing him to Lady Hambledon.

By the time Mrs. Rockingham was preparing to serve the picnic dinner to her guests, Madeline still had not exchanged even two words with Sir Roger, nor had she had the opportunity to make the introductions to Lady Hambledon. There had been so many activities in which all

the guests participated, including a display of horseman-
ship from a traveling troupe who had at one time
performed at Astley's Amphitheatre in London, that she
had been separated from him completely.

She did, however, chance to speak with Lady Hambledon briefly and mentioned that she hoped to present Sir
Roger to her. Lady Hambledon was a petite woman with
brown hair graying but only slightly, gentle brown eyes,
and a sweet disposition. For all her kindness, however, she
was very strict in her principles, so that when Madeline addressed her concerning Sir Roger, her smile grew quite
reserved.

"I have heard you were attempting to introduce him to
Chilchester society. I could only wonder why, when I have
known you in the past to be quite set against it."

She explained that given the castle's proximity to
Chilchester and Sir Roger's evident intention of settling
permanently in the valley, that the only proper thing to do
was to extend every courtesy and hospitality to him. "After
all," she said, "he was knighted by George III some nine
years past for extraordinary services to the crown. It
seemed a small thing, in light of such royal patronage, to
open the societal gates of our neighborhood."

Lady Hambledon frowned heavily. "I believe you may
have taken too much upon yourself, Miss Piper."

"I have no doubt of that whatsoever," she had responded
sincerely.

"Well, thus far I am quite impressed with your achievements. First, Mrs. Crawley is to host a Christmas ball at
Pelworthy and now, if I have understood correctly, Mrs.
Rockingham is to create a historical society for the castle
itself. Commendable efforts, indeed."

"A historical society?" she inquired, surprised.

"You have not heard? It is all Albinia can speak of. I
must say, Sir Roger certainly knew precisely what to say

to his hostess to win her favor, although I can't help but feel he might come to regret his overture, since she is already speaking of conducting private tours of the castle herself."

At that, Madeline could not help but smile. She gave Sir Roger a great deal of credit in having laid the woman's feathers with so noble an offering, but she could not conceive of two people more likely to cast a rub in one another's way than Sir Roger and Mrs. Rockingham. However, if it was truly his wish to enter Chilchester society, then he might as well become accustomed to the exigencies of it sooner than later. She could only wonder if he would in the end regret his having purchased Pelworthy and forced the issue of his acceptance in the region.

When Lady Hambledon moved away to join her husband for the alfresco repast, she searched out Georgiana and sat down to table with her. The meal was a fine blend of roast beef and chicken, pigeon pies, boiled leg of lamb, and a haunch of venison, every manner of summer's ripest vegetables, pickles, salad, mince pies, orange pudding, and a very fine plum cake. Champagne was served all around, as well as lemonade for the children.

If Madeline thought Harris, Mr. Calvert, and Captain Bladen were all drinking a trifle too heavily, she said nothing. Though they frequently cast darkling glances at Sir Roger, at least she had nothing to feel ashamed of in his conduct. He was behaving admirably, just as he ought. Presently, he sat between Cressida and Randolph Crawley, both of whom were laughing more often than not in his company. Yes, she was greatly pleased indeed.

After the excellent meal, she rose from the table and, without knowing from which direction he had come, Sir Roger was suddenly upon her. "Come," he said, offering his arm. "Have you solved the maze yet?"

She took his arm readily. "Of course. When I was nine."

"Excellent. Then I rely upon you to direct me to the center. I have tried three times and have become lost on each occasion. One of the children had to lead me out."

Madeline smiled up at him and moved happily by his side in the direction of the maze.

"You look quite beautiful today, Madeline," he whispered, leaning close to her.

"Thank you," she returned, her heart picking up its cadence. His breath had brushed her cheek and a spattering of gooseflesh was rippling down her side.

"You should leave off wearing braids entirely. They give you a somewhat austere appearance, which I am increasingly persuaded does not comprise even a jot of your true temperament."

"Did you think me *austere* heretofore?" she asked, dismayed. She had never viewed herself in this manner, but it would seem many others did—her father, for one.

"Yes, of course. But then I have held the same opinion of nearly everyone in the valley. However, because of this delightful picnic and the soiree at Wistfield Hall a sennight past, I must say I have a much nearer view of my neighbors. Some I believe I could grow quite fond of."

She could not help but smile. "Like Arthur Spight?"

"Yes. He is a good lad, if a trifle demanding. I understand his father perished some time ago. I should think his uncle would do well to involve himself more readily in his life."

Madeline thought of John Calvert and frowned slightly. She had never given this aspect of his temper a great deal of thought, but it now occurred to her that she rarely saw him evince even the smallest interest in his nieces and nephew, even though they resided beneath his roof. "I believe you may be right in that."

By this time, they had reached the maze and would have crossed the remaining four or five feet to the entrance, but they were stopped by Lord Anthony, who came rushing around the corner in a state of panic. Little Peaches followed hard on his heels, yipping for all she was worth. Madeline wished she might have been more polite, but the sight of a grown man in obvious terror of a dog smaller than a rabbit was more than she could bear. She burst into a peal of laughter.

"Anthony, you could fit that dog in your pocket," Sir Roger called to his quickly retreating back.

"The beast already ate my pocket!" he exclaimed as he ran in the direction of the house.

"Your friend seems to be suffering from a terror of dogs, or am I mistaken?"

Sir Roger nodded. "I believe they sense his fear and attack regardless of the benignity of their object. I cannot seem to persuade Anthony that he is not in the least in danger." He then glanced up at the tall, clipped yew hedges that formed the structure for the maze. "Shall we?"

"Indeed, yes. It has been several years since I attempted to reach the center. Now that I think on it, I begin to wonder if I will get us lost as well."

She led the way, but his voice, whispered against her bare neck, sent another shivering of gooseflesh down her side. "I should not mind becoming lost for a pleasant hour or two."

She glanced back at him and saw the warm, interested light in his eye. For the slightest moment she knew an instinct to turn around and suggest they try the swings at the far end of the grounds, but when he smiled and her heart picked up its cadence a little more, her feet moved further into the opening. A few steps more, and she made her choice of right or left. This much she knew: the solution was to the right.

For the next several minutes, however, she made mistake after mistake. Sir Roger teased her mercilessly, joking with

her time and again, so that she was more often than not
laughing heartily and begging him not to be so provoking.
He would tease her a little more, she would laugh, her
heart would grow easier than it had in years, so that in the
end she found herself hoping she would never solve the
maze, that she might be trapped in its twistings and turn-
ings forever with Sir Roger by her side. An odd thought,
indeed, except that she had not been so content in a very
long time.

At last some half hour later, since it covered no less than
a half acre, Madeline led him into the center of the maze.

"This is quite lovely, but it cannot be. Is it Roman?"

Madeline smiled, looking up at the tower. "Yes, it is."

"Why was I not told of it? I vow had I known I should
have attacked the maze first." He began walking about the
perimeter of the tower, touching the weathered stones.
"Imagine how many centuries have passed since this structure was laid."

"It is extraordinary."

Madeline began walking slowly in the opposite direction around the crumbled remnants of the tower, her hand
sliding over the stones. She tried to sense just how many
hands had worked together, laying one stone after another.
Once more, however, Sir Roger was upon her, only this
time he did not speak but rather slid his arm about her
waist and pulled her close. She planted her hands on his
chest. Her heart was now thrumming with fear. She should
not let him hold her thus, even if they were all but betrothed. It was very wrong, and what if someone should
discover her so scandalously in his arms?

There were no sounds nearby to indicate the imminent
arrival of other guests, and even the sounds of general rev-
elry were dimmed by the distance of the various games
and activities from the center of the maze. Oddly, she felt

as though she was a hundred miles from everything that was familiar to her.

"Will you permit a kiss, Madeline? I will not trespass your mouth without your permission."

Her gaze fell to his lips, and she felt as though a spell were descending on her, robbing her of the will to speak, to stand, certainly to refuse him.

"Of course you may kiss me," she whispered. "We are to be husband and wife."

At that he grinned. "You are so certain of success, then?" he asked, his voice low. "You are confident that you will be able to get the required invitations to Lady Cottingford's harvest ball?"

"I must," she responded, her gaze drifting to his eyes, to the sculpted line of his cheek, to his lips again, which were still smiling.

"You still desire my fortune," he stated.

Her arm stole suddenly about his neck. "I don't give a fig for your fortune. I merely wish to keep my sisters from falling into disgrace. Is that so wrong?"

His arm drew her closer still. "It is quite noble, only I wish that you did not feel you were sacrificing yourself in our union."

His lips were but a breath away. "Kiss me and make me forget, then," she returned, unable to comprehend how she had come to speak to him so boldly.

He bruised her mouth, so forceful was the kiss he pressed on her. She could not breathe, she could not think, her feet lost all sense of being connected to the earth. Tears darted to her eyes. She did not understand in the least what was happening to her, or why she was not at all appalled by how closely he held her or how his tongue had begun to explore her mouth in the most sensuous of ways.

She was stunned by the sensation, ripples of gooseflesh flowing over her in wave after wave of the most intense pleasure. Both her arms were now clasped firmly about his neck, and she felt the entire length of him, so closely was he pressed to her.

When we are married, she thought, *he will kiss me thus every day.*

How pleasant that thought was. Minutes passed, and the kiss continued on and on. His hands kneaded her back and her waist, her fingers slid through his hair. She found her breath coming in little gasps, for she still could not breathe at all properly.

He drew back, whispering, "Do you think a Roman soldier once kissed a British maid here beside this tower?"

"Undoubtedly for I am convinced the tower is charmed."

"You are charmed, my beautiful Madeline." He drifted his fingers through the curls beside her face. "And I believe you have charmed me as well." He smiled suddenly. "Do you think one day you might be able to love a Scot?"

Madeline was confused by the question. What did he mean by it? When understanding dawned on her, suddenly she was filled with a thousand former doubts and disgusts about making an alliance with the man still holding her captive.

She began drawing back from him, her arms sliding down his, her heart compressing painfully in her chest. Could she love a Scot? Why had he felt obliged to pose such an odious question to her? Why had he seen it necessary to disrupt their charmed embrace with such a horrid notion?

"Good God," he murmured. "Even after this, you find the thought of wedding me, of perhaps even loving me, offensive to you?"

"No," she cried. "Yes . . . I do not know."

His face turned a ruddy color and his mouth worked strongly. She felt his anger pass through her as though it were a tangible thing. She took a step backward, but he took hold of her arm and would not let her leave. "You would say this to me," he stated, "the man whose fortune you hope to possess? You ought at least to learn to disguise the truth of your sentiments, of your prejudices, of your innate hatreds, particularly if you mean to share my bed."

With that, he dropped her arm and stalked away from her, his expression rigid with contempt.

Madeline sank down upon the grass at the base of the ancient stone tower. She covered her face with her hands and began to weep. Tears poured forth, unbidden, unwelcome. She did not know why she cried, or why the thought of Sir Roger holding her in the smallest disdain made her feel physically ill.

Yet how could he know what the teachings of her childhood had been—her grandmother's hatred of the French and all foreigners, her mother's strict sense of propriety and what she believed the daughters of a fine, ancient lineage such as the Pipers enjoyed owed to their ancestors?

She had been bred from the first to wed an Englishman and a gentleman, a man of property and, if possible, of rank. Madeline had listened to tales of presentations at court, of London Seasons, of young ladies making the very best match possible. If love were to accompany such an alliance, so much the better, but in Lucretia Piper's view, love was never to be the object.

"Did you love Papa?" Madeline had asked, sure of the sweet answer her mother would give.

But no such welcome response had slipped from her mother's lips to warm Madeline's heart. Instead, her mother had said, "Ours is a marriage of like ideals, property, and dowry, and two fine lineages. I cannot tell you how proud I am of our family, Madeline, and of my dear daughters." She had been counting the linens at the time and setting aside those in need of repair. Madeline could still smell the fresh, clean lavender scent of them and of her mother. But there had been no love between her parents.

And then her mother had died.

Could Madeline ever love a Scot? Could she ever give her heart, her soul completely to such a man, a man who represented everything her mother and grandmother despised? Could she ever betray her mother's memory in such a horrid fashion? No, a thousand times no. And she wept more violently still.

A half hour later, Sir Roger was cursing Mrs. Rockingham's maze. He still had not found his way out of the deuced tangle of pathways and was just about to begin shouting for assistance when, as if by magic, the opening appeared before him and he emerged onto the picnic grounds.

He was relieved and frustrated at the same time. He had heard Madeline weeping. He had even at one point wanted to return to her, but he could no more find his way back to the Roman tower than he could to the exit. By the time he quit the maze, he half expected her to be awaiting him and asking what had taken him so long.

Glancing around, he saw that many of the guests had already departed. Even the fair-like tents were being dismantled, and a servant was lining the boats up on the grassy shore and cleaning them for storage. He searched the remaining figures scattered about for signs of Lord Anthony and finally saw him far away, sitting on a swing with his legs drawn up and Peaches awaiting his descent. He might have laughed had he not still been so aggravated by his intended.

He waved at Lord Anthony, beckoning him to come to him, and turned to begin making his way to Mrs. Rockingham in order to thank her for her hospitality, when three gentlemen, each half-foxed, approached him.

"Look, Calvert, 'tis the Scotsman," Harris Rockingham cried, his voice a trifle slurred. "What do you say to that?"

Calvert, his eyes red rimmed, huffed his displeasure. "I say the picnic was poorer for it because of his presence. And you, Bladen? What is your opinion?"

Captain Bladen, his dark, mole-like eyes focusing sharply on Sir Roger, sneered, "We should have rounded up all the Scots a century ago and shipped the lot of them to the Colonies, when we had the chance. Now see what comes of it? We are condemned to living side by side with them."

Sir Roger knew the gentlemen had been fortifying their courage with ale and champagne most of the day. Now, it would seem, they were sufficiently prepared to do battle. He turned away, intent on ignoring their taunts, but Captain Bladen moved swiftly in front of him, though tottering on his feet. "Look how the Scot tries to run away, like all his kind, cowards to the last." He poked at Sir Roger's chest.

Sir Roger caught his hand hard and, with a swift movement, twisted it backward, holding him immobile. "You would do well, Bladen," he whispered harshly, "to find a comfortable chaise and sleep off this haze of ale that has clouded your mind. You can't seriously mean to challenge me at Mrs. Rockingham's picnic. Where are your manners?"

Revulsion similar to the kind Sir Roger had seen cross Madeline's face a half hour earlier twisted Bladen's mouth. "How dare you speak to me of manners, you whose mother was an English whore."

Time slowed for Sir Roger. He knew that several guests were drawing near, that even two or three of the older gentlemen were running in his direction, but this vile slur on his beloved mother's name robbed him of his ability to see anything but Captain Bladen's mouth. A red film cloaked his eyes. Still holding his hand in a tight grip, he slapped

Bladen across his mouth three times quite hard, then landed a flush hit on the same spot. Captain Bladen fell hard to the ground and lay there groaning, rolling his eyes and holding his jaw.

Sir Roger turned to Harris, whose complexion had become a lovely chalky color. Harris backed away, his fist at his side as though holding a pretend sword or something. As for John Calvert, he mumbled, "I should not have expected a Scot to hold his temper." With this weak shot, he walked away.

By now a large group had gathered about him, many whispering questions, the remainder staring at him. He glanced about him and said, "Would anyone else care to speak badly of my parentage? I believe the moment to be propitious."

Madeline had emerged from the maze in time to see Captain Bladen struggling to sit up, blood pouring from his mouth, his neckcloth already smeared with blood. She was appalled and slightly ill from the sight of it. As she looked up, however, another sight struck her eyes. Lady Hambledon stood opposite Sir Roger, a severe expression on her face. A moment later, the baroness lifted her chin and moved away.

By now, everyone was silent and staring—at Sir Roger, at one another, at poor Captain Bladen bleeding profusely. It was as if no one could move.

At that moment, however, a high-pitched yipping was heard and a moment later, a harassed Lord Anthony raced toward the circle. His expression was wild, but seeing Captain Bladen struggling to right himself, he moved quickly forward, hurriedly lifted the captain to his feet, then sped on his way as Peaches rounded the maze and headed toward him.

A chortling began that quickly became a hearty laughter. Captain Bladen tottered on his feet and Squire Crawley slung an arm about his neck and hauled him away. Madeline watched her father attempt to speak with Sir Roger, imploring him to apologize to the captain, but the cold stare Sir Roger offered him in response silenced her father immediately.

Sir Roger then trailed after his friend and Peaches.

For herself, with all her sennight's effort having been reduced to ashes, Madeline walked wearily toward the house.

Nine

Two days later, after allowing herself all of Sunday to forget Saturday's debacle, Madeline walked slowly about her mother's rose garden. She had refused to ponder any of her difficulties until this moment, hoping that her mind, if given a respite, would be better able to find solutions to her numerous problems.

She held several fragrant rose petals in her hand and sniffed them every now and then, taking in the honeyed perfume. Finally, she let her thoughts tumble about at will, permitting a first evaluation of all that had happened at Mrs. Rockingham's picnic.

Images of Sir Roger filled her mind first, of how handsome he had appeared in buckskin breeches and a blue coat which he had shed the moment he began playing with the children. She had admired how readily he had given himself to the spirit of the picnic, entering into the various activities as well as any number of conversations with Mrs. Rockingham's guests. She remembered feeling relieved that he had done nothing to cause embarrassment to her family and yet that throughout the day she had been so fearful he would do just that.

Then he had guided her into the maze and she had led him to the Roman tower, where he had kissed her. She tried to recall just how the kiss had come about. The memory returned to her and her cheeks began to burn. What

was it she had said to him? *Kiss me and make me forget.*
How could she have said anything so bold to him, as
though she had been begging for a kiss? What had she
been thinking? What sort of madness had taken hold of her
in that moment?

If only he had not obliged her and kissed her. How much
simpler would everything be right now, particularly when
merely thinking about that kiss caused her heartbeat to
quicken? She had truly never known anything so sublime
in her entire existence. Even now, she could feel his lips
pressed hard to hers, as though he meant to keep her forever. When he had kissed her before, every touch had been
so gentle, but what had occurred between them on Saturday had been something quite different, indeed. And he
had kissed her over and over, not ceasing for what felt like
an eternity. She realized with a horrified start that just for
the pleasure of that kiss, she would do the whole thing
again. Could anything be worse?

Then he had asked her teasingly if she could love a Scot.
How she wished that question undone, a millionfold. She
paused in her steps, the rose petals falling to the gravel
walk at her feet. Could she love a Scot? Or perhaps a more
significant form of the same question: was she already
tumbling in love with a Scot?

No, a thousand times no, her mind cried. It was not possible. She had been trained from infancy to a different
standard, one of purity and loyalty. The Scots killed the English and the English killed the Scots. The two cultures were
wholly disparate, and if she had required more proof, Sir
Roger had provided it when he sent Captain Bladen reeling
to the earth, having planted him a facer. Sir Roger had a temper he could not master, a Celtic temper of ruddy faces when
the heat of their rage overtook their complexion.

Her mother would have been dumbfounded that any man
would have so crossed the bounds of propriety as to enter

into a bout of fisticuffs with a fellow guest at Mrs. Rock-ingham's picnic. There would have been no other subject spoken of within the confines of her traveling coach from the time she quit Mrs. Rockingham's drive until the horses were safely returned to the stables. Her diatribe would have been long and pointed, probably beginning with, "What more could one expect from a man of Scottish descent but manners of the most offensive in every respect?" Even after all these years, Madeline could still hear her on the subject of the odiousness of foreigners.

At the far end of the garden, Madeline spied a familiar stone bench to which she immediately directed her feet. Once there, she sat down with a sigh. Her thoughts were still full of Sir Roger. She clasped her hands tightly in her lap and sighed heavily. And yet she could not wholly blame him. Though she had heard little of the exchange by the time she left the maze, she saw that her swains to the man were quite in their altitudes. She knew that each of them was particularly vehement on the subject of not per-mitting Sir Roger to enter Chilchester society, and that they had already made his time at Mrs. Crawley's soiree exceedingly unpleasant. She had little doubt Sir Roger had been sorely provoked.

Who, then, could blame him completely for having lost his temper as he had? And yet, could she really bear being married to someone who had not learned to master himself?

She buried her face in her hands as the final horrible as-pect of the encounter slipped into her mind, of Lady Hambledon having been witness to the spectacle and of her subsequent expression, swamped as it had been with utter disgust. Herein lay the rub, she thought unhappily. Even if she could forgive Sir Roger for his conduct, she doubted Lady Hambledon ever would. Of the three women she had thus far dealt with, Lady Hambledon was the most intractable of all the high sticklers.

Her spirits sank so low in this moment that Madeline doubted she would ever be happy again. The whole situation, so intolerable in nearly every aspect, was proving disastrous, from the reasons for her pursuit of Sir Roger in the first place to how difficult the task of bringing him into fashion was proving at every turn. Was she being punished, she wondered?

"Maddy, my dear?"

Madeline looked up and saw that her father had somehow managed to come upon her without making his approach known. She had been greatly lost in thought, indeed. "Papa," she responded, leaning back and shading her eyes with her hand. The day was beautiful, the sky blue, the sun shining brightly.

"I have not seen a sadder face in my entire life," he said, taking up a seat beside her and possessing a hand with his own. "Thinking of the picnic?"

"Is there anything else I could be pondering?"

"Your wedding day."

She laughed outright. "Oh, Papa, but you are hopeful even in the bleakest of circumstances—or did you not see Sir Roger attack Captain Bladen on Saturday?"

Mr. Piper patted her hand. "Of course. I saw it all. I had meant to prevent it, but I was too far away. I only saw your three most dogged suitors approaching him at the very last moment. I had known they were in their cups—indeed, everyone was painfully aware of it. But even running as I did, I could not prevent either Captain Bladen from speaking such terrible words or Sir Roger responding with a perfectly comprehensible swing of his right arm. I thought the blow would have finished Bladen for good."

"The good captain was not in Sunday services," she observed.

At that, Mr. Piper barked his laughter. "No, indeed he

was not, nor will we be seeing much of him anytime soon. I wonder if his jaw has been broken."

"Was the blow that severe?" she asked, aghast.

"It ought to have been. He called Sir Roger's mother a whore."

Madeline could not have heard correctly. "I beg your pardon?"

"Oh, come, come, Maddy. You will not be missish with me for saying it when it crossed Bladen's mouth first."

She still did not understand. "Do you tell me, Father, that he spoke of Sir Roger's mother in so vile a term?"

Mr. Piper nodded.

"Good God. No, I did not hear. I arrived just after the blow was delivered, not a moment sooner. Had I known! I am so very shocked and so deeply disappointed in the captain. How could he have been so vile, whatever his prejudices?"

"There, there, Maddy, don't climb onto your high ropes. Do but think a moment. Captain Bladen has been sitting in your pocket nigh on two years. He had hopes that you would one day give him the encouragement he needed to offer for you, but you have not. Then, without his comprehending why, you suddenly take up Sir Roger's cause and disappear with the fellow into the maze for over an hour. Believe me, even if he had not been in his cups, he would have had reason to have had his anger stirred up a bit. All three of your beaus did. Or are you such a ninnyhammer as to not understand that each one of those men fancies himself in love with you?"

"I have not been indiscreet, have I? I mean, yes, of course I have known of their respective *tendres,* but I hope I have not been so insensitive as to have offered hope where there was none."

"You could never be so cruel. I suspect much of their present aggravation is because they sense Cupid at work in his mysterious ways and are become threatened, not unjustly."

"I do not know what you mean," she stated uneasily.

"Stubble it, Maddy, you know deuced well precisely what I mean. You can't but look at Mathieson without your face turning pink, and not from displeasure, either, so don't think to tickle my nose with that feather. No, my dear, you are half in love with him and, were you to permit yourself, you could tumble the rest of the way without the smallest difficulty. My only concern is that you do restrain yourself, and all because of a ridiculous scruple or two that you learned at your mother's elbow—a dictum, I might add, that is as outdated as panniers in a ball gown."

At the picture of the wide hoops worn several decades past, Madeline could not help but smile.

"There, that is much better. Now, don't be in the mopes a moment longer. Life is too precious and too short for such a long face, especially on such a beautiful morn."

"Perhaps you are right, but are you not in the least concerned that I shall fail in making this match? Then where will we be?"

"In the river tick, of course, but I don't give a fig for that. I am one and fifty, my darling daughter, but I vow until this past month or so I had not been alive for the last—well, for a very long time, even before I met your mother. Should our fortunes fail completely, then we shall start over, no matter how hard it might prove to be."

Madeline stared at her father as though she had never known him before. "You speak with such conviction and such confidence. Papa, what has happened to you? I vow I have never seen you this way before."

"Are you displeased?"

"Not in the least. Indeed, your strength of spirit has quite restored me. Well, a little, anyway. But I hope all will be well."

He slipped his arm about her shoulder, gave it a squeeze, then rose to his feet. After clearing his throat and frowning slightly, he said, "I shan't be home for dinner this evening. I have an engagement."

Madeline smiled. "This sounds rather intriguing? May I inquire with whom?" She sought about in her mind for several unattached ladies, whether in Chilchester or the surrounding villages, whom her father might be courting, but no one in particular came to mind.

"No, you may not, puss," he said, smiling in a naughty fashion as he chucked her chin. "I shall merely say that I will be in Elsbourne for the evening."

"Elsbourne? But that is nearly ten miles distant."

"So it is," he responded cheerfully. Without another remark, he sauntered away.

She lifted a hand, remembering she had meant to ask him about the brood mare he was reputedly purchasing from Mr. Calvert, but by then he was too far away. Besides, the moment seemed to have passed anyway.

"And where, might I ask, is Lord Anthony?"

Sir Roger frowned slightly at the plump form of Mrs. Rockingham, who had taken great pains to call on him this afternoon. He still could not credit that she had actually come to Pelworthy after he had created such a horrid spectacle at her picnic two days past, nor that she seemed not the least bit overset in any other manner than in the fact that Lord Anthony was not present to greet her as well.

She settled herself in a comfortable chair near the fireplace and, snapping her fingers, brought Peaches leaping sprightly onto her lap.

Sir Roger eyed first the little dog, then his own Churchill, who sat on his haunches not three feet away, tongue lolling and a quite amorous expression on his canine face as he watched the female make herself comfortable on Mrs. Rockingham's ample form. "He is in Chilchester, ma'am, visiting his tailor," he responded at last. "He has, I fear, a number of pockets that require mending."

"Cannot his valet manage the business?" she asked brusquely.

Sir Roger chuckled. "I fear not. The damage is too great."

"I take it your Churchill was the cause?"

"Just so."

She shook her head vigorously several times. "I cannot think what he was doing provoking Peaches as he was at my picnic. The man has no sense at all."

"No, ma'am, he does not."

"Ah, just as I suspected. Well, well, you are a good man to have befriended him."

"Nonsense. What Lord Anthony lacks in sense he more than makes up for in sweetness of disposition and kindness. He is the best friend I have ever had."

Mrs. Rockingham smiled crookedly, and then she began to chuckle. "I shall never forget how he rounded the maze and, without comprehending even a mite of what was going forward, lifted Captain Bladen to his feet. I have awakened in the middle of the night only to laugh at the recollection."

When he remained silent, she asked, "Did you chance to speak with Mr. Rockingham on Saturday, engage him conversation?"

"Aye, ma'am. He is a very knowledgeable gentleman, on many subjects. I was quite impressed with him."

"As he was with you, which is in part the reason that I am here. He insisted I come, despite your conduct on Saturday, which I agreed to, because what was said to you was so very unforgivable that I can hardly bear to think of it without the greatest shame."

"You have no reason to be ashamed," he said. "You did not speak the words."

"No, but I did nothing to foster a more accepting manner toward you. In that, I consider myself culpable and can only be grateful that it was not Harris who so badly offended you. Indeed, though dueling has long been outlawed, I would not have been in the least surprised had you challenged Captain Bladen as he lay at your feet."

"As to that," he said, smiling, "I would never issue a challenge to a man so deeply in his cups, if you will forgive the expression. I knew him to be foxed and responded in what was the quickest and best means of putting an end to his insults."

"So you did," she responded. "Well, well, best it is all forgiven and forgotten. May I rely on you not to take this matter further?"

"You mean, not to engage your son in a duel for his part?"

She sighed heavily. "Precisely. Georgiana Bladen told me of your reputation as one of the finest shots to have practiced at Manton's in London. Indeed, I believe you hold several records there. For that reason, I hope you will take Harris's age into consideration."

"I will, if you will listen to a suggestion."

At that, he saw her bristle, but waited until she nodded her acquiescence.

"A pair of colors, ma'am, would do the boy a world of good. Have you not noticed that he is perpetually holding an imaginary sword hilt?"

"It is the greatest annoyance, and no amount of correction on my part could break him of the habit. As for a pair of colors, I have no interest in that subject at all."

"What does your husband say?"

At that, she narrowed her eyes. "There is something else I would discuss with you," she said, giving the subject a hard turn, a rebuff he accepted without batting an eye. "I wonder if I might see some of the documents you referred to at the picnic—or were you merely attempting to turn me up sweet with a whisker or two about just how you have been managing your repairs here at Pelworthy?"

"I am not a stupid man," he said, smiling. "I would never tell you a lie about which I could so easily be found out. Though I can see now why you paid this call without the smallest warning of your intentions."

"And I am not a stupid woman," she responded, lifting an imperious eyebrow. "The documents, if you please, Sir Roger."

He excused himself and, after ordering peach ratafia for his guest, which he knew she preferred, he went to the room located in the north curtain wall which housed the architectural plans and the various archival letters which he had gathered over the past year since his purchase of Pelworthy and which contained references to the castle over the centuries. Upon returning to the drawing room, he bid Mrs. Rockingham join him at a central round table and began laying out the letters and original plans. She settled Peaches on the floor and joined him directly.

He was surprised by how quickly Mrs. Rockingham became engrossed in the various papers. He brought forward a chair for her, settling it close to the table, and watched as the older woman seated herself in a slow manner, her gaze fixed to a yellowed parchment. He then retrieved her glass of ratafia and settled it at her elbow.

After half an hour of reading and perusing, she leaned back in her chair, her eyes misted. "Where did you get so many wonderful letters and architectural renderings? Really, it is quite amazing."

By now he was seated in his own chair and sipping a glass of sherry. "You approve, then?" he queried, smiling.

"You know I do. But how? Where?"

He had never thought he could warm to the lady before him, but he did so now. "When I settled upon purchasing Pelworthy, and relieving who I now understand is a cousin of yours of his considerable, er, embarrassments, I also contacted the British Museum, as well as Oxford and Cambridge Universities. All three establishments were diligent in researching what documentation they could concerning the history of Pelworthy and obligingly forwarded such papers to me, though I must admit I did pay a rather large sum for them."

She chortled. "Annuities."

"At the very least."

"Well, well, then I am glad you have come to Chilchester, though I suspect you never thought to hear me say so. I knew Sylvester was in dun territory—"

"Again, to say the least—"

She inclined her head in acknowledgment of this truth. "And since it would seem your purpose in purchasing the castle was with so evident a design to do what is right by Pelworthy, then I lift my glass to you."

He accepted the accolade and partook of his sherry as she sipped her ratafia.

She fingered a nearby document and shook her head. "I suppose it is only natural. Nothing remains fixed and settled, even though we strive so diligently to preserve things the way we believe they ought to be preserved. You must forgive us, Sir Roger. Our little neighborhood does not easily accept anything new or different."

"So it would seem."

"But Madeline will be of great use to you, see if she won't." When he smiled perfunctorily, she leaned forward in her chair slightly. "Why so downcast? You cannot be regretting our dear Madeline?"

"The shoe, I fear, is on the other foot, and I am not at all convinced for that reason that we would suit."

She pierced him with her knowing stare, her brown eyes sparkling. "She offended you. No, I beg you will not protest. I can see it in every line of your exceedingly handsome face. I recommend, however, that you pay no heed to it. She'll come about. You'll see."

"I have my doubts, ma'am, if you will forgive my contradicting you."

She merely grunted in response, then took to examining the documents once more.

Sir Roger rose from his seat and, with glass in hand, took a leisurely stroll about the tall, expansive chamber which he knew had once been used as an audience room by Henry VIII. It was one of the few decent chambers to have remained intact after decades of neglect, and he had had it fashioned into his principal receiving room. He sipped his sherry, and after a time his thoughts turned to Madeline. As always, his first recollection was of standing before her near the Roman tower in the center of Mrs. Rockingham's maze and being wholly unable to restrain himself from taking her in his arms.

He turned away from the round table and moved to a window overlooking the keep. He truly believed that had he not kissed her as he had and had she not responded as though she had always belonged to him, he would not have been so upset by her subsequent expression of horror and distaste when he had asked her if she could love a Scot. He shook his head while at the window, still unable to credit that the experience had even happened. He had kissed her before, so it was not as though he was unprepared, but something occurred in that moment which he still could not quite comprehend.

He had felt as one with her, as though in the mysterious ways of life, she had simply come back to him from having been gone on a long voyage. Everything about kissing her had felt ancient and familiar, yet like nothing he had ever before experienced. How was that possible? What did it mean? He had never known such simple happiness in all his existence.

So when he drew back and asked her if she could love a Scot, he had meant the question most sincerely, but had expected a completely opposite response. He had expected her to gush over him, to ply her own kisses over his face, to say, 'With all my heart, my beloved Roger.' Instead, would he ever be able to forget the cold revulsion on her beautiful face?

He thought not.

"You make too much of Madeline's bewilderment," Mrs. Rockingham called out.

He turned slightly and saw that she was watching him with a sympathetic smile on her face.

"Trust me in this," she added. "She will come about. Oh, and I do believe that Lord Anthony is returned, for Churchill has moved to the doorway."

Sir Roger turned around and saw his dog seated in an alert position, ears forward, his tail wagging happily with future prospects. He was soon joined in his vigilance.

"Do but look," Sir Roger called out, gesturing to the doorway.

Mrs. Rockingham glanced in the direction of Churchill and chortled again. "I have never known Peaches to take to another dog as she has to yours. I believe it to be an omen, and a good one at that."

"Not for Lord Anthony, if I apprehend the matter."

Lord Anthony, however, had tricked Churchill, and arrived stealthily at the opposite end of the chamber. "Where is your dog, Roger?" he asked, whispering, for from his vantage point, he could not see Churchill.

However, he should not have spoken, for both Churchill and Peaches, once having heard his voice, bolted in his direction. Hearing the scattered clicks of their combined nails on the stone floor, he uttered a cry and disappeared down the hall. The dogs followed swiftly after.

Mrs. Rockingham, holding two letters on her lap, lifted her brows. "I still do not understand why he plays such games with either of the dogs. He will wear them out."

"I fear it is worse than you know. He is afraid of them."

"Afraid of them? What nonsense is this, when my poor Peaches has never hurt a single creature in her entire life?"

"There is no understanding it at all, ma'am."

On Tuesday, Madeline received an enormous bouquet of flowers with Sir Roger's card inscribed with, *Forgive me, R.* She sat for a long time on the edge of her bed, staring at the card and thinking that it was absolutely perfect, for no lengthy explanation of his conduct could ever suffice to make her happy about what had happened at Mrs. Rockingham's, and yet a complete absence of any form of atonement would have been quite beyond the pale.

She could only chuckle as she turned the card over and over in her hands. Had these been Sir Roger's thoughts as well?

She was just tidying the last few curls about her face and thinking that she would probably never wear her braids again, when a scratching sounded at her door.

"Come," she called out.

A maidservant appeared in the open doorway. "Beg your pardon, ma'am, but Lady Bladen is come to call. Shall I show her to the drawing room?"

"Yes, of course. Thank you. I shall be down directly."

A few minutes later, she found Georgiana seated on a sofa of pink silk damask, examining a nearby embroidery hoop.

"Good morning. How nice to see you. I had thought you would have returned to Somerset by now."

"On no account. Once having escaped, I meant to enjoy a little holiday and will be staying through my mother's fete. Mama, of course, would not forgive me otherwise."

"Of course."

"This is a lovely pheasant. Charity's work?"

"Indeed," she said, taking up a seat opposite her. "Is not her work perfection?"

"I must say it is, and though I fancy myself an accomplished needlewoman, her efforts quite put me to the blush."

"I shall relay your compliment to her, but what brings you here this morning? Your mama cannot like having you far from her side."

"No, she does not. She is quite attached to me and has never really forgiven me for having tumbled in love with Sir William."

"She cannot have any true objection to him."

Georgiana chuckled. "Only his holding his land in Somerset."

"Of course."

Georgiana then shifted her attention to Madeline. "So how do you fare after Saturday's excitement?"

Madeline shrugged. "Well enough, I suppose. In truth, I have not allowed myself to dwell on it overly much, and therefore I still do not know what I ought to do next to make things right. I imagine your mama has waxed long on Sir Roger's iniquities."

"Nearly as long as she has concerning my brother-in-law's conduct. Really, Madeline, what he said to Sir Roger was shocking. I for one cannot blame him at all for responding as he did. Richard deserved far worse than a blow to his chin, of that I am convinced. If Mrs. Rockingham chose to invite Sir Roger to her picnic, then there was no cause for anyone to have the smallest objection to his presence, whatever their private opinions."

"That is all very well and good, but Sir Roger lost his temper. That, I think is equally as unforgivable."

"Mama quite agrees with you, but for myself, I approve of Sir Roger's conduct. I think there is to a degree a certain hypocrisy in our society about such matters and I would like to see a more direct, more honest resolution to such conflicts. Believe me, Richard will think twice before ever challenging another man in such a fashion again. If we are to speak of tempers, Captain Bladen's is quite horrid."

"Indeed?" Madeline was surprised to hear say as much. To her, he had always been a perfect gentleman.

Georgiana nodded. "I know that he has been a favorite of yours for some time, but I must confess I have worried incessantly that you would accept an offer of marriage from him. I fear he is not all that he appears to be."

Madeline was shocked, but felt that given Georgiana's close association with that family through her marriage to Captain Bladen's elder brother, she was privy to a much deeper knowledge of his character than most of the ladies of her acquaintance. "I do not know how it was," she said, "but my heart could not truly warm to him."

"Not as it has to Sir Roger?"

Madeline felt a blush creep up her cheeks. "I do not understand how you have drawn such a conclusion," she cried, even though her father had already said something similar to her.

Georgiana grinned and tossed her head. Laughter bubbled in the air. "Oh, my dear Maddy, if you could but once see your face when you look at him. It is as though you are seeing into another world entirely, to which you desire more than anything to belong. I believe you are beginning—now, do not take a pet!—to love him."

Madeline pressed a hand to her stomach. She felt dizzy and slightly nauseous. "Am I?" she asked, feeling hopelessly confused. "But that would be such an impossibility. You can have no notion."

"But why?" her friend cried.

Madeline stared at her. "Because of his heritage, of course."

"Oh, pooh!" she returned with a dismissive wave of her hand. "What nonsense is this? These are modern times, Maddy. All that unfortunate history is forgot between our peoples. Clearly his mother had already come to that conclusion, being English."

"It is not so simple for me."

"Why?" she asked again.

"Because I hear my mother's voice in my head, her strictures on the subject of marriage and what I owe to our lineage."

"Though my own mother's beliefs are not dissimilar, our generation, yours and mine, has a greater responsibility here."

"And what would that be?" she asked, hoping against hope that her friend might present an argument that would help relieve her of her distress on the subject.

"To our hearts, of course. I have never told anyone this, but when I was in London several years past, the Marquess of Saye made me an offer of marriage. He was young, handsome, a gentleman of good fortune, but my heart was not touched in the least. Mama was beside herself that I insisted upon refusing him, but there was nothing for it. I was in love with William, and I have never regretted for one moment refusing Lord Saye."

Madeline found herself dumbstruck. "You refused a marquess?" she asked. What her own mother would have said on this subject, even though it was quite different from the heinous notion of marrying a Scot, would have resounded through the halls of Fairlight for a full twelve month. "Is this true?"

"Yes," she said, smiling. "And had William been Scottish, or even Irish, I would have married him regardless."

Madeline grew quiet for a long moment as she pondered her friend's revelations. She appreciated her openness as well as her opinions, but she still could not escape the nagging sensation that in either wedding or in possibly developing an affection for Sir Roger, she was committing a most disloyal offense.

She pressed her hand to her forehead. "In truth, what my sentiments toward Sir Roger may or may not be are not my first consideration, as you may recall."

"That's right," Georgiana murmured. "Your father's debts."

"Why do you smile in that manner?" she asked, suspicious suddenly.

Georgiana giggled. "It is nothing. I always liked your father. He could be such a devilish creature at times. I remember once when I had come to visit you, he hid my muff and told me if I wished for it I would have to find it. Do you remember? I walked all over Fairlight and finally found it under a cushion in the drawing room."

Madeline shook her head. "He can be amusing and charming and quite annoying all at the same time, but for the present I am quite put out with him for having placed me in this wretched predicament."

Georgiana rose to her feet. "Wretched, indeed!" she exclaimed facetiously, as she began preparing to take her leave. "You are being courted by a very handsome gentleman, to whom you are not the least indifferent, who has more guineas than Golden Ball Hughes—"

"Golden Ball Hughes?" she cried.

"Well, very nearly as much."

"Wealthy, indeed," Madeline murmured, awestruck. "I had no notion."

"And he is head over ears in love with you."

"He is not."

"Now who is speaking nonsense?"

Madeline doubted quite sincerely that Sir Roger had any such depth of sentiment toward her. Regardless, however, of the state of either of their respective hearts, she still had to somehow finagle an invitation to Georgiana's mother's fete in four day's time.

"Now what has wrinkled your forehead?" Georgiana asked.

"I have told you of Sir Roger's conditions to the marriage, but the only means by which I believe I will have even the smallest chance of getting an invitation to Lady Cottingford's harvest ball is by making the introductions at your mother's fete. Only how will I ever get your dear parent to grant such a favor?"

"I have not the smallest notion," Georgiana responded. "But come. I must away, or she will come the crab when I return to Hambledon Court. Walk me to your door?

"Of course." Madeline rose, caught up her friend's arm in her own, and strolled with her into the entrance hall.

"I promise I shall do what I can," Georgiana said, "to encourage Mama to relent in inviting Sir Roger to the ball. Perhaps you could bring him to call. I believe he might be able to charm my mother if given the chance. Say tomorrow for nuncheon? I shall pretend I forgot that I asked him to join us, but I will have already made arrangements with Cook. Will that do?"

Madeline felt tears spring to her eyes. "Thank you," she gushed. "Yes, that will do famously, as well you know."

"Tomorrow at noon for nuncheon, then." She kissed Madeline's cheek and was gone.

Madeline closed the door, a relief so profound sweeping over her that for a very long moment she felt dizzy again. Regaining her balance, she immediately penned a note to

Sir Roger and had a footman deliver it posthaste. An hour later, she received a response of acceptance.

> *I shall call for you at half past ten o'clock, which*
> *should give us ample time to arrive at Hambledon*
> *Court at the appropriate hour.*
>
> R.M.

Madeline smiled as she read the missive for the third time. At least he was punctual. At least she could rely on him in that. Now if only he could learn to manage his temper.

Ten

The next day, Madeline sat beside Sir Roger within the elegant confines of his crested traveling coach. Though the roads were well tended with gravel and the vehicle nicely sprung, she could not be at ease. She did not know what to say to him, how to begin an impossible apology, or whether such an attempt ought even to be made. She found her tongue to be utterly immobile, the silence within the conveyance disrupted only by the patter of a summer shower on the roof of the coach.

The first part of the four-mile journey had therefore been accomplished in silence.

Finally, when she could bear the situation not a moment longer, she turned toward him. "Sir Roger," she began, her hands trembling.

He shifted an appraising gaze to her, his blue eyes speculative but not unkind, as he waited for her to speak.

She drew in a deep breath. "I feel I must apologize for what happened on Saturday last."

"I see." A frown split his brow. "Are you referring specifically to having begged for a kiss from me—or something else, perhaps?"

She tried to read his expression, but could not, at least not entirely. One aspect of it was clear. "You are angry," she said.

"Yes, a little. Of course."

"You have every right to be. I behaved abominably, and for that I do most sincerely beg your pardon."

"This will not do," he responded. "I must know in some explicitness to what you refer."

She felt deeply ashamed. "For having asked for your kisses and, once having taken delight in them, to have allowed my prejudices to have surmounted everything. It was wrong of me."

He was silent, searching her eyes carefully. "You acknowledge only that you regret your prejudice having surmounted the moment, but do you feel any remorse where your beliefs are concerned?"

She had known him to be an intelligent man, but in this moment she realized he was a great deal more perceptive than made her in the least comfortable. "I wish you might understand, Sir Roger. I was taught so very differently concerning our respective lineages that from the first I have struggled to accept that I will not be able to honor my mother's wishes and wed an Englishman. As for Saturday, in that moment when you asked me if I could love a Scot, I was reminded not only of your heritage but of the whole of my situation as well, of my father's enormous debts, of my pursuit of your fortune, which is utterly abhorrent to me, and of having to face the dragons of Chilchester one after the other, that I reacted far too strongly—indeed, so badly that I am mortified when I think of it. Everything about our arrangement is repugnant to me."

He turned away, his jaw working strongly.

She continued. "I realize you have every right to think ill of me, certainly to end our agreement this very moment if you desire, but I hope you will instead be patient with me, particularly since I have known of my father's distressing circumstances for scarcely a fortnight. I beg you will believe that I am attempting, with my whole heart, to come quickly to terms with all that is required of me in this situation."

He glanced at her, eyeing her thoughtfully for a long moment. A smile touched his lips. "Just how long, might I ask, have you been preparing that speech?"

She smiled ruefully in return. "Since Saturday. It has undergone at least a hundred revisions and still it does not seem in the smallest way adequate for the offense I have given."

He took sudden possession of her hand and lifted her gloved fingers to his lips. "Ours is a difficult and unusual courtship. We have both made it so for our respective and frequently unworthy reasons. You have been honest with me, I will grant you that much, and if you have spoken truly, then I suppose I must grant you the favor of patience—though I am, as you know, a rather impatient, hasty, quarrelsome fellow. I will only do so upon the condition, however, that you forgive me for planting Captain Bladen what I have come to understand was a damaging facer."

At that, she shook her head. "Though I was horrified to learn what he had said to you, I beg you will understand how seriously our local hostesses take these matters. Lady Hambledon will not forgive you so easily."

"But will you?"

"The point is moot if Lady Hambledon does not, for if we do not garner her blessing today, you will not be invited to the fete, and then there will be not the smallest opportunity of making Lady Cottingford's acquaintance."

"You have not answered my question." He still held her hand tightly, a circumstance that was causing her heart to increase its cadence. She felt by this gesture he was expressing his claim on her. Oddly, she found she rather liked it.

"As to that, I hope you will endeavor to gain command of your temper. Of course I can forgive you, I must forgive you, but if we are to be husband and wife, I would be very unhappy to be always fretting for fear that someone should say the wrong thing to you and you would be unable to keep from entering into a bout of fisticuffs."

"I was wrong to have struck Captain Bladen. I admit it freely. It would be of equal value, however, if the neighborhood in general learned not to insult my mother or my father's name. I know I cannot promise perfect acquiescence in this, Madeline, but I will do my best."

Madeline thought that never had two people forgiven with such restraint nor promised better conduct with less certainty or enthusiasm than she and Sir Roger Mathieson. She chuckled.

"Why do you laugh?" he asked, his fingers flexing about hers.

"Because we neither of us have granted the other a great deal."

He laughed as well. "No, I suppose we have not." He then shifted toward her sufficiently to catch her gaze once more. "In truth, Madeline, I would have ended our secret betrothal entirely on Saturday had I not been so completely bowled over by the kiss we shared. I am still not persuaded we shall suit, not in the least, but I could not entirely relinquish all hope after having held you in my arms as I did."

"Indeed?" she queried, not understanding him precisely. "You place so much importance, then, upon a kiss?"

"Not just any kiss. *That* kiss."

She felt a blush climb her cheeks. She recalled the kiss vividly, as she had innumerable times since Mrs. Rockingham's picnic. She doubted that as long as she drew breath she would ever be able to forget it. She still grew quite dizzy when she dwelled for even a minute or two on how extraordinary it had been. Yet not once had she thought it a proper basis for a marriage.

When she remained silent, he gave her fingers a gentle

squeeze. "The kiss was passionate, wholly and inutterably. I have never before experienced anything of the like. You astonished me, which was what caused me to ask you if you could love a Scot, because if I were to ascertain the answer to that question by how you kissed me in return, then I would have said you already did love me."

She stared at him in disbelief. "Because of a kiss alone you presumed I loved you?"

His smile was crooked. "No, I was simply hopeful that you had developed some measure of affection for me. How do you account for the kiss, if not love or affection?"

She shook her head. "I do not know. I had not considered the matter before, save that you are quite handsome and for some reason when I am near you my heart tends to race. But I had thought this was merely some bizarre animal sensation."

"It is," he whispered, leaning into her, his breath drifting over her cheek. He smelled of shaving soap and she nearly lost her own breath entirely . . . again.

"But such sensations often prove transitory and deceiving," she answered hastily, afraid of what she was feeling.

"Perhaps." She felt his lips touch her skin. Her eyes closed of their own volition. She was back in the maze, her body pressed tightly against his. Oh, dear, this would not do.

When she tried to draw away, he caught her opposite shoulder and turned her toward him, holding her gaze fiercely. "There is great passion in you, Madeline. I have felt it from the first, from that very day I found you on my property February last. I cannot explain it, but never has a lady hidden such passion more assiduously than you. Only you need not any longer, because I am here now, willing to hold you, to kiss you, to husband you."

His words felt like warm water all over her skin, as though she was sinking down into a spring that bubbled from the hot depths of the earth. She wanted him to say more, but the subject disturbed her. She wanted to think clearly about these matters and not just respond physically. "What are you suggesting?" she asked. "Would a passionate embrace, a kiss, a marital bed be sufficient for you? You have expressed your doubts today of our ability to make one another happy. How could a kiss, then, change that?"

"Not change," he responded. "Reveal. That is what I hope. That somewhere couched in the sweetness of your lips is a truth about you not yet revealed that might be the undoing of my heart."

She realized she loved the way he spoke of these things. "A revelation."

He nodded. "As much for you as for me. Let these things speak to you as well, Madeline. Do not dismiss the passionate nature of our kisses as being representative of only one facet of our beings. Rather, if you will, allow that these experiences might be gateways to something greater, in every respect, between us. If I have hope, that is the basis for my hope."

"I will allow it," she responded.

"Good," he said, a slow smiling stealing over his face. "I would kiss you again, even now, had we not just turned down the drive to Hambledon."

"We are arrived?" she asked, glancing about her, stunned.

"So it would seem."

"How did the time disappear?"

"It always seems to, quite inexplicably, when we are together."

Hambledon Court sat majestically on a swell of ground in the center of a vast park. Of all the local manors, Madeline had always felt that Hambledon shone most brightly

in the simplicity of its landscaping, which had all the hall-
marks of Capability Brown's inspired hand. The park
appeared as though it had always meant to enhance the
manor, with scattered lakes, stone bridges, and large, elegant trees all placed to give the most natural appearance
possible, yet she knew that the immediate grounds had
seen an entire renovation some ten years, past including
the difficult relocation of several large, established trees.
The effect was truly sublime.

Once within the manor, the decor felt ancient, warm and
familiar, like comfortable half boots that served the feet
year after year, requiring mending perhaps, but always fit-
ting to perfection. Georgiana swept into the entrance hall,
greeting them both with her gentle but effusive welcome.
Madeline was exceedingly grateful for this attention, since
she had no way of knowing precisely how Lady Hambledon or her husband would respond to Sir Roger's presence
in their home.

Once in the drawing room, decorated *en suite* in a buff
and robin's egg blue silk damask, Madeline comprehended
the lay of the land quite clearly. Lady Hambledon offered
a stiff nod of her head, while Lord Hambledon came forward and shook Sir Roger's hand warmly. Madeline
breathed a sigh of relief. Whatever her ladyship's displeasure, it did not extend to her husband. Half the battle was
won already.

She made the introductions, since Sir Roger had not
been properly introduced to Lady Hambledon. He bowed.
Again, she offered him a slight inclination of her head. She
had not been a leading hostess of Chilchester Valley for
nigh on two decades without having learned a thing or two.
Lord Hambledon poured a glass of sherry and shoved it
with enthusiasm into Roger's hand. Madeline accepted a
cup of tea gratefully.

Lady Hambledon swung a graceful arm to her right. "I

thank you for the flowers, Sir Roger. A very thoughtful gesture."

Sir Roger smiled faintly. "A necessary one, my lady, since my conduct on Saturday had the unforgivable result of placing you in dreadful proximity to Captain Bladen. For that, I am truly sorry."

She narrowed her soft brown eyes and met his gaze unflinchingly. She was a petite woman, but what she lacked in height she made up for in strength of spirit. More than one unheeding person had mistaken her stature for a measure of her determination and ability and had paid for it severely. Madeline watched over the rim of her teacup to see if Sir Roger would be so foolish. She found that her heart was hammering nervously against her ribs.

Sir Roger, however, would not be foolish today, it would seem. There was no arrogance in his manner, nor did he begin babbling in a foolish fashion. He politely waited for her to speak, manners Madeline knew Lady Hambledon would appreciate completely.

Finally, her ladyship said, "Had I not actually been present and heard for myself in what manner you were so sorely provoked, you would not be here today. I do not countenance gaming hell manners in the fine salons and beautiful grounds of our neighborhood families. Everything that we do, Sir Roger, from our gracious attitude one to another, is meant to set an example for the next generation, which leads me as well to say this, you did very right in taking some of the children under your wing. These picnics in which even the youngest of our members are permitted to frolic are meant for just these purposes, to instruct in the midst of gaiety. Fortunately, there were no children present at the time of Captain Bladen's assault on your parentage, but you must understand that I will not countenance another lapse of judgment from you, even if the memories of both your parents are damned in the presence of Chilchester society. As for Captain Bladen, he received my own thoughts on his conduct and will not be welcome in my house for some time to come, until I am persuaded he has been properly chastened. Do you understand what I am saying to you, Sir Roger?"

"Yes, my lady. Perfectly."

"And will you make every possible attempt to keep your temper tightly restrained?"

"Yes, I will."

Madeline breathed a very deep sigh of relief and offered Sir Roger a smile in response.

His lips twitched, but he gave his attention to Lady Hambledon who, like any good hostess, moved the conversation in a new direction entirely, asking after the progress of work on the castle.

Sir Roger spoke at length about the repairs he was making, dwelling in particular on his architect's attention to the various documents he had been using as his guide in order to preserve historical integrity. He referred casually to Mrs. Rockingham's visit of Monday and to the sense of gratification he felt in being able to include a descendent of a previous owner of the castle in his efforts. Lady Hambledon watched him, her brown eyes shrewd.

Lord Hambledon slapped his knee. "Damme, but don't I wish that at least part of it, the keep for instance, might retain some of its antiquated appearance." He smiled tenderly upon his wife. "One of the happiest of my memories was on the top of the keep tower. Do you recall, my love?"

Madeline watched in fascination as a faint blush stole upon the baroness's cheeks. A smile played at her lips, and she tossed her head. "This is hardly the moment to bring forward such a subject. I am certain neither Sir Roger nor Miss Piper have the smallest interest in the matter."

"But I do," Georgiana stated. She was seated adjacent to Madeline and addressed her father. "Pray tell us, Papa, to what you refer. I am all agog to know, for I can see that it is of a romantic nature, and, if you must know, your wife is terribly dull on the subject."

"If you mean by dull, discreet, then I most certainly am guilty," Lady Hambledon cried. However, her daughter would not meet her gaze but instead kept hers pinned expressly upon her father.

Lord Hambledon swirled his sherry in the small the glass. "The day was blustery, even cold. But my heart was as warm as a snug fire flanked by screens. Your mother's hand was tucked in mine and she smiled at me that day as though I had the moon in my pocket and meant to give it to her. We stole up to the top of the keep tower and I begged for her hand in marriage. By Jove, but didn't she accept me and make me the happiest of men."

"Oh, Peter," his bride chided, but there was a tear in her eye.

Madeline glanced at Sir Roger and noted an arrested expression on his face, even a faint frown. She wondered what he was thinking and hoped she might be able to ask him later. He sipped his sherry, then offered, "I first met Miss Piper at the castle. I had come to take possession of it and found her trespassing. I thought it an omen, a very hopeful omen, indeed."

Madeline now felt a blush on her cheek and hurriedly explained, "I was wont to go there as a child. I was forever listening to Mama's strictures on the subject of the need to forego my frequent explorations of the ruins. I heard rumors that the castle had not only been sold but was to be refurbished by the new owner. I desired more than anything to see it before it began changing. Like you, Lord Hambledon, my recollections are the sweetest of the ruins themselves."

"I was wondering," Sir Roger interjected, addressing Lady Hambledon, "if you would allow me to include in the castle documents the history of your husband's proposal. In centuries to come, I would like future visitors to know not just its warrior history but also the reality of all the lives that are touched by a building so majestic and ancient as Pelworthy. Would you allow it, my lady?"

Lady Hambledon seemed torn, but her husband encouraged her. "I should like it above all things, my pet. Please permit it, for my sake?"

"I must confess that I do not comprehend in the least why you should wish it so, but I shan't prevent you from having your way. However, since it is your desire, then I request that you compose the tale yourself and see it delivered to Sir Roger."

"As you wish, my love." He swirled his sherry a little more and grinned like a schoolboy.

The subject was let drop, and when Lord Hambledon began making inquiries of Sir Roger's adventures in India, Georgiana took the opportunity to draw the ladies into an adjoining parlor, where apparently there was an exquisite arrangement of roses to be seen. Madeline followed behind, glancing once at Sir Roger and Lord Hambledon. The last she heard was Lord Hambledon's query asking if Sir Roger had ever been caught in a hurricane.

Madeline would have liked to have heard his answer, but she slipped into the antechamber and Georgiana guided her to a seat at some distance from the doorway. Since Lady Hambledon was already seated, and the arrangement of flowers consisted of a meagre three roses and a tall fern, she found herself wary. She wondered what her good friend meant by it.

She did not have long to wait.

Georgiana, her hands clasped before her, spoke hastily. "I beg you will tell Mama of your circumstances, Maddy. I believe it would be of some use in our present situation."

"You mean of Father?" she asked.

"Yes, of course."

Madeline had not been prepared in the least to once more tell the story of her father's wretched perfidy in Brighton, but since Lady Hambledon was clearly prepared to hear it all, she felt she had no recourse but to begin. She spoke succinctly of having learned of his extensive losses and of her father's belief that Sir Roger was the solution to the salvation of the Piper's lands and standing in society.

At the end of the history, Lady Hambledon wrinkled her nose, which gave her a momentary appearance of a young girl. "Horace Piper lost his fortune in Brighton?"

"Yes, my lady."

"I am dumbfounded. Indeed, I am loath to believe a word of it and would not have, had you not been the author of the story, Madeline." She shook her head vigorously. "But are you certain?"

"Quite. He was extremely remorseful and had no need to lie to me."

"I must confess I am shocked. Why, then, does he mean to purchase Randolph Crawley's racing gig?"

"I beg your pardon?"

"At the picnic, Randolph was telling me all about it— that your father rather fancied learning how to drive a racing gig and was he of a mind to sell his. Since Randolph had had his made especially in London, the price he was asking was rather dear, at least for one who had so recently suffered a reversal of fortune as it would seem your father had."

Madeline lowered her gaze for a long moment. She found herself deeply disappointed in her parent yet again. First she learned he was purchasing Mr. Calvert's mare and now Randolph's gig. For a man who was in the basket, he was certainly behaving as though all was well. "I cannot credit he would be pondering such a purchase so hard on the heels of his losses. Nothing is for certain, as well he knows. Sir Roger is courting me, for he wishes to know if we might suit, but we have signed no papers of engagement. Nothing has been promised as yet. I must say, Papa has been behaving quite strangely of late, purchasing things when he ought not, and he has even taken to driving to Elsbourne without explanation. What could possibly be his reason for going to Elsbourne?"

She lifted her gaze and saw that Lady Hambledon was looking at the ceiling, her expression conscious. "What is it?" Madeline asked. "You must tell me what it is you are thinking, or what you know."

Lady Hambledon met her gaze. "Perhaps he is tumbled in love," she suggested.

"I must confess that that particular thought has crossed my mind, but with whom? Do you know anyone in Elsbourne to whom my father might have become attached?"

Lady Hambledon cleared her throat. "I believe that question would be best put to your father, my dear. No, no I will not discuss that subject further. It would, I believe, be most improper."

With that, Madeline had to be content. "As you wish."

Georgiana, who had been standing by the window, swished past her mother's chair and took up a seat on the ottoman at her knee. "Mama, will you now grant the favor I requested of you earlier? Now that you know of Madeline's most wretched dilemma, will you not support her in this time of trouble, if not for her, then for your affection for her mother?"

Madeline glanced at Lady Hambledon hopefully. Though she was a trifle taken aback by Georgiana's sudden request, she felt she had reason to hope.

Lady Hambledon narrowed her gaze yet again. "I must confess, Madeline, that had my daughter not been hounding me for days, I would not have countenanced even receiving Sir Roger today. I admit I am pleased with his general demeanor and conduct, but I doubt that I shall ever forget the horror of seeing Captain Bladen laid out at my feet."

Madeline nodded in agreement, since she had been of a similar mind in that moment. Hope dimmed as suddenly as it had risen.

"However, having heard Captain Bladen's provoking remark, I am not without sympathy for Sir Roger. There is something, however, I should like to know. Why have you been working so strenuously to introduce Sir Roger to Chilchester society?"

Madeline considered telling Lady Hambledon of the precise nature of her arrangement with Sir Roger, that only an invitation to Lady Cottingford's harvest ball would do for him, but she thought the better of it. Instead, she responded, "He desires above all that his children be accepted fully into the local Society. Anything less is wholly repugnant to him. He required of me, therefore, to prove to him that it was possible before he would agree to seal the bargain."

"I see," she murmured. "I believe he may be right in this."

Madeline could see that this was the moment on which her future yet again turned. She could see in her hostess's brown eyes the weighing and calculating of the decision before her. If she said no, there would be no hope at all of charming Lady Cottingford, since Madeline was but a very distant acquaintance of that great London hostess. Her heart began to race and she felt a warmth upon her cheeks. Oh, dear, what if she said no? What then?

She would not think of that.

"I believe," Lady Hambledon began slowly, "that I will help you. You have done nothing wrong, Madeline, and it seems to me that your father is the true culprit here. I will send Sir Roger and Lord Anthony an invitation to my fete on Saturday. Will that suffice?"

"Exceedingly so," Madeline responded. "You have no idea."

"Oh, but I believe I do. Come, you may kiss my cheek, and then we shall enjoy a nice nuncheon."

Two hours later, after the meal had been consumed, Madeline felt Georgiana slip her arm about her waist. She returned the gentle embrace as together the ladies strolled in the direction of Sir Roger's traveling chariot.

"It is a fine carriage," Georgiana remarked.

"Quite beautifully sprung, as it happens," Madeline responded. "Oh, dear friend. How shall I ever repay you?"

"Well, there is something you might do for me."

"Anything within my power."

"Name your firstborn, either male or female, after me— George or Georgiana."

Madeline smiled. "But it is not a Scottish name," she responded, glancing at the carriage beside which Sir Roger stood conversing in some animation with Lord Hambledon.

Georgiana shrugged. "It is not English, either, but German."

Together the ladies laughed heartily. "George or Georgiana it shall be."

On the return trip to Fairlight Manor, Madeline remained in a glow of relief and happiness. In truth, she had not expected so much support from any of the ladies or gentlemen of her acquaintance. But Mrs. Crawley was content in making her plans for Sir Roger's Christmas ball, and it would seem Mrs. Rockingham was already deeply committed to establishing a historical society for Pelworthy. Even Lady Hambledon had been fair in her assessment of the culpability for the disaster at Dallings Hall when Sir Roger struck down Captain Bladen. She felt hopeful as she had never felt hopeful before.

"You are beaming. Do I apprehend that you have once more achieved the impossible?"

"Lady Hambledon will be sending an invitation to Pelworthy within the hour," she declared. "I dare say it shall be awaiting you when you arrive."

He smiled and shook his head. "I must confess I enjoyed myself very much this afternoon. Your neighborhood continually surprises me, you know."

At that, Madeline chuckled. "No less than myself, I assure you. I begin to believe I have been much mistaken in many of my acquaintances. What did you think of Lord Hambledon's proposal of marriage?"

"I thought it charming, though I was quite astonished. I had not expected such openness, nor such a genuine display of affection as Lady Hambledon's tears."

"You had thought all of us as dull as dogs."

He chuckled. "Perhaps."

"What do you think now?"

"That Chilchester society keeps the very best of itself hidden most of the time. It is a pity, for I have never been more charmed than I was today."

"So were you caught in a hurricane?" Madeline asked.

"Yes, off the coast of India. I do not know how the ship survived. The masts and timbers creaked and groaned like you cannot imagine, and all the while the wind howled around the ship. Of course we were crippled afterward, severely, but a Dutch ship carried us a day's journey to the coast."

Madeline looked at him, wondering suddenly why he was settling for the tameness, indeed often insipidity, of English country life and said so.

He laughed. "I suppose one needs to have a survived a

hurricane to be able to say that a dull country existence is highly underrated."

Madeline smiled but then said, "I envy you your life abroad. There was a time when I longed very much to have adventures."

"Why do I have the sensation that was a very long time ago?"

"Because it was."

Eleven

Madeline drew her cape more closely about her shoulders and smiled. She was seated in the family coach, opposite Charity, Hope, and her father. Prudence sat next to her. Though she was quite anxious about the forthcoming fete at Lady Hambledon's, she was also exhilarated. Over the past fortnight, she had achieved the impossible in guiding Sir Roger through what had proved the rocky shoals of Chilchester society, an accomplishment of no small merit and of which she felt very proud. Of course, she had had Georgiana's support in this latest momentous effort. Without her help, Lady Hambledon would have scarcely allowed a social call, let alone granted of an invitation.

"I have not seen you so happy in months, Maddy," her father said. "Though I can guess the cause of it. May I also say that it is a delight to see you smiling so very much?"

"I am happy," she announced.

"And you look so very pretty!" Hope exclaimed. "Your hair has never been lovelier."

"Thank you," she said, regarding her youngest sister with considerable affection. "You do not think I am sporting too many curls, do you?"

All three of her sisters disclaimed this in such loud accents as even the smallest possibility so that she could only laugh. Yes, she was quite content, indeed, and even felt excited at the prospect of attending Lady Hambledon's fete, an excitement she had not felt in a very long time. She wondered why precisely, although the moment an image of Sir Roger Mathieson came to the forefront of her mind, she knew at least one reason. In truth, and this much she was able to admit to herself, she was looking forward very much to seeing him again. Even parting from him on Wednesday, after their joint visit with Lady Hambledon, she had known the strongest desire to beg him to call on her the next day. She had restrained herself, however, permitting him to drive off in his coach with but a farewell and a wave of her hand.

So it was that tonight, as the coach rumbled its way toward Romsbury Village and Hambledon Court, she found herself rather longing to see him again, a circumstance she could not quite explain. She had come to enjoy his society when they were not brangling, but the feeling she was experiencing presently seemed to indicate that she had to some extent come to depend on his society, however strange the notion.

"Maddy," her father said, interrupting her reveries her again.

"Yes, Papa?"

She glanced at her parent and watched him draw a deep breath, a perplexed frown settling over his forehead. "What would you say if I told you that I fancied a Frenchwoman and meant to wed her?"

Madeline stared at him for a long moment, as did her sisters, each with mouth agape. However, she soon realized he was poking fun at her predicament of being betrothed to a Scotsman. "A Frenchwoman," she cried. "How absurd!" She began to laugh and laugh. She did not know why the notion struck her as so ridiculous, but so it did. Her sisters joined in her merriment. "Oh, Papa," she added, seeing a smile disrupt his former frown. "What would Mama think of that? I believe she would think her entire household had gone mad!" She laughed harder still and did not stop until tears streamed down her cheeks.

"I do not think it was that funny," he offered, appearing a little sheepish.

"I suppose . . . it was . . . not," Madeline said, wiping at her cheeks from a kerchief she had withdrawn hastily from her beaded reticule. "It is merely that . . . given my situation . . . you must admit that were you to do anything so absurd, how much the entire neighborhood would be given to gossip exclusively about the Pipers."

She watched him shrug his shoulders and turn to stare at the passing landscape, the downs cloaked in evening's twilight. After a mile had passed, she glanced once more at her father, intending to tease him about joking her as he had, but something in his expression—which seemed quite despairing, she thought—arrested her tongue in mid word. She felt uneasy suddenly, as though she had stumbled upon the subject for his sadness, and should not have done so. She quickly turned to Charity and broached a different and quite innocuous subject by asking if she had finished her beautiful pheasant yet.

Charity responded that she had not, and the subject now shifted to more domestic issues, continuing until the avenue leading to Hambledon had been reached. From that point, the occupants of the coach fell silent as every gaze scoured the grounds.

"I have never seen so many Chinese lanterns!" Hope exclaimed. In these few words she gave utterance to the general feeling of awe now prevalent within the coach. It would seem Lady Hambledon had created a fete, indeed.

Lady Hambledon's imagination had been captured by the east. Her home had been decorated with palm trees, an enormous array of flowers of every kind undoubtedly obtained from the London markets, and thousands of lanterns casting her gently rolling park into a fairyland of light. At odd, unexpected moments, fireworks would suddenly burst from one vantage or another, setting the crowd of guests into surprised cries followed by applause. The male servants paraded about in Morrocan slippers and garb reminiscent of the east, their heads covered in turbans. The serving maids wore glittering gold tunics over muslin gowns, their curls and faces covered by flowing scarves and veils. Champagne flowed, and fruits, sweetmeats, a variety of nuts, tartlets, and smoked fish were offered innumerable times to guests traveling from one intriguing location to the next. The pathways were punctuated with gypsies telling fortunes, with jugglers and magicians teasing the youngest of the ladies, and in the center of all, well into the heart of her land, was an enormous tented ballroom in which an orchestra could be heard playing a constant stream of familiar melodies.

Madeline walked with her sisters until one by one they were drawn off by their friends or beaus. Her father disappeared early on, heading in the direction of the billiard room with Squire Crawley. By the time she was alone, Georgiana found her, taking her by the arm and confessing that even she felt her mother had surpassed herself in the exotic and wondrous scope of her fete.

"Have you seen the lions?" her friend asked.

"I beg your pardon?" Madeline responded, stunned.

"Yes, there are two lions in cages. The handler steps inside and the huge beasts perform tricks."

"I must see them at once," she said.

Georgiana guided her in to an eastern path well lit with swaying lanterns, a delightful breeze adding to the charm and gaiety of the festivities. "I hear them," Madeline cried. "What a dreadful sound!"

A servant bearing a turban, his skin darkened by what

Georgiana had told her was walnut juice, bowed and offered a glass of champagne and apricot tartlets. Madeline
could not resist, nor could her friend. On they moved,
heading in increasing fright toward the roar of the African
beasts.

Madeline's happiness grew, as well as her pride in her
accomplishment. She was here at Lady Hambledon's fete,
as were Sir Roger and Lord Anthony, though she had seen
neither gentlemen yet.

A young lady Madeline immediately recognized as Arabella Lindfield darted across her path, causing both ladies
to stop abruptly. She was squealing with laughter, the
cause of which soon made itself known as a rather wild
young man from the village of Balfriston, Thomas Pid-
dinghoe, followed quickly in her wake.

Madeline was disgusted and lifted an eyebrow. Georgiana, however giggled beside her. "Oh, to be young and
in love."

"I doubt they are in love," Madeline returned severely.

She felt her friend give her arm a squeeze. "Oh, Maddy.
You are too prosy at times."

"How can you say such a thing? Were any of my sisters
to act in so hoydenish a manner, I should be mortified beyond words."

Georgiana sighed but let the subject drop, an easy thing
to achieve since another roar, closer now, had captivated
their attention completely. No, Madeline could not agree
with her friend in the least. What strictures her mother
would pronounce were she to have witnessed such an
event!

Madeline smiled. Her mother had been very particular,
indeed. Her words returned to her: *A lady always rises
above the ignorant, the coarse, the foolish.* Madeline suddenly realized that was how she felt in all her dealings with
Sir Roger and how it was she had been able to overcome

much of her dislike of being courted by him. She had risen above his unfortunate birth. In this, too, she felt a great deal of pride in herself. After all, she had been forced into the odious situation completely against her will, her wishes, her true desires for the future. But she was thereby doing her duty to her family, and in this she took immeasurable comfort and, yes, pride.

When the path opened to reveal two red and black cages settled amongst spreading oaks, the ladies gasped to witness the trainer's hand held captive in the mouth of one of the lions. A crowd was gathered in stunned awe at the man's courage, Madeline no less so. He removed his hand, at which time the crowd applauded him fiercely. The lion sat quietly until a series of fireworks exploded nearby. The lion roared, causing even the trainer to jump slightly. Several cries went up. The trainer took the chain at the lion's neck and gave a tug. The lion immediately lay down.

Madeline was watching, her gaze riveted to the trainer, when suddenly she felt hands on her waist and a pinch that followed so swiftly that she was sure she was being attacked. She shrieked and whirled about only to find Sir Roger grinning at her.

"Oh, what a devilish thing to do!" she exclaimed.

"It was awful, and I would beg your pardon, except that now you are smiling, so you cannot be too overset. How do you do, Lady Bladen?"

"Very well, thank you." An exchange of pleasantries followed, but only for a handful of minutes, after which Georgiana excused herself, saying that she had just caught a glimpse of Julia Rockingham and needed to speak with her at once.

Madeline did nothing to prevent her leaving. How could she when Sir Roger was standing next to her looking resplendent in a black tailcoat of superfine, a finely embroidered burgundy silk waistcoat, black breeches, silk stockings, and black leather shoes? His neckcloth was tied in a simple manner, his shirtpoints were of a medium height, and in every respect he gave the impression he had taken Brummel's dictums on fashion quite seriously. She approved warmly of his appearance, another reason she felt quite proud tonight, for unless one was knowledgeable about Sir Roger's parentage, one would think he was an English gentleman and nothing less.

For some reason, these thoughts, however noble in her own mind, suddenly brought her father's image back to her of how he had appeared when she had laughed so heartily at his saying he was in love with a Frenchwoman. She could recall vividly the despair in his eyes and on his face. Only why on earth was she thinking of that now, when everything was going so well for her?

She therefore pushed the thoughts aside, and when Sir Roger asked if she would honor him with the next waltz, she agreed readily. He offered his arm, and together they walked in the direction of the tent.

"How are you enjoying Lady Hambledon's decorations?" she asked, smiling up at him. "It must please you in its familiarity."

"Very much so, you can have no idea. My thoughts more than once have been given to memories of having resided in India. I found myself grateful for her choice of theme. What did you think of the lions?"

"They frightened me. I cannot imagine how their trainer is able to command his own fears."

"That I suppose we shall never know."

Lord Anthony came into view, with Cressida Crawley on his arm. He was looking down into the young woman's face, his expression deeply affectionate.

"A love match?" she queried softly, as the couple disappeared down another brightly lit path.

"I believe it may be, particularly since I know for certain that Mrs. Crawley told him she never permits the squire to bring any of his dogs in the house."

Madeline chuckled. "Then it is a match for certain."

As they made their way toward the tent, Madeline surveyed the scattered groups, her gaze seeking the tall, elegant figure of Lady Cottingford. Thus far, she had not encountered her ladyship, and even now she did not see her among the guests. She released a small sigh. However much she might be enjoying the fete, she was still cognizant of one quite necessary deed she must accomplish, the most difficult of all, in fact. Not only must she introduce Sir Roger to the viscountess, but she would also have to begin the delicate process of procuring an invitation for herself, her father, and Sir Roger to her ladyship's prestigious harvest ball.

Her heart skipped a beat several times in response to the truth that though she had accomplished a great deal, the largest dragon to slay was yet before her. Only where was Lady Cottingford?

Sir Roger glanced at the lady beside him. He saw the slight frown marring her forehead and knew that she was hunting for Viscountess Cottingford. His conscience smote him as he recalled the truth of his situation. He knew he was using her badly in this regard, and for the barest moment he debated telling her she need no longer fret about procuring the harvest ball invitations.

Only for a moment, however. Some instinct warned him against the idea, at least for the present, something perhaps yet unknown to him about Madeline Piper.

"This is by far the most elaborate of Lady Hambledon's fetes," she commented.

"I begin to think we have been transported to Olympus."

The lady beside him chuckled. "She would like to hear you have said as much. She is very fond of a compliment."

"Most people are, I believe."

"Indeed, I think you have the right of it."

The open air tent, which amounted to an enormous canopy, was lit with equal dazzle by scores of Chinese lanterns. Here, palms and flambeaux flanked every taut, supporting rope so that no guest would be tripping over unseen lines. Sir Roger was impressed, for every detail had been attended to with thought and care. At an opportune moment, he would offer his compliments to his hostess, for in his vast experience, particularly having enjoyed the last three London Seasons, he had seen any number of rather spectacular events. Lady Hambledon's fete surpassed most of them.

He found he was enjoying himself prodigiously and had done so as well at both Mrs. Crawley's soiree and Mrs. Rockingham's picnic. He was very fond of Society. "I want to thank you, Madeline, for your strenuous efforts on my behalf."

At that, she looked up at him and smiled. "You do not accuse me of doing so merely because my family has need of your fortune?"

He could see that she was teasing him, and the candid reference to the purpose of their imminent betrothal made him smile broadly in response. "I believe I can be grateful whatever your motivations. I would not have come to know Chilchester society without your exertions. You are to be commended."

"Thank you," she responded in a manner that let him know she was fully aware of her achievements as well.

Nearing the tent, a servant passed by, bearing empty champagne glasses. He leaned near her. "Did I tell you that I have received confirmation of my order for the wine? Five hundred bottles. A small fortune, actually."

She shook her head. "I have told such whiskers over the past fortnight. I still blush when I think on it."

"You blush very prettily, too."

She glanced at him, her lovely green eyes lit with laughter. She had never appeared more beautiful than now, with the flambeaux near the tent ropes casting flickers of light over her face. A powerful sensation gripped his chest, and had not the present country dance been ending and a waltz announced, he might have suggested a long walk into the less frequented pathways.

As it was, he led her onto the ballroom floor, took her in his arms, and smiled down into her face. "Do you realize this is the first time we shall have danced together?"

Madeline felt peculiar. Sir Roger's hand was upon her back, his other holding hers in a gentle clasp. A dizziness assailed her. She blinked, wondering if she would be able to manage the steps and whirls of the dance when she could not feel her feet precisely.

The music commenced. With a firm pressure on her back, he began guiding her about the floor, up and back, round and round. All the while, she found she could not shift her gaze away from his.

She felt as though the lovely summer night, the luminous fete, the dizzying whirls of the dance were all combining to cast the most inexplicable spell over her. She knew there were at least a score of couples also engaged in the waltz and circling the floor, but they were only a blur.

Up and back, round and round.

Nor did Sir Roger speak. Instead, he continued to hold her gaze with his, his blue eyes intense, his lips parted, his expression unreadable. She felt the strength of him in that moment, of his spirit, his willfulness, his stubbornness. She had not known a man like him before. There was perhaps in his Celtic nature an untamed vitality that the gentlemen of Chilchester lacked generally. She felt, even believed, that he was the sort of man who could accomplish anything were he to put his mind and shoulder to it. Had he not done so already in India?

The music of the waltz seemed to play on and on forever. The more he turned her and whirled her, the more she fell beneath his spell, so that when the dance ended, she felt as though an entire eternity had passed.

He hurried her away into the darkness of the night, stealing her along first one pathway, then the next, always the brightly lit island of the waltzing tent drifting farther and farther away from their small little ship. She continued to look at him, surprised and overwhelmed. She still did not comprehend what she was feeling, except that when he suddenly drew her into the deep shade of a sprawling oak and took her roughly in his arms, all of life made sense to her in that moment.

She gave herself to his kiss the way she had surrendered to the waltz, as though he alone existed on the earth and no other. She clung to him, captivated completely by what was transpiring in a powerful flow between them, of mystery and passion. He had told her he had felt that together they were capable of great passion, but until now, until he was holding her so tightly against him, until his tongue was piercing her mouth so sweetly, she had not comprehended his meaning.

Now, it was as though all the secrets of heaven had been revealed to her. Was this love? Her mind cried to know. Her heart responded in a thousand affirmations. This must be love—yet how was it possible?

"Dearest Madeline," he whispered against her lips. "Only tell me, could you love a Scot?"

She leaned back to look into his face, the blue of his eyes nearly black in the deep protective shadows of the oak tree. Did she love him? Could she? "I am believing it more every moment I'm with you," she whispered in return.

Without waiting for him to respond, she made a small cry and kissed him hard.

Nor was he hesitant as once more he embraced her roughly, kissing her thoroughly, wantonly, until she was breathless. The dizziness she had felt while waltzing with him increased tenfold. She was floating and delirious, happy beyond measure in the warmth and excitement of being kissed by him.

Only after a time did he finally release her and then with a chuckle against her cheek. "I fear ruining your lovely curls. I find I can scarcely keep my fingers from sinking into your locks."

She laughed as well. "I think there is some madness at Lady Hambledon's fete tonight."

"Madness, indeed," he murmured, "of the very sweetest kind." Straightening his coat and waistcoat and smoothing down his hair, for her fingers had been less restrained than his own, he guided her back onto the lighted path and gradually began returning her to the party.

As he walked beside her, the glow of having kissed her clung to him like a gentle summer rain. He was happier than he had ever been before, happy that he was with her, that she walked beside him, that she had kissed him so passionately. He understood in this moment that he loved her. The thought came to him in such purity and simplicity that he did not question it in the least. He loved her. He believed he had loved her from the first, from that cold winter's day when he had come upon her at the castle and she had been so lost in thought and appeared like an angel to him. Yes, he loved her very much, indeed. Only was she beginning to love him? Could she love him? If her kisses were any indication, the answer was a resounding yes and yet something within him still felt uncertain, though why he could not say.

He held her arm tightly, feeling a strong impulse to tell

her she had no need to bother about procuring invitations to the harvest ball. He looked down at her and opened his mouth to speak, but her expression arrested the words at the tip of his tongue. "What is it?" he asked.

"There, near the pond. They are watching us."

"Who?" he asked, his gaze sweeping hard across the shadowy landscape. Finally, he saw the source of her troubled expression. Mr. Calvert and young Mr. Rockingham stood in frozen, condemning judgment. Harris once more had his hand to an imaginary sword hilt.

"Do you think they saw us emerge from the woods?" she asked.

"Undoubtedly."

"Oh, dear. I trust Mr. Calvert to keep his temper, but Harris—"

Sir Roger glanced about quickly and saw to the west that a rather large bank of fireworks was being readied for display. "Come," he said. "There is a group gathering near the fireworks. If either of the gentlemen desire to confront me, let them do so in a crowd." He felt her arm trembling beneath his own. "You have nothing to fear. I beg you will trust me in that."

Madeline chuckled nervously. "I do not fear for you, Sir Roger, but rather for either of the gentlemen should your temper be aroused once more. Harris would dearly love to fight a duel, and it has been made known to me that you are a true marksman."

"I would not think for a moment to accept a challenge from Mr. Rockingham. He is fully twelve years my junior. It simply is not done."

"I shall hold you to that, sir," she responded uneasily.

"Come, the fireworks await us."

The ploy was sufficient to keep the hostile gentlemen at bay. A large crowd had quickly gathered in a semicircle before the fireworks, and Sir Roger maneuvered their relative positions several times to keep an adequate distance from Mr. Calvert and Mr. Rockingham. Madeline entered into the spirit of the game and for the next hour, as they moved swiftly from one small vignette of entertainment to the next and finally back to the well-lit tent, Sir Roger was able to avoid a confrontation with the men.

Eventually, he was separated from Madeline, as such large events were wont to separate any two persons. He let her go, doubting he would be in such intimate company with her again. Indeed, besides going down a country dance with her, then being whisked away to the house for a game of billiards with Squire Crawley and Lord Hambledon, he did not see her again the remainder of the evening.

So it was late that night, or rather in the early hours of the morning, he found himself back in his drawing room alone. Lord Anthony had retired for the night, expressing a profound unwillingness to confront Churchill when he had had so many iced cups of champagne. He sat therefore alone, swirling a snifter of brandy and pondering all that had happened. The kiss beneath the oak tree had been profound and revealing, at least for him. He had come to recognize the truth as well as the depths of his feelings for Madeline Piper. However, he was left with an equally profound uneasiness, wondering about her true sentiments or certainly whether she had softened at all in her dislike of anyone not of English descent.

The brandy swirled and swirled. His thoughts bent round and round the puzzle of who Madeline really was. He could form no conclusion, save one. He would tell her soon that she no longer needed to labor to get the invitations to Lady Cottingford's ball. That at least he owed her for all her efforts.

The night had been wondrous indeed. He had enjoyed himself prodigiously, and not just because of Madeline.

The game of billiards with Lord Hambledon and the squire had been precisely what he enjoyed. There was always a political flavor to any gathering of gentlemen that soon sparked a spirited debate. Just such a discussion had ensued and any number of rousing sentiments were brought forth that only served to enhance the competitive nature of the game.

Yes, he had enjoyed the evening from beginning to end. He had been able to spend a great deal of time with Madeline, to dance with her, even to kiss her, which always pleased him. This was a critical truth. He enjoyed her company, he delighted in her kisses, and he loved her. Yes, he loved her more than he could possibly express. He understood now that he had always loved her, from that first meeting so long ago, and that he always would.

How happy his mother would have been had she witnessed all that had transpired, even that he had tumbled in love with an Englishwoman.

He sat forward suddenly, a frown pinching his brow. He understood something in that moment which he had not before, that his mother would not have given a fig for any of it save that he was happy. These were his objectives and the things that brought joy to his life, not anything that she would have, in themselves, applauded. Perhaps he had begun the whole venture, of forcing his way into Chilchester society, in order to somehow make reparations for his mother's sufferings, but in truth, she had not suffered. She had never once evinced the smallest regret at her decisions or even in being ostracized. Sadness, yes, but only a little. Regret, no. Rather, he was the one who had suffered.

He tossed off the remainder of his brandy, chuckling softly at how greatly he had deluded himself. No, he had entered Chilchester society for one reason only, to make up for the sufferings of his youth.

Even as the awareness came to him, another truth surfaced: however much he loved Madeline, however much he enjoyed being part of Chilchester society, he could not enter into a marriage with her unless she reciprocated his feelings completely. That was the legacy of his mother's life. She had loved his father truly, and theirs had been a happy union. He wanted no less for himself and his children.

Twelve

Madeline awoke on Monday morning with a start. She sat straight up in bed, a certain terrible realization striking her—she had forgotten entirely to make certain that Sir Roger was introduced to Lady Cottingford at Lady Hambledon's fete! How could she have been so stupid, so thoughtless, so forgetful? But even as these thoughts pierced her head, another one, much more delightful in nature, flowed over her, the very same thought which had dominated her mind all through Sunday, that Sir Roger had kissed her again and this time she vowed she had been transported to the heavens. She was not certain she had as yet returned.

Surely after that kiss Sir Roger no longer cared about invitations to the harvest ball. Surely he had been as passionately moved and changed as she had. Surely.

She nibbled playfully at her fingernails, smiling all the while. She had never been so happy, never in her entire existence. Only when was she to see Sir Roger again? When would he kiss her again, and would he hold her to getting the invitations?

Well, there was only one thing to be done. She must ride over to Pelworthy and ask him herself. With this thought taking command so readily of all other thoughts, she leaped from her cosy, warm bed and immediately began dressing for the day.

By the time she had descended the stairs, the hour was sufficiently advanced so that she felt it would not be at all improper to call upon her neighbor immediately. She might have done so, even without the benefit of breakfast, but her father called to her just as she was leaving the front door.

"Madeline, will you delay for a moment? There is something of great import I would say to you."

She thought nothing could be more important of the moment than that she see Sir Roger right away, but she could hardly say as much to her father. "Of course," she responded, closing the door. "What is it? Your color seems rather high. Are you well?"

"Indeed, yes," he cried. "Come into my office where we might speak privately."

Madeline became curious. Her parent seemed quite agitated yet at the same time rather elevated in spirits. "What is it, Papa?" she asked.

"Do sit down."

When he gestured to the wing chair by the fireplace, she took up her place thinking he would do the same. Instead, he began pacing back and forth, so much so that she became alarmed. "Papa!" she cried. "Whatever is the matter?"

Suddenly, her father stopped and turned to face her. With his hands flung outward in a helpless gesture, he cried, "It was all a hum!"

Madeline frowned slightly, then laughed. "What was a hum? Of what are you speaking, Father?"

"Of Brighton. It was all a hum!"

"What?" she asked again, chuckling. "That you did not go? Are you saying you did not go to Brighton a month past?"

"No, I did go to Brighton, but I . . . oh, dear . . . how shall I say this?"

Madeline was on her feet instantly. "Papa! You cannot

possibly have wagered more, lost more, than even Sir Roger's entire fortune?"

At that, he began to laugh and could not stop. "No . . . no!" he cried between chuckles. "It is nothing of the sort. It is the . . . the opposite. Do you not see?"

Madeline shook her head and frowned a little more. "No, Papa, I do not see."

"I never lost even a farthing in Brighton. Not even a tuppence. Actually, I believe I was about fifty pounds the richer for that journey." He wiped his eyes and took up the seat Madeline had just vacated.

Madeline stared down at him, trying to make sense of what he had just said to her. "You won money while gaming in Brighton?" she asked. "You . . . you did not lose at all?"

"Precisely." He put away his kerchief and looked up at her in a speculative manner.

"You . . . you lied to me?" she asked, a slow indignation beginning to spread through her veins.

He nodded.

"About your losses, all your losses, all your *supposed* losses?"

He nodded again, this time more deeply.

"The Piper family is not in dun territory?"

"Not in the least."

Madeline was overcome by two pressing sentiments at precisely the same moment and of equal intensity. The relief she felt was so profound that she felt giddy. Yet the anger, the sense of having been duped and betrayed, nearly exploded through the top of her head. For the longest moment, she did not know which of the two would come to dominate her mind. In the end, her anger at her parent was decidedly more profound. "How could you have done this horrible thing to me?" she cried, incredulous.

Though he opened his mouth to speak, to explain his reasons, she lifted an imperious hand. "Do not say a word!" she exclaimed. "I should not believe a thing you told me in this moment. Oh, Papa, how could you have done anything so wicked, so vile?" The tirade which flowed from her mind, her heart, her mouth waxed long. Her trip to Pelworthy was entirely forgotten. All that she could see was her wholly unrepentant parent leaning back in his favorite chair, completely unmoved no matter how precisely or logically she pointed out his horrid perfidy. She grew hoarse before ever she completed her thoughts on the subject.

Exhausted at last, she sat on the edge of his desk shaking her head in complete bewilderment. "Why?" she whispered, her throat raw. "Why ever would you do such a thing to me?" Tears filled her eyes.

At that, her father looked down, his expression grim. When at last he appeared to have sorted his thoughts to his satisfaction, he met her gaze anew. "One day last May, you and I and your sisters were having tea at The Bear in Chilchester. You probably do not recall the occasion, for I am certain in your mind it was minuscule. Regardless, it became fixed in my head. I could not shake what I saw that day as though it took roots in my brain and grew into a huge, thorny shrub."

Madeline could make no sense of this. "Of what are you speaking, Papa?" She wondered briefly if he had gone mad.

Mr. Piper gave himself a shake. "I saw you," he cried. "Looking at Sir Roger in such a way. He appeared in the doorway with Lord Anthony and stared at you. I wondered if you were meeting him by design and turned toward you, meaning to pose the question, but there was such a look on your face, my dear, that must have given all heaven pause in that moment."

Madeline frowned. She had no particular recollection of

the event. "Papa, are you certain you were looking at me? Not one of my sisters or some other lady present?"

He smiled, and that so warmly, that she began to believe him, a circumstance that caused her heart to beat unevenly. "No, my dear, I was not mistaken in that. You appeared as smitten as if Cupid himself had struck you with one of his arrows."

"And upon this, a moment's admiration, perhaps—if I was admiring Sir Roger in that moment—you chose to play this trick on me?"

Again he shook his head. "No, that was but the first time I realized you fancied him. After that, I watched you closely whenever the man appeared unexpectedly, and even arranged a few forays into town when I had heard he would be there. God knows there was enough gossip about Sir Roger to have plotted his every move since his arrival in February. The look on your face was always the same. You have had a *tendre* for him these many months and more."

"Why did you not come to me with your suspicions? I could have told you it was no such thing. I was probably merely appreciating how handsome he is. Everyone acknowledges he is a fine-looking man, despite his unfortunate birth."

"There!" he exclaimed, rising abruptly from his chair. "That is the reason I did not tell you. I meant to force your hand to a purpose. I knew your stubbornness in holding to your mother's ridiculous strictures on the subject of birth and breeding, and I wanted you to have a chance to follow your heart instead of your head!"

She slipped from the edge of the desk and met his gaze squarely. "By pretending to have lost your fortune in Brighton?"

"Precisely."

"Of all the absurd starts!" she exclaimed.

He placed a hand on each of her arms. "Only tell me

this, Maddy, do you love him? Now that you know him, now that you have been in company with him, are you in love with him as I believe you to be?"

Madeline meant to respond in the negative, but the words would not pass her throat. Did she love him? Oh, dear God, was that what had been happening to her over the past fortnight?

"There, you see!" he cried, victoriously. "You are in love with him. Of course, if you were not, I should feel obliged to tell you it is not at all the thing to go about kissing a man when you do not love him."

"You know of that?"

"Everyone does, foolish child!" But his expression was soft, even tender.

"Papa, the truth is I do not know how I feel about Sir Roger. All this time, I had felt it necessary to allow an intimacy or two because we were engaged or very nearly so, and I did enjoy kissing him, but now that I will not have to wed him—"

He gave her a small shake. "Maddy, do not tell me I have erred! I would have said nothing if I had thought there was still the smallest doubt in your mind about your sentiments toward the man! Tell me you love him."

She straightened her shoulders. "I do not know that I do, Father."

"So formal," he responded, wincing, his hands dropping back to his sides. "Just like your mother." He seemed deflated suddenly, like a hot air balloon having drifted back to earth and no longer in need of fire-laden air. "Well, I suppose I can always take comfort in having made a push."

"You seem so disappointed," she said.

"I am. There is no man I should like to call a son-in-law more than Sir Roger Mathieson. Well, do as you will, Maddy. You always do." With that, he turned on his heel and was gone.

Madeline remained in the office for several more minutes, not knowing exactly what to do next. She was experiencing such relief at not being obligated to wed anyone at present that she could scarcely think of Sir Roger at all. At last, however, she came to know one thing for certain: Sir Roger had a right to be informed of her change of circumstances, as well as her father's chicanery, as soon as possible.

A half hour later, she stood in his drawing room, having removed her bonnet and turned in a large circle to take in the massive stone walls, the fresh flowers, the heavy furniture, which seemed Italian in origin, covered in tapestried fabric. She wondered what the chamber would look like once Mrs. Crawley had adorned the room with decorations for the Christmas ball. She smiled and shook her head in bemusement. How much had changed in little over a fortnight's time. In one way, she felt as though she had lived an entire lifetime. In another way, she wondered if the past fortnight had even existed at all.

"Madeline," Sir Roger called to her, his voice tender.

She whirled about and her breath caught. He was an extremely handsome man. Undoubtedly that was what her father had seen in her that day in May. She had looked at him, and her breath had caught in her throat because he was so very handsome. Undoubtedly he had mistaken her admiration for true interest.

"Sir Roger," she responded, offering him a formal bow, her bonnet still clutched in tight fingers.

"To what do I owe this visit—though at the moment, I confess I do not care why you have come, only that you *have* come." When she took a step backward at his advance, she saw a frown dart through his eyes. "May I order you some tea or ratafia?"

"I thank you, no. Actually, I have something of a serious nature to tell you, and in truth I do not know how you will feel about it."

"I see. Then I beg you will be seated." He gestured toward the sofa.

She sat down, finding that her hands were shaking. She kept her bonnet on her lap, or meant to, but in his politeness, he took it from her and placed it on a table by the door.

When he returned and took up a seat opposite her, he queried in a soft, almost beguiling voice, "Only tell me what has overset you. I do not like to see you so unhappy."

Though the words first came in a wretchedly halting manner, she told him in full what her father had revealed to her an hour earlier.

Sir Roger listened in some bemusement to her revelations. He could not credit that Mr. Piper had gone to such lengths to throw them together. When at last she fell silent, he thought for a moment, then said, "So the entire charade was merely to force you into my society?"

"So it would seem."

"What would have prompted him to do so?"

He watched her glance about nervously. "He thought I had already formed a *tendre* for you, even in May."

"And had you?" he inquired softly, watching her every gesture with great care.

She lowered her eyes and shook her head. "Of course not."

There it was, he thought unhappily. He understood her. He had from the first. "So what do you intend to do now?"

He watched a smile suffuse her features, and his heart sank further. "I do not know," she said. "You cannot imagine the relief I have felt since learning the truth. I never wanted a marriage of convenience, as I am certain you did not either."

"You have the right of it."

"I suppose, if you are of a mind, you may continue to court me." She tossed her head, and he lost his temper.

He stood up. "I suppose this means that my having kissed you on Saturday had no particular effect on you. Is that what I am seeing in your countenance, in your present demeanor?"

She appeared startled and very young. "No . . . yes! Oh, I do not know. I do not know what to think."

"I believe you have already formed your opinions on the subject," he stated harshly, his feet beginning to march a line in the carpet between them. "You are glad to be out of a bad bargain and may now resume your life, keeping your three beaus in your pocket and casting the past fortnight aside as though it was but a fleeting scourge. I am happy for you, Madeline. Indeed, delighted and thrilled."

"Why are you so angry?" she asked. "I would have thought you to have been grateful to be rid of me as well."

"What on earth, may I ask, would have led you to believe anything so heartless of me? And just why do you think I would have agreed to court you in the first place?"

"You made the conditions of our betrothal so difficult, I had always presumed that you wished to punish me."

"Of course I desired to do so. You had all but given me the cut direct. But, Madeline, I have been in love with you since last winter. Do you not see that? Could you not fathom in all the times I kissed you how passionately I felt about you?"

At that, she appeared dumbstruck, her mouth slightly agape, her eyes wide with shock. "Y-you love me?" she asked.

He turned away from her. He was deeply hurt. He moved to the round table at the end of the sofa and picked up Lady Cottingford's invitation. He returned to stand before her and extended the first sheet of paper to her. "I had meant to come to Fairlight today to give you this. I have had it for a sennight now. I had thought that everything was all but settled between us on Saturday, and I had wanted you to know the truth."

He watched her take the invitation and scan the contents quickly. "But this is an invitation for my father and me to attend Lady Cottingford's harvest ball. I do not understand. How did you get it?"

He snorted. "Oh, my dear. Are you so insular? How can you be?" He threw up his hands and returned to his chair. He felt resigned in a manner that drove every loving sentiment he felt for her straight out of his heart. "As it happens, Lady Cottingford is a most excellent friend of mine. I was used to attend all her soirees, fetes, and balls in London. This past spring, I made her a promise that since I was taking up residence in Chilchester Valley I would attend her harvest ball, having had to refuse the two years prior. When I gave you the task of procuring an invitation yourself, I took the liberty of securing one for you and your father."

"You have been invited to her ball three times?" she asked, ignoring the latter portion of his explanation.

He nodded.

"Good God!"

"Just so, Madeline." He removed his snuffbox from the pocket of his coat and took a pinch. She sat staring at the invitation as though it were a sparrow that would suddenly fly away should she move even the smallest muscle.

"And you have an invitation for yourself?"

"For myself and Lord Anthony, of course."

"Then you do not need my help in Society."

"In Chilchester, your recent efforts have been very helpful. I suppose once it was known that Lady Cottingford received me, the rest would have followed."

"But you must have visited her at Ovinghurst Hall on occasion, surely."

He nodded.

"Why have I not heard even the smallest bit of gossip to that effect?"

"I cannot say. Perhaps her servants are more loyal to their mistress than others in the valley. Of course, I did ask her to remain discreet, since I wished to be accepted in Chilchester on my own merits."

By now, her complexion was rather white. "I should be going," she said, rising to her feet, the invitation falling to the floor without her awareness.

"Yes, I suppose you should."

She moved slowly, as one in a dream, toward the table upon which sat her bonnet. "You may call upon me if you like."

"I shan't do so," he stated, snatching up the invitation and following in her wake.

She picked up her bonnet and turned to look at him, a deep frown on her brow. "But why? I thought you loved me."

"After today, I have every confidence those ill-placed sentiments will dissipate soon enough. You have many fine qualities, Madeline, but your belief in your superiority because of your birth will always be a wedge between us, and that I could never tolerate. I wish you well, but please understand that I have no intention of continuing this misbegotten courtship." He extended the invitation to her.

She took it in hand, though rather blindly. She said nothing more, but in a dazed manner settled her bonnet over her curls and tied the pretty yellow ribbons beneath her left ear.

"Come, I shall see you to your carriage."

A half hour later, Madeline arrived home feeling as though she had been struck down by a mail coach. Her heart was a stone in her chest that seemed to grow heavier by the minute. Sir Roger loved her. He loved her, but he hoped never to see her again. Sir Roger was on an intimate footing with one of London's leading hostesses, the august Viscountess Cottingford. Sir Roger had been in love with her since she first met him in February.

Entering the house, she heard a woman's lilting laughter in the drawing room. She had guests and must strive to put a smile to her lips. How stiff her features felt as she gave herself a shake and forced her lips to curve up, to expose her teeth, to evince some measure of contentment she did not in the least feel.

She strolled into the drawing room, hoping she appeared reasonably content, and was surprised to find seated beside her father on the sofa a woman she did not in the least recognize. Her father was on his feet instantly, his expression glowing. "There you are my dear!" he cried. "I have someone I wish you to meet."

Madeline moved forward, her father took up her arm and gave it a squeeze. He said, "Madame Charbonneau, my I present my eldest daughter, Madeline Piper."

The Frenchwoman. Of course, the Frenchwoman from Elsbourne! But what was she doing here? How did her father know her? By habit of long training, Madeline offered her best bow.

The lady inclined her head. "How do you do, Miss Piper?" Though her words were spoken in perfect English, they were laced with a beautiful accent. "You look like your father when he was young."

"You knew him then?" she asked.

"Mais oui. We have been *amis* for a very long time. How long has it been, Horace?"

Madeline could not believe the woman had addressed him by his Christian name. She turned to look at her father and saw his face so softened by affection, by love, that she gasped.

Her father moved forward and took up his seat once more beside the woman, this time taking her hand gently in his and lifting her fingers to his lips. "Thirty years now."

Thirty years. Then he must have known her before he knew her mother, or at least during the same time. Thirty years would have placed her here in England just before the advent of the French Revolution. She was a refugee, then, having escaped imprisonment and likely death.

"We are to be wed, my dear," her father said, disrupting her calculations.

"Who is to be wed?" she asked like the simpleton she felt she was in this moment.

Her father frowned, but spoke firmly. "Madame Charbonneau and I are to be wed in a month's time, once the banns have been posted properly."

Madeline glanced from one to the other several times. It was too much. First her conversation with Sir Roger, and now this. What would her mother say to such dreadful doings? She weaved on her feet and then felt nothing at all.

When she awoke, she was in her bedchamber, with Prudence stroking her hand lightly, Charity pressing a cool damp cloth to her head, and Hope holding a vinaigrette beneath her nose. "What happened?" she asked.

Hope, ever bouyant, cried out, "You swooned. We had just come in from the garden to bring Madame Charbonneau a bouquet of roses for her to take back to Elsbourne, and the next thing we see you crumpled in a heap right in the center of the room. I do not believe you have fainted in your entire existence."

Madeline tried to sit up, but her head ached, so she lay back down. "No, I have not. Never, in fact."

"Hope, that will do." Her father's voice boomed from the doorway. "Feeling better, Maddy?"

"Yes, thank you, though my head aches fiercely."

"I am not surprised. You did not look well when you entered the drawing room."

"I was not, Papa. I was, in truth, greatly overset."

He nodded, moving forward. He then bid his younger daughters to allow him a moment's private speech with Madeline. The girls wished her to get better soon, then filed out of the bedchamber.

"I do not trust them," he whispered, closing the door. A series of muffled groans were heard from without, giving firm evidence of his suspicions.

Madeline smiled, if faintly, as he drew near.

She looked into his face and wondered if he was indeed real, for nothing of the past two hours could possibly have actually have happened. She had never before swooned in her life. Had Sir Roger actually told her he loved her, and who was this Frenchwoman her father had announced he was wedding in a month's time?

"I can see by your expression," he said, gently dabbing the cool linen over her forehead, "that you are still in shock. I did try to warn you, however, if you may recall."

"In the coach, on the way to Lady Hambledon's fete?" she asked.

He nodded.

"You were serious, then?"

Again, he nodded.

"Oh, Papa. I laughed so. I do hope you will forgive me, but I had thought—I was convinced—you were joking me."

"I know. At the time it was most lowering, but I believe I had hoped you had overcome some of your mother's prejudices."

"My prejudices," she murmured.

"As you will one day, I am certain. Only I do hope you

do not mean to swoon every time you are in Eugenia's company."

"I shan't," she murmured. "It was just such a shock after having—" She could not complete her thought.

"What, my child?" he queried gently. "Did you have a row with Sir Roger?"

"Worse than that. There will be no betrothal now."

"I see. You must have offended him very badly."

"I did, but not as you might think. I am always guarded in my speech, but he saw my belief in the superiority of the English in my face, the set of my shoulders, I daresay even in my smile."

"Yes, I have seen it there as well."

"You have?" she asked, astonished. "But, Papa, do you not hold any such belief, even in part."

He shook his head very slowly. "No. Never. Even though it was a favorite subject of my mother's and yours."

She held his gaze and understanding dawned quite suddenly. "You have been in love with Madame Charbonneau for a very long time, have you not?"

"Ages," he replied simply.

"Thirty years?"

"And a little more. I had meant to wed her, but it was forbidden by both my parents on pain of disinheritance. I had no cause to disbelieve either my mother or father, and perhaps I should have been stronger, but I chose my birthright, and Mama chose a bride for me."

A cold, hollow feeling stole into Madeline's heart. She tried to picture her father as a young man, perhaps violently in love, and faced with the severe aspect of losing Fairlight and a considerable fortune. She could understand his choice quite easily. He would not have had a feather to fly with otherwise, yet how he must have been tormented. "You never stopped loving Madame Charbonneau?"

"Never. She in turn married as well, but has been a

widow for nearly twenty years. Is it wrong of me to confess as much to you, my dear? I know you loved your mother very much. I only hope that you will forgive me and take what lessons you can from my life and from the extraordinary opportunity before you."

"What would that be?"

He chuckled. "Why, to break with tradition and end these horrible prejudices forever."

He quit her bedside soon after, and Madeline was left to ponder all that had transpired on the beautiful August morning.

After an hour of difficult ruminations in which her headache remained steady and determined, she finally rose from her bed. She thought a walk might be of some benefit and began ambling in the direction of the nearby village of Stanham and to the church. There was a vault on the property which had belonged to the Piper family for three hundred years. She entered the sacred, cool stone crypt and sat on the bench at the far end. She had come, it would seem, to say good-bye to a beloved parent and to the strictures which had kept her imprisoned for the past decade of her life.

She wept for some time, for the loss of her mother, for her disrupted childhood, for so many teachings over so many generations that had kept her father from wedding the woman he loved, and finally for the truth that she might have lost Sir Roger's love forever. As the afternoon waned, she began to dwell most particularly on this last point, Sir Roger's love.

He had said he loved her, that he believed he loved her from the moment he found her at Pelworthy, that their shared kiss beneath the oak had only confirmed what had been in his heart from the beginning. She let herself dwell upon that moment, of being kissed so wondrously, so passionately. She recalled that she had felt so dizzy she had been unable to feel her feet, that she had felt transported into the heavens. But was this love, these passionate, transient feelings?

It came to her that such manifestations were just that, a surface glimpse of deeper waters, of love unrecognized, unseen, even unfelt until now, when she allowed herself to truly feel.

Yes, her soul cried loudly within the sacred tomb, she loved him. She loved a Scotsman. She believed she always would.

The tears came quickly now, seeping from her eyes in a long stream of painful regret. She had been so proud earlier when she had suggested to Sir Roger that he might court her if he wished to do so. How she shuddered at the memory of it. How much she had meant to say by the way she addressed him that he was unworthy of her but she would consider his suit, among others.

He had been so right. She had thought herself superior. She lifted her gaze and wiped her eyes, staring at the brass plate upon which was engraved her mother's beloved name. *And marry an Englishman, Madeline. Only an Englishman will do, could ever do for a Piper.*

How wrong she was, Madeline thought. How very wrong, indeed, for only a Scotsman, in all his passionate strength, would do for her.

She rose to her feet and shed her prejudices in that moment as though she had dropped a heavy, cumbersome cape from her shoulders. She left the strictures of a dozen generations behind her as she walked slowly from the crypt, still wiping her eyes, yet feeling more at peace than she had in a very long time.

Only one difficulty plagued her now: how to prove herself worthy, if that was even possible, of Sir Roger's love.

Thirteen

That same day, Madeline's first thought was that she must speak with Sir Roger, but she doubted very much that he would be receptive to her sudden change of heart, at least not so readily. For that reason, she spent the remainder of the day and evening cloaked in her own thoughts and often separated from her family so she might more perfectly comprehend all that had happened, both in the miraculous nature of her having tumbled in love at last, but, not less importantly, the complete revision of her scruples on the subjects of birth and breeding.

By the following morning, she felt ready to address Sir Roger, yet still she delayed. She sensed that his heart was not to be won overnight and certainly not by a hasty enumeration of her prior unfortunate beliefs and her present, more gracious new ones. So it was that she resisted putting quill to paper and begging his forgiveness and instead agreed to go to Chilchester with her sisters and father to enjoy a nuncheon at The Bear and to do a little shopping.

After a fine meal had been consumed and all the packages stowed safely in the family coach, Madeline was about to follow her sisters within when three gentlemen on horseback suddenly pulled up before her and dismounted.

"Mr. Calvert. Mr. Rockingham," she said offering a polite bow. "And Captain Bladen. You are looking well." A bruise, accentuated by the white of his shirt point, was still quite visible on his jawline.

The gentlemen gathered round the family and exchanged civilities for several minutes until Harris requested that the gentlemen have a private word with her.

Her father nodded his acquiescence. "But only a minute, mind. We've kept the horses standing long enough."

"Aye, Papa. I won't be but a moment."

Mr. Calvert spoke first. "We are all concerned for you, Miss Piper, and trust that all is well."

"Very much so, thank you."

"But are you certain?" Harris asked intently, his dark brown eyes flashing.

Madeline frowned. "To what do you refer?" she asked.

"To Lady Hambledon's fete, of course. It escaped none of our notice that Sir Roger led you into the woods."

"Only to an oak tree," she answered, trying not to smile at the memory of that wondrous kiss. She felt a blush steal up her cheeks, and in order to keep from succumbing to a sudden embarrassment, she bit the inside of her lip.

"He overset you," Captain Bladen cried. "I can see it in your countenance even now, the cur!"

"It is no such—" Her gaze became fixed some fifty yards past the gentlemen. Just approaching the door to The Bear Inn was the man himself. Her heart became trapped in her throat, and she could hardly breathe. What an exquisite sight he was dressed in a finely tailored coat of Russian flame, buff breeches, and glossy top boots. She felt an odd wish that she might merely look at him forever.

"You need not demur," Mr. Calvert said quietly.

"Demur?" she queried, her gaze flitting to him, but for only a moment. She did not know to what he was referring. Her gaze sought out Sir Roger again. She smiled when he caught sight of her, but he merely nodded coldly and went inside. Her thoughts were instantly overcome by sadness.

Harris's hand reached for his imaginary swordhilt again. "He should pay for this! He must pay."

"Just as you said earlier," Captain Bladen said, addressing Mr. Calvert. "We should put a fire under Mathieson. Would you not agree, Miss Piper?"

"Agree to what?" she asked, having heard only one word in two.

"A fire under Sir Roger."

Madeline blinked several times. "Yes," she murmured absently. She should build a fire under Sir Roger, only how? How to help him see that she was changed, that she loved him and that he could love her again, if only he would deign to speak with her? Yet how to gain that audience with him?

"Madeline," her father called to her. "We must go."

"Yes, Papa." She turned to her beaus and offered her hand to each. Though Captain Bladen and Mr. Calvert each were satisfied merely to press her fingers, Harris could not resist the opportunity to salute her fingers with a lingering kiss. She finally had to withdraw her hand from his firmly.

"It is rumored," Mr. Calvert said, "that Sir Roger has been invited to attend the harvest ball."

"Yes, it is true."

The gentlemen exchanged glances.

"Madeline!" Her father's voice was sharp.

"I must go."

The gentlemen prevented her no further, but bowed her away.

Once aboard the coach, Madeline watched intently as the conveyance swept past The Bear. She searched the windows carefully for the smallest glimpse of him, but her efforts went unrewarded. She leaned back against the squabs, her mind wrapping itself instantly about the task ahead of her. She felt it absolutely requisite that she beg for a minute or two of his time to lay her case before him. If he could but see her remorse and her misery, he would more readily believe what she had to say to him.

She set a servant to keep watch on the lane leading from Chilchester to Pelworthy so that she might know when Sir Roger returned to his home. Once the servant arrived at Fairlight with word that Sir Roger had indeed been seen heading in the direction of Pelworthy, she had the same servant take a brief note to the castle, requesting that Sir Roger meet her at the bridge at Halland Creek. Once the servant had disappeared into the lane, again on horseback, she began the one and a half mile march to the bridge.

She waited there over an hour, her heart in a constant state of fretting mingled with the sweetest sensations of lovesickness, until finally she saw a figure coming toward her. How desolate she was when she recognized not Sir Roger but his liveried servant, bearing a note in hand. He approached her in the self-conscious manner of a person delivering unhappy news. He bowed formally, gave her the missive, then turned abruptly on his heel and began walking back up the hill.

Madeline fingered the fine vellum, but even before she broke the seal, tears had already plopped onto her name, the ink immediately smearing and running. Her heart was so heavy that it seemed to have weighed down her feet in equal measure, for she had never felt so lethargic as she turned in the direction of Fairlight and began retracing her steps. She did not open the missive at once, already certain of its contents, but only did so after a half mile had been crossed. She sat on a fallen log beside the grassy lane, broke the seal, and began to read.

Dear Miss Piper,
    I hope you will forgive me for not agreeing to meet with you, but I do not believe there is anything that

*can be said at this juncture to alter the very deep
truths of our situation. I wish you every happiness.*
                                            S.R. Mathieson

Worse and worse, she thought. He was convinced she
was beyond redemption and she had little doubt that with
every day that passed, his heart would grow increasingly
dead to her. She must do something, and for a moment she
considered laying seige to the castle until he did agree to
speak with her, but this she dismissed. Her words, it would
seem, would not be nearly sufficient to persuade him that
she was different, changed. Of that she was convinced. No,
words would not suffice. She must make a grander gesture, something that would snag his attention fully,
something that would demonstrate the nature of her new
heart, something that would allow for discussion and
hopefully renewed trust.

Only what? Denied the opportunity to see him or speak
with him, how was she to win his heart anew?

She left the log and continued her journey home. For
much of the trip, her mind remained completely unre-
sponsive, and only the most banal notions occurred to her,
like sending her father to speak to him, or writing him a
succession of letters which he might or might not read, or
even waiting by the barbican until he should chance upon
her.

In the end, she dismissed them all, wondering if she
would ever concoct precisely the right method by which
she might reveal her reformed thoughts and attitudes. She
did not despair precisely, but how was she to win the heart
of a Scot?

The moment her mind brought forward his heritage, a
notion so stunning followed that she nearly tripped in her
steps. She knew now precisely what she must do, and the

moment she arrived at Fairlight, she went to her father, begging permission to travel to London immediately.

When he heard her reasons, he smiled broadly, nodded his assent, and bid her good hunting. "But will you have returned in time for Lady Cottingford's fete? We should not offer a slight on this, our first invitation to her harvest ball."

"Never fear, Papa," she responded gaily as she quit the room. "I shall run all the way home if need be!"

"I shouldn't do that!" he cried. "You will be too exhausted to dance otherwise."

As it happened, Madeline returned on Saturday from London with but two hours to spare. She was sore from having been jumbled about in a carriage for so many rigorous miles on end, but had succeeded in her object so much to her satisfaction that she could not complain. Her sisters were all agog to see what it was that had sent her to the metropolis in the first place, so much so that when the footman brought a large package into the entrance hall and handed it to her, they clustered about her like hens gathered about a fresh throw of seed.

Prudence began plucking at the brown paper.

"You may not look!" Madeline cried, gathering up the bulky package more securely in her arms and beginning to mount the stairs. "But if you will send my maid to my room, you shall very soon have your curiosity satisfied."

She heard her sisters groan behind her and made her way to her bedchamber.

An hour and a half later, she emerged, bathed, coiffed, and gowned, to make her way to the drawing room, where she knew her family awaited her. She was horridly nervous, for what she had done was beyond daring, even perhaps beyond the pale, but as she thought of Sir Roger and the manner in which she had used him so very ill over the past three weeks, her resolve strengthened. He would understand this particular gesture, even if no one else did. That her abigail had nearly fainted at the sight of the gown had not helped to calm her nerves, but what was done was done, and unless she actually incited a riot or gave extreme offense to her hostess, she meant to attend the harvest ball as she was.

When at last she arrived on the threshold of the drawing room, she waited until all eyes turned upon her before advancing farther. She saw the gaping stares and heard the gasps of shock. She was not surprised.

Her father, however, hushed any comments that sprang to her sisters' lips with a quickly lifted hand and instead rose to greet her. "I think it perfection. Absolute perfection. I only wonder how you had it made up in time."

"It was something of a difficulty and, though I hope you will not faint, I fear it cost you two hundred pounds."

Though he gulped visibly and her sisters gasped anew, still he did not hesitate, but held his hand out to her and said, "Now let me see you move in a circle, for I believe it sports a demi-train."

Madeline took his hand, and he guided her in walking in a large circle so that all the Piper sisters could see the pleated train. One and all, they marveled at the workmanship of the unusual gown.

"But it is made of wool," Hope said. "Will you not be dreadfully hot this evening?"

"Only the overdress is in wool," she responded. "The rest is silk, so I should not be too uncomfortable."

"And you did this for Sir Roger?" Prudence asked, her eyes glowing.

Madeline smiled. "Yes, of course. I believe I owed him that much for all the insults I have given him during the past six months."

"I would wager a thousand pounds you never spoke a harsh word to him," Charity cried, frowning. "So how do you say you insulted him?"

How, indeed? "With every gesture, every pause in a given sentence, every toss of my head. Insults are not always delivered exclusively by the tongue."

Charity, the least able of her sisters to grasp subtleties, nodded several times, then finally said, "You love him, then."

"Yes, very much."

Hope, the youngest cried, "Well you must, to be making such a cake of yourself tonight!"

Having summed up the entire purpose of wearing a gown with an overdress made up exclusively of wool tartan in as close a match to the tartan of Sir Roger's kilt as she could find, Madeline burst out laughing. "You are so very right, Hope," she responded, "You have no idea!"

With that, the family enjoyed a dinner together, after which Madeline joined her father in the traveling coach and began the nearly ten-mile journey to Ovinghurst Hall.

"Good God!" the Duke of Wellington cried.

Sir Roger had been conversing with the duke when he suddenly saw something to his right that took him vastly by surprise. "What is . . . it?" Sir Roger queried, but the words faded on his tongue. He had never been so shocked, so stunned in his entire existence.

Madeline had arrived with her father, and they were presently being announced at the top of the ballroom's flight of stairs. "Mr. Horace Piper, Miss Madeline Piper." The butler's sonorous tones alone might have brought all conversation in the expansive ballroom to a halt, but there was no doubt in Sir Roger's mind that it was Madeline, or more precisely her gown, that had caused every mouth to fall agape and every sentence to drop unfinished to the floor.

"What does she mean by it?" Wellington asked.

Around him Sir Roger heard a humming of similarly posed questions from, it would seem, the entire assemblage.

"I believe it may be an apology," Sir Roger said. "And a very grand one, at that."

"Is this the lady of whose beauty I have heard such extensive accounts?" he inquired, eyeing Sir Roger with a smile.

"She would be the one."

"Then I say you are a fool to let her go."

"I begin to think you may be right." Still, he did not move forward to greet her. He watched, stupefied, as she made a very regal descent into the body of the revelers. Her father leaned near her more than once, undoubtedly to whisper encouragements, but she did not seem to be in the least overset. Instead, she let her gaze drift in some indifference over the crowd, all watching her and murmuring still, until she found him. Only then did she smile.

"My God," Wellington murmured, "I should have taken the Peninsula five years earlier had I such a smile to return to."

Sir Roger could only chuckle at the absurd remark, and yet he himself had observed more than once that when Madeline Piper smiled it was as though the whole heavens began to sing.

The crowd parted for them. He doubted she knew many of Lady Cottingford's guests, so to him was given the pleasure of greeting her.

Madeline's heart was fairly pounding in her chest. Certainly she was a trifle agitated at having caused such a stir, but that was not the source of her increased heart rate. Indeed, the poor organ seemed to have been having some difficulty in being restrained within her chest from the moment her gaze settled upon the man she loved. Her eyes were only for him, her feet could have made their way in no other direction, and her pulse sang exclusively for him.

She responded politely to his greeting and was even able to manage a proper curtsy and a civil, "Your grace," when presented to the Duke of Wellington. Even meeting this most famous soldier, her nerves were steadier than when she but looked at Sir Roger Mathieson.

The duke seemed amused, though she was not certain why. She watched him give Sir Roger a nudge, which prompted the knight to speak. "I beg your pardon, Miss Piper. I believe his grace has reminded me of my duty. Would you honor me with the next dance? It is a waltz, I believe."

"I should be delighted," she said. When he offered his arm, she took it happily. She had achieved at least this, then—by wearing a shocking gown of tartan, Sir Roger had been sufficiently moved to ask her to dance. The trip to London had been worth, she was certain, at least a score of apologetic letters that would have undoubtedly been returned to her unopened.

As he guided her toward the ballroom floor, he murmured, "I believe you have nearly caused at least a dozen ladies to faint. However did you manage to summon the pluck to actually wear that gown?"

"I was resolved, sir," she responded quietly. "I was convinced you would not speak to me again unless I showed you how greatly my sentiments, indeed, my opinions have been altered by my having known you."

He led her to a place on the floor in which several couples were now positioned, waiting for the waltz to commence. If their eyes were fixed not on each other but on her, upon the demi-train she had gathered up with the loop attached for that purpose at the side of the gown, upon the pleated swirl of tartan her maid had fixed earlier among her golden curls, upon the man taking her in his arms who was known to be of Scottish descent, she could hardly proclaim her surprise.

However, in this moment, Madeline found she did not care. She was in Sir Roger's arms, if only dancing, and there was no place else she wished to be, now or forever. She tried not to think of the future or whether though he might value this gesture he would still remain untrusting of her heart. Instead, she concentrated quite profoundly on enjoying every moment of the swirling, up and back, round and round, of the progress of the dance, of the color of his eyes, and the way he always looked so fiercely at her.

"Your thoughts, Sir Roger?" she asked bravely at last.

His smile was slow and determined. "That you are either one of the bravest ladies I have ever known or you have gone mad."

She laughed. "Neither, I fear or hope as the case warrants. I had but one object, as you must know, to demonstrate that your words have had an effect, a very profound influence, upon my thoughts and beliefs."

"So it would seem," he murmured, gazing deeply into her eyes.

Up and back, round and round. The swirling movements heightened the exhilaration now coursing through Madeline's veins. He did not seem angry. Speculative perhaps, questioning, of course, as was to be expected. However, her gown of tartan had achieved so much more than she had expected. At the very most, she had hoped for a conversation, but this, being swept about Lady Cottingford's magnificent ballroom beneath the glow of three enormous chandeliers and in the arms of the man she loved, was almost beyond bearing in the sweetest sense possible.

He did not speak the remainder of the dance, but guided

her perfectly about the floor, all the while looking at her, smiling at times and at others searching her face intently. For herself, she rested in the knowledge that she had done all she could for the present to ingratiate herself with him and that regardless of what happened in the future, she would have this moment of dancing with him to remember always.

At last, however, the dance drew to a close. Taking her firmly by the arm, he led her from the ballroom floor, through several antechambers, nodding to several acquaintances along the way, until the French glass doors to a broad terrace came into view. Madeline's heart began to sing. He desired, for whatever reason, to be alone with her right now. She could not have asked for more than this, an opportunity to explain the purpose of her unusual gown and the exact nature of her present thoughts. She longed to tell him that she had since discovered how desperately she loved him, but she still was not certain if he would truly welcome the idea or not.

So it was that when he led her to the far end of the stone terrace, cloaked by several potted conifers, her heart had again begun to pound in her chest. She glanced at the countryside, the downs rising to the north. Even a glow of lights from Pelworthy was visible in the distance.

"Madeline," he said, calling her attention back to him. When she turned toward him, he took her hands in his. "I must know," he said, "what is in your heart that you would have risked so much in appearing in Society in Scottish tartan."

She was not certain precisely where to begin or even when the words were spoken whether he would believe her or trust her. Tears filled her eyes, and a concerned frown slipped over his features. "I hardly know what to say to you, except that when you last spoke with me, you opened my eyes. I did not know, I did not understand the depths to which my mother's prejudices lived within me. To say I have shed them completely would be a falsehood only in that I do not know the extent to which my beliefs have been penetrated by her outmoded strictures. I can only promise that I have worked steadily, and will continue to do so, to change for the better how I view my heritage and the heritage of others."

"This change seems so sudden. You must forgive me if I do not readily accept that it has happened. Indeed, I am tending to believe it now because of this extraordinary gown. However did you conceive of the notion?"

"You will find it a great irony that my mother once told me that before the new century, she had heard of some famous Scottish ladies, the Misses Maxwell, who had had tartan gowns created for the purpose of showing Scottish patriotism. I can still see the twist of disgust on her face as well as her animadversions on the subject of the stupidity of the 1782 repeal of the 1746 Act for the Abolition and Proscription of Highland Dress. It was from their example that I chose to have this gown made up."

"You could not have found tartan in Chilchester?" he asked, incredulous.

She chuckled. "No, not at all. I went to London."

"Indeed?" His gaze grew increasingly intent. "All the way to the metropolis merely for a bit of Scottish plaid?"

"I can think of few better reasons to have gone," she responded, smiling, "particularly since you refused to meet me at Halland Creek. I had so much I wished to say to you, but I do not blame you in the least for being unwilling to hear me. My conduct was horrid in the extreme. I cannot think of it without feeling the worst mortification, for you were right on every score, and I would not have blamed you had you never acknowledged my existence again."

"You have no particular obligation to me, Madeline.

Ours was a private, discretionary courtship. We had no commitments to one another, then or now."

Her heart sank. What was it he was saying, or meant to say? She could not be certain. "If you think I did this because of a sense of obligation, I fear you are greatly mistaken. As for what you owe me, I am perfectly cognizant that you owe me nothing, if that is what you fear."

"No, my concerns do not lay in that direction. But I would know, Madeline, I desire to know why you have done this thing."

She understood what he wanted to hear her say and yet her heart quailed at the thought of revealing her affections lest he despise her, even laugh at her by being so presumptuous in speaking them when he had already made it clear, Monday last, that there could never be a betrothal between them. She drew in a deep breath, her heart once more hammering wildly against her ribs. She had never been in love before, nor had she ever told a man that she loved him. The words did not come easily. Could she even speak them? She did not know.

However, she stiffened her spine and gathered her courage. She sensed rather than knew for a certainty that this was the hour to speak, to not hold back, to let her sentiments be known in their entirety. To do less would be to continue to dishonor the man still holding her hands in a tight clasp.

"When I left you that day, I discovered that somewhere betwixt having met you for the first time at Pelworthy last February and that wretched conversation five days ago, I had come to desire, indeed to long for your company more than anything else on earth. I realized that I loved you, that I had tumbled quite violently in love with you. When you refused to meet with me, I knew I had to do something to both prove the worthlessness of my former opinions and to tell you that my heart now belonged to you."

Sir Roger stared into her lovely green eyes, still glittering with tears, and could not credit the transformation of the lady before him. Gone was the arrogance he had witnessed on Monday that had seemed to seal his heart from her forever. She was a creature changed, and yet he did not entirely trust her. After all, was it possible for someone to alter their beliefs so quickly, so simply?

He watched her smile, if ruefully. "You owe me nothing," she stated firmly.

He was grateful she had said as much. He needed time now to think over what she had said, to place in some sort of rational perspective the exceptional gesture she had made in wearing a gown of tartan to a purely English harvest ball. Yet at the same time he could not quite bring himself to release her hands, not when she was looking so very beautiful and vulnerable, not when tears danced on her lashes, not when she had humbled herself so completely before him.

"Oh, the deuce take it!" he cried. He gathered her up quickly in his arms. "I should not—Madeline, what is it?" Her suddenly wide-eyed, almost panicked, gaze was fixed beyond him.

"There!" she cried, dipping her chin to the north. "I believe—oh, dear God—it must be Pelworthy!"

He whipped around and saw what it was that had brought such an expression of horror to her face. "My God, I believe you are right. My home is in flames! I must go!"

Word spread in lightning flashes that Pelworthy was ablaze. Madeline flew beside Sir Roger as he hurried to the entrance hall and, after issuing the orders to have his curricle brought round, suddenly cried. "Never mind! I shall see to it myself!"

"Sir?" the butler cried, greatly shocked.

"I know where the stables are."

"May I come with you?" Madeline cried.

"If it pleases you, yes, but you must come now."

Madeline begged Lady Cottingford's butler to summon her father and explain that Pelworthy was on fire and that she had accompanied Sir Roger to his home.

"Very good, miss."

With that, Madeline ran beside Sir Roger, the tartan demi-train dragging the gravel as it moved over the walkway until she caught up the dancing loop and swept the overdress across her arm.

The head groom of Lord Cottingford's stables was one of the finest in the county. He was known for precision and care, and after tonight undoubtedly would be known for his speed as well. Within five minutes, Sir Roger's horses were harnessed to his curricle and the fine team was trotting quickly down the avenue. Once in the lane, he used his whip and the team began to plunge ahead at breakneck speed.

Madeline braced her feet, slung one arm about Sir Roger's waist and held on for dear life. Pelworthy was a distance of seven miles from Ovinghurst, and she was certain she would be well-bruised after so quick a jaunt over occasionally uneven terrain and uncertain roads.

Fourteen

Madeline still had her arm pinned about Sir Roger's waist as he drew the curricle up to an abrupt stop some hundred yards from the barbican. Much of the outer, southern portion of the castle was ablaze, which represented to a large extent the scaffolding placed securely against several portions of the stone wall. The largest flames, however, shot out from the barbican itself, much of which was made of wood, including the ancient drawbridge.

She stared up at the leaping flames, unable to credit the ferocity of the blaze. "Whatever can be done?" she cried.

Sir Roger handed her the reins and leaped down. Several of his servants ran to and fro, some carrying water brought up from the creek the others attempting to determine if everyone had been able to make their escape once the fire took hold of the edifice. He called out to one of his manservants. "You there! Is everyone safe?"

"Yes, Sir Roger. We have just made certain of it. We are now searching for more buckets."

"Carry on," he murmured.

Madeline watched his shoulders slump. The foundation and the exterior walls might be made of stone, but there was a great deal of wood that could easily burn in the interior walls, upper floors, and roofs, which would keep a castle engulfed in flames for a long time. She watched as

Churchill approached from behind and nuzzled Sir Roger's hand. He immediately bent down and ruffled the dog's fur and rubbed his ears. What he said to the beast could not be heard, but there was obvious relief in Sir Roger's expression that his dog was safe.

He stopped another servant and the pair of them, with Churchill following behind, approached the carriage. Sir Roger gestured for Madeline to descend and the servant led the horses and the curricle away.

"What can be done?" Madeline asked, her throat constricted with tears. She could imagine what Sir Roger was feeling in this moment, but to see Pelworthy shooting flames was more than she could bear with even the smallest equanimity.

"Not a great deal, I'm 'fraid," he responded, his voice nearly lost in the roar and the crackling of the fire. "We would need an entire army to extinguish these flames."

Madeline turned away from the barbican, her heart still sitting harshly in her throat. After she permitted several tears to slip down her cheeks, her attention was caught by the sight of lights bouncing in the distance both from the lane at the bottom of the hill to the east as well as the lane to the west. The lights converged as they began a progress up the rather steep, final ascent to the castle.

She turned around, her eyes filling with tears anew. "Sir Roger," she called to him, his gaze still fixed on the mountain of flames before him.

He glanced at her, hopelessness visible in his blue eyes. "Yes?"

"I believe your army has just arrived."

"What?" he cried, a quick frown splitting his brow.

"Do but look!" She gestured to the southern lane.

"There must be hundreds coming. How is this possible?"

"In part, I am certain, because Pelworthy is a great part

of our local history and in part because I am convinced the new owner of the castle is a greatly respected man, particularly with the tradesmen and villagers throughout the vale."

"Whether you have the right of it or not, especially as concerns your last opinion, I am so grateful I hardly know what to say."

"Well, then, I would suggest you begin formulating a plan of attack as to precisely where a battle might be staged to stop the fire."

He chuckled and cupped her face. "Thank you," he said.

"For what?" she cried. "I have done nothing."

"For being beside me in this moment."

She smiled in return then glancing about queried. "I have not seen Lord Anthony. Do not tell me he was within?"

At that, Sir Roger shook his head. "No. He was spending the evening with Squire Crawley. I believe his intention was to beg for Miss Cressida's hand in marriage tonight, if I did not much mistake the matter."

Since the villagers, tradesmen, and farmers would soon be upon them, Sir Roger began to organize his own servants, giving them orders as to where the line of buckets and water carried from Halland Creek would best be laid over the flames, in some cases thirty feet ahead of the flames to drench roof and floors in hopes of preventing further spread of the fire.

Once the brigade of water laden buckets began, so did a night of exhaustive labor. It was several hours before signs of victory began to be seen. By then, the barbican was a hollow, smoking, wet shell and gave a stench to the area which Madeline believed probably extended for several miles in every direction. Two score of women had brought food for the laborers, which Madeline helped to dispense with great regularity along with a large quantity of coffee.

There was a rhythm to the work, to the efforts to save as much of the castle as possible, that settled into each grim, determined face.

When it was clear that the flames were growing smaller and lower with each passing minute, a rousing cheer went up. Sir Roger, his face soot-covered, went about thanking many of those nearest the castle, but the older and wiser of the men spurred on the effort saying that many a fire, when not properly extinguished, would burst to life again. On and on, therefore, the drudgery continued until all the flames were gone. Only then was there some relief as the several lines which had led to the creek resolved to only two. Even then, those men who had had experience with fires began checking the perimeters over and over for any sign of hidden flames.

When at last dawn's light came and not a single tendril of smoke curled from even the smallest burnt ember, the laborers and the many women who had kept them fed through the night began a long walk home. Fifty, however, remained behind, where they were given sustenance and places to sleep in case an undetected beam or floor joist once more erupted into flame.

Madeline, exhausted, approached Sir Roger to bid him good-bye, when a servant, red-faced and perspiring heavily, approached them.

"What is it? Has another fire been discovered?" Sir Roger asked.

"Nay. I come from Lord Anthony. He begs you to accompany me, along with Miss Piper if possible." Here, he bowed to her, then continued, "There is something he desires both of you to see at once—that is, now that the fire is controlled."

"Of course," Sir Roger said. "I shall come directly, but I believe Miss Piper needs to see her bed."

At that, the servant became distressed. "Begging your

pardon, but Lord Anthony was most specific and repeated the order, that is, the request, at least a dozen times that Miss Piper must attend you. Begging your pardon, miss."

"I shall come as well, of course. I am certain if his lordship has requested my company, then he must have good reason."

"Aye, miss, that I believe he does."

With that, Sir Roger gave orders to his head groom to keep his eye fixed to the continuing inspections of the charred portions of the castle. When he proffered his arm, Madeline took it gratefully. She smiled up into his sooted face. "I would not know you at a distance, sir," she said cheerfully.

"Nor I you."

"Indeed? And is my face as black as yours?"

"Very nearly, I am sure."

With such light banter, the journey, surprisingly brief, was accomplished. Madeline was still smiling as the last bend in a small, hidden ravine was achieved. Her general lightheartedness died on her lips, for there, in bondage, were John Calvert, Captain Bladen, and Harris Rockingham. Poised over them, a hunting rifle in hand, was Lord Anthony and two more servants, also keeping watch. Madeline recognized one of them, having given him several large portions of coffee, bread, and ham, which she had thought he meant to take to the laborers. She had wondered at the time, quite vaguely, that his clothes were still so clean, but now his purpose was made clear to her. He had been feeding his master's friend and probably the gentlemen still bound at their ankles and hands.

"What is this meaning of this, Anthony?" Sir Roger asked.

"I returned early from Wistfield, for Miss Cressida was not at all feeling well. The castle had just been torched, and I saw three men running in this direction. Your servants were not far behind, one of them carrying this gaming rifle, and naturally I joined pursuit. I was shocked to find these gentlemen at the end of the chase."

Madeline stared at her beaus, trying to comprehend what it was they had done. She did not understand. "You must be mistaken," she said to Lord Anthony.

"For your sake, Miss Piper, I wish I were."

"But do you know for certain? Have they admitted as much?" She glanced at Harris, who met her gaze, but who quickly looked away, wearing an expression of the most profound guilt. She understood in that instant that the accusation was true. "Oh, dear God," she murmured, lifting a hand to cover her mouth, for she was greatly shocked.

Captain Bladen said, "I do not see why you pretend your surprise, Miss Piper. We would never have done so without your blessing!"

"What?" she exclaimed, astounded. "I never . . . I would never . . . how can you say such a thing?"

Mr. Calvert interjected. "In Chilchester, on Tuesday, you agreed quite readily that a fire should be lit under Sir Roger."

What she might have said was interrupted completely by Harris who cried out. "What the deuce? Are you wearing tartan, Miss Piper?"

All three men then took in the sight of her soot-covered gown and each expression grew quite dumbfounded, indeed shocked.

"Yes, I am," she responded. At the same time, she sensed that something else was amiss. Glancing at Sir Roger saw a speculative, even suspicious expression on his face as he watched her as well.

"More to the point, Miss Piper," he said, his voice cold, "did you perhaps wear the tartan to keep me distracted? Was this your purpose?"

Madeline was so stunned that her mouth fell agape. For

a long moment, she could not answer him. That he would think her capable of such a horrific act of destruction against him, not to mention against Pelworthy, was so disturbing that no words came to her tongue.

"There, you see!" Harris cried out. "She knew precisely what we meant to do and clearly used the tartan to help us."

"No, Harris," she said at last. "You are mistaken, utterly and completely."

She could see that Sir Roger was not convinced and a deep chagrin came over her, not so much that he disbelieved her, but because of all the ways she had made her former feelings of superiority made known to him, so much so that he could not in this moment trust her. Tears started to her eyes. "I know you will not believe me, but I had no hand in this, no notion of what these men intended to do."

"Why do they say you sanctioned their actions, then? What did you say to them in Chilchester that would have given them cause, even justification?"

"I cannot recall precisely, because when I was speaking with them, for that much I do remember, Papa was hurrying me to take my leave, and then I saw you. You were just entering The Bear and I smiled at you, but you gave me the coldest nod. I admit I was but half listening to them and, yes, I do recall something about 'lighting a fire under Sir Roger,' but I wasn't paying the least heed."

Mr. Calvert snorted his disgust. "We all heard you say, 'Yes, a fire should be lit under Sir Roger.'"

"But I was not referring in any manner to the torching of Pelworthy," she cried. "I was speaking of his heart. I have been in love with him for ages, and yet he had found me wanting, but not unrightly so." She turned to Sir Roger, tears still brimming in her eyes. "You must believe me. I was thinking of your heart, not your home, and even if I had been as mad as fire, though I beg you will forgive the use of that particular aphorism, I would never, never in a thousand years sanction such an act as we have witnessed tonight. Never."

"I wish I could believe you," he said.

Madeline was exhausted from the night's labors and could not stem her tears. She could not believe this was happening, neither that some of her dearest friends had committed so heinous an act against Sir Roger, nor that somehow she had become culpable in his eyes.

She was sunk again and knew it. She had believed herself out of the woods, but here, at this moment, she was in the darkest part of them all over again. Even her gown of tartan could be turned against her. A stronger question arose: even if he believed her in this situation, would he ever be able to truly trust her? Perhaps not. If not, then what basis was there for an enduring love?

She did not know what to do, yet to protest further seemed a hopeless avenue, so she remained silent. The gentlemen fidgeted on the ground, each appearing haggard.

"What would you have me do, Miss Piper?" Sir Roger asked.

She turned to look at him, hope dawning, if slowly. "What do you mean?"

"Whether or not you are innocent remains to be seen, but for the present, what shall I do with your beaus? I suspect the destruction of an ancient castle might be considered by an English court to be a hanging offense."

Madeline started. The consequences of their horrid crime had not yet occurred to her. Now that Sir Roger had offered the first course of action as a possible one, she shuddered. "I had not thought of that."

"Perhaps you should have," Harris cried, "when you told

us to light a fire under Sir Roger." He was shaking and near tears.

Captain Bladen interjected. "She did not *tell* us to do anything."

"She did so!" Harris exclaimed sounding a great deal younger than his two and twenty years.

Madeline stared at him for a long moment. Suddenly she knew, at least in part, how to respond to Sir Roger's question. "Were the matter of passing judgment left to me, I should have Harris sporting a pair of colors before the year was out."

"A pair of colors!" he exclaimed, his eyes brightening. They dimmed as quickly. "M'mother would never permit it."

Madeline ignored this quite pathetic response. Instead, she turned to the older gentlemen. "As for you, Captain Bladen and Mr. Calvert, I am persuaded you knew quite well I meant no such thing as the burning of Pelworthy. Harris, I will allow, might have believed it because he is young. However, even if I disliked Sir Roger, which you knew very well from my conduct with him on Saturday past that I did not, you also knew of the devotion I have always felt for the castle. Therefore, I believe your actions were based solely upon your jealousy of the man you knew I had come to love." She turned to Sir Roger. "As for you, I fear you will be required to forgive all three of them for that. How could they have known that you would steal my heart as you did? I did not imagine such a thing would be possible myself. To sentence them to death, therefore, because each fancied himself in love with me would be foolish beyond permission, given your desire to raise your children among the finest of Chilchester society. However, there are reparations to be made."

She shifted again to look Captain Bladen in the eye. "You, sir, I would banish forever from a thirty-mile radius of the valley. I would forbid you to purchase Maresfield, for I have heard other opinions of your character in the past sennight which lead me to believe you would not always be welcome in Chilchester." Since he merely eyed her uneasily and did not in any manner protest, she knew that Georgiana's warnings to her about the captain had not been far off the mark.

She turned once more and met Mr. Calvert's sullen gaze. "Your task will be the more difficult one, I believe. I could hardly sentence you to banishment or to the army, for you are the owner of a fine estate. Were I to do so, I should start a war, even if your nefarious deeds became known. Your atonement, therefore, will be to fund the necessary reparations for the damage to Pelworthy caused by the fire." His eyes bulged in his head, for he was a notorious pinchpenny, but he kept his mouth clamped shut as well. Here she smiled. "Were you to refuse, I would make it known that you were the author of the fire. You would be forgiven among many of your peers, but not all, and certainly the common folk would look with great disapprobation on last night's crime."

She drew in a deep breath and turned to Sir Roger. "These would be the judgments I would pass. These *gentlemen* could, of course, be held up to the scrutiny and chastisement of the law, which I believe would be severe, but if you hope to remain in Chilchester, I think it would be a great deal wiser for you to soften the blow. If you are not entirely enchanted with my ideas about how best to proceed, I would advise you to consult Squire Crawley, who seems to have a peculiar adroitness in handling such matters." Without waiting for him to approve or disapprove, she simply excused herself, saying she was quite fatigued, and left the ravine, scrambling with some difficulty up the path, since her limbs had begun to shake. She was as unsettled by the night's trials as she was by the sure knowledge that not only had three of her closest friends been the authors of the burning of Pelworthy, but that Sir Roger undoubtedly believed her equally as guilty.

Returning to the castle, she found that her father was awaiting her with his coach. She boarded the fine vehicle with some difficulty, as though great weights had been attached to each ankle. Finally, however, she was seated beside him. Without a single thought having entered her head, she burst into a hearty bout of tears, which did not cease until she had arrived home, been bathed and rid of all the soot, clothed in a warm nightdress, and tucked between the sheets.

When she awoke several hours later, she turned toward the window and watched as sparrows flitted about the thick ivy encroaching on the window frame. She smiled, though wearily. Her eyes felt swollen and scratchy, a swift reminder of all that had transpired in a fragile four and twenty hours.

Her maid brought tea to her at five o'clock, for which she did not leave her bed, but rather propped herself up on several pillows and cradled the cup in her hands. "How did you know I was awake?" she asked softly.

Her maid, who had begun busying herself by checking the condition of every pair of silk stockings in Madeline's possession, smiled. "I was told to awaken you if you were yet abed. I would not have liked to have done so, but Mr. Piper requested it most particularly, so I felt obliged to come to you."

"I suppose he does not want me to sleep too long, then awaken at midnight and be awake through dawn."

"Actually, miss, he told me to tell you that his solicitor is downstairs and there seems to be a problem with your dowry that needs discussing. He was hoping, if you were not too fatigued, that you would be able to receive him."

Madeline could not make sense of this. She could not

imagine in what way her dowry would have even the smallest complication, since it had been settled in her mother's marriage papers so many years ago. Besides, there was something more. "My father's solicitor has called on a matter of urgency on Sunday evening?" she asked, greatly surprised.

Her maid shrugged and appeared not to comprehend the meaning of it either, but a faint smile clung to her lips that made her suspicious. Whatever game was afoot, if indeed there was a game, Madeline felt the need to see for herself in what way her dowry had become a point of concern.

A half hour later, wearing a gown of embroidered muslin and her hair caught up in a simple knot atop her head, she entered the drawing room and found not only her father and his solicitor present but Sir Roger and an unknown gentleman in attendance as well.

At the mere sight of Sir Roger, her heart began to hammer, and she felt near to fainting all over again. What was the meaning of his visit? Her father, perhaps seeing her quick discomfiture, immediately went to her, catching her arm in his and holding her firmly. He led her to a wing chair near the fireplace, which she sank into gratefully. Her legs were trembling again. She was still greatly fatigued, and her nerves were in a tender state. Her father then brought her a glass of sherry, which she began to sip in hopes that she might become more at ease.

However, the unhappy and truly distressing thought occurred to her suddenly that the man with Sir Roger was his solicitor, as well, and that somehow he was holding her responsible for the burning of Pelworthy. She almost began to weep anew, so certain she was that she was to be tried for the crime instead of her three friends, which she had to admit held some merit. She gulped her sherry instead and came up sputtering.

"Madeline!" her father cried, a little shocked.

"Another glass please, Papa? I am not feeling at all the thing, and I believe that whatever it is you have to tell me will certainly require at least another small glass of wine."

"Madeline, I think you misunderstand," he began.

"Please, Papa, I would be most grateful."

"Allow me," Sir Roger said. He approached her quickly and took her glass from her trembling fingers.

He was clean shaven and appeared rather well-rested, though faint circles rimmed his eyes, evidence of his night's exertions. He was as handsome as ever, and as usual she felt dizzy just looking at him. When he smiled in an amused manner, his blue eyes strangely tender in expression, she was able to offer an unsteady smile in return. In a trice, she was holding a second glass of sherry.

He addressed her father. "Perhaps it would be better if I spoke with your daughter alone, to *soften the blow."*

These words, precisely the same ones she had used when suggesting the manner of punishment for her beaus, nearly caused her to faint.

"Of course. Use my office." He waved an arm in the direction of the entrance hall.

She saw that Sir Roger's expression had now turned rather grim. Perhaps he had been polite in bringing her a glass of sherry, but she could see how it was. He had, indeed, come to lay the charge at her door. She must therefore be brave. She must accept. She must die at Tyburn Tree for the torching of Pelworthy.

When he extended his hand to her, she lifted her chin and rose from her seat holding herself as proudly as she was able, given the circumstances. She would go to her death with every measure of courage she could summon.

"There, there," he murmured, patting her hand which was presently holding his arm. "This will not be too painful, I promise."

"Not for you, perhaps," she returned on a half sigh, swallowing with some difficulty.

"That much is true," he said. "I am finding this interview remarkably easy."

"Then I have meant so little to you?" she asked quietly, as they passed into the hall. "All is forgotten, then? The love of which you spoke, even the kiss we shared on Lady Cottingford's terrace?"

"Oh, I shan't forget any of those, I promise. Your father spoke of his office?"

"Oh, yes, there. The door opposite."

He led her inside at which time she again sank into a chair, the same one she had occupied when her father had lied to her about having lost his fortune. So the whole business had come to this: Sir Roger, though saying he would never forget his love for her, found it remarkably easy to set aside his affections because of the present horrible circumstances. He clearly blamed her completely for the fire. She lifted her gaze to him, and waited.

He frowned slightly. "My dear, you do not need to look so very sad, unless you mean to refute the evidence."

She swallowed hard again, and straightened her shoulders. "You have heard all the evidence. I suppose, therefore, the judgment must belong to you."

"There is something I must know, however, before I continue. Can you love a Scot?"

Tears darted to her eyes, but she did not waver her gaze from his, not even a bit. "More than you could ever imagine," she responded. "Just as I said last night."

His expression softened anew, and the former look of tenderness suffused his eyes once more. "That is all the evidence I require," he stated.

"For sending me to Tyburn Tree?" she asked, much shocked, as well as thinking he had perhaps become addled from being too near the fire last night.

He moved toward her, took strong hold of her arms, and lifted her to her feet. "No, my silly goosecap," he said, pulling her into a warm, tight embrace, "for asking if you would do me the honor of becoming my wife."

Madeline placed her hands on his shoulders and blinked at him several times. "You . . . you wish me to become your wife?" she asked, incredulous.

"Yes, my darling Madeline. The sooner the better, though I suppose proper form requires that we wait an entire month."

"I do not understand," she said, tears beginning to roll down her cheeks. "I had thought you despised me. I was certain you believed me responsible for the fire."

"For some time I questioned it, but my doubts were resolved at the nature of your judgments. There was nothing in them of prejudice either toward them for the nature of their crime or toward me in favoring them above any culpability at all."

"Yet you said nothing and you did not stop me from leaving. Why?" She swiped at her cheeks.

"Because I knew you were exhausted, and I had to deal very quickly with the culprits, before anyone else was apprised of the truth."

"And did you?" she asked, astonished.

"Yes. My solicitor has already resolved matters with Mr. Calvert, who has agreed to assume the cost of the repairs for Pelworthy. Captain Bladen, for his part, has left town with intentions of making his home in Somerset. Lastly, Mrs. Rockingham has finally agreed to purchase a pair of colors for her son."

She stared at him in some wonder. "You accomplished all this today?"

He nodded.

After a moment, she asked, "Did you actually tell Mrs. Rockingham what her son had done?"

He shook his head. "No, Harris informed her himself."

"But in your presence?"

"Yes."

Madeline sighed. "Then I am happy for him. He should have been in a cavalry regiment all these years instead of suffering through several unproptious terms at Oxford. But, Sir Roger—"

"Please, Roger will do."

She could feel a blush stealing up her cheek. "Roger, are you certain you wish to marry me? Could you truly love an Englishwoman?"

He smiled, again so tenderly that her heart melted and she leaned into him. "With all my heart," he responded.

He kissed her, so sweetly, so lovingly, that Madeline heard a series of coos which she realized must have come from her own throat but which seemed a thousand miles away. She was lost, as she had been so many times before, in the wonder of his embrace and in the sure knowledge that she loved and was loved and that somehow she was being permitted the truly remarkable joy of marrying a Scot.

Much later, when Sir Roger opened the door to the office, a bevy of faces stared back at Madeline—her father, both solicitors, all three of her sisters, Lord Anthony and Cressida Crawley, and her father's betrothed, Madame Charbonneau.

"Is it all settled?" Hope cried, her face lit with excitement.

Madeline nodded and was immediately swamped by her sisters, who flocked about her, hugging her and exclaiming how happy they all were. Lord Anthony kissed her cheek and Cressida admitted that she was betrothed as well. Madame Charbonneau kissed both her cheeks and wished her every happiness. Her father, the solicitors, and Sir Roger retired to the office to finalize the marriage agreement after which the legal representatives left and those who remained enjoyed a quiet dinner, though one served with a great deal of champagne, with a little music and dancing afterward.

Madeline marveled, as she stood opposite Sir Roger for a country dance, that her first encounter with him so many months ago at Pelworthy could have ended so wonderfully. She remembered the shock at the time of realizing that a Scot had actually taken possession of her dear Pelworthy and that now nothing pleased her so much as the thought of being married to him in the near future. How much had changed.

When Lord Anthony had left to escort his betrothed home and her father had settled Madame Charbonneau in his coach by which he meant to see her safely to Elsbourne, when her sisters had discreetly retired to their bedchambers, she was alone at last with Sir Roger once more. She requested that a small log fire be built in the grate, an unusual occurrence for the summer months, and together they sat before the leaping flames, her head on his shoulder.

"I wish we did not have to wait a full month, my love," she whispered, tilting her face to his and receiving a kiss in return.

"Well," he murmured, sweeping a stray curl away from her face. "We could always elope."

She began to giggle. "To Gretna Green," she said, still chuckling.

"Why so amused?" he asked.

"Because it is in Scotland!" she cried, laughing harder still. "I thought the notion would please you above all things."

"Actually, it does. There would be some wonderful irony to it, I think."

"Yes, and if you truly wish to go, I shall pack my portmanteau even now." Part of her was suddenly completely in earnest.

He kissed her again. "Darling Madeline, how you tempt me, and how you delight me by saying so. But no, ours shall be a stodgy betrothal, a stuffy marriage, and *my*—that is, *our*—children will have every advantage of going about in Society as much as they desire. I would be foolish to succumb to your entreaties, and I beg you will stop looking at me in that wicked manner! You shock me, dearest!"

"I mean to shock you," she said. "A great deal!" With that, she kissed him full on the mouth and spoke with her lips all the intentions of her heart for the coming months and years.

"If you are not careful, we will be forced to Gretna Green," he said, pushing her away slightly.

"I want to go," she said abruptly. "More than anything else in the world. Roger, take me to Gretna, this instant!'

"Madeline!" he cried, obviously shocked.

"I am quite serious. You do not know what it is to have lived in the confining Society that I have. You have had your adventures. You had the wondrous pleasure of living in India for fifteen years, while I was afraid to smile very much lest I give the wrong impression. There may be something to be said for discretion, but not in this moment, not now. Will you take me to Gretna?"

He searched her eyes for a very long moment. "I will," he said. "Everything is settled with your father, the papers have been signed. You will leave a note saying that we will return in a year."

"A year?"

"Well, you do want to see India, do you not?"

Madeline leaned away from him. "Tell me you are not

teasing me—for if you do, I vow I will not marry you at all. Of course I wish to go, more than you could ever know."

"Then pack your things, Maddy. We leave tonight."

Madeline did not hesitate. She packed a portmanteau just as she said, wrote four letters, one to each of her sisters and one to her father, and bid her maid good-bye. Sir Roger had brought his coach round and was awaiting her in the entrance hall.

"If you are having the smallest doubt," he said, "we do not have to go."

"The truth of it is, Roger, that I have no doubts at all, not even one."

She took his arm and, beside him, drove from Fairlight and into the future.

"But how did you know?" Madame Charbonneau whispered to her betrothed in her lilting accent. His coach was secreted in the shadows of a great oak down the lane, and Sir Roger's coach had just passed by, beneath the light of a full moon. Visible within was Madeline. Visible without was her baggage.

Mr. Piper swiped at a tear. "Because until the events of the past three weeks, she had been her mother's daughter exclusively, but now she is mine."

"So it would seem," his long lost love said to him. "But you may not see her for a very long time, if I have taken Sir Roger's measure."

"I hope not. I hope she will see something of the world before she retires to Pelworthy and to the wonderful, if confining, joy of raising children of her own."

"I believe this wish you have has already been granted."

**Discover the Thrill of
Romance with**

Lisa Plumley

__Making Over Mike
0-8217-7110-8 $5.99US/$7.99CAN
Amanda Connor is a life coach—not a magician! Granted, as a
publicity stunt for her new business, the savvy entrepreneur has
promised to transform some poor slob into a perfectly balanced
example of modern manhood. But Mike Cavaco gives "raw material"
new meaning.

__Falling for April
0-8217-7111-6 $5.99US/$7.99CAN
Her hometown gourmet catering company may be in a slump, but
April Finnegan isn't about to begin again. Determined to save her
business, she sets out to win some local sponsors, unaware she's not
the only one with that idea. Turns out wealthy department store mogul
Ryan Forrester is one step—and thousands of dollars—ahead of her.

__Reconsidering Riley
0-8217-7340-2 $5.99US/$7.99CAN
Jayne Murphy's best-selling relationship manual *Heartbreak 101* was
inspired by her all-too-personal experience with gorgeous, capable . . .
outdoorsy . . . Riley Davis, who stole her heart—and promptly skipped
town with it. Now, Jayne's organized a workshop for dumpees. But it
becomes hell on her heart when the leader for her group's week-long
nature jaunt turns out to be none other than a certain . . .